SUSAN EDMUNDS is a business journalist by day and a fiction scribbler by night. She lives in Whangarei, New Zealand, with her husband Jeremy and their two children, Liam and Olivia. Most of Susan's non-work writing relates to motherhood and the crazy experience of being left to take care of a child when you have no real idea what you're doing. When she gets the chance at some time off, she spends it with her children, exercising and trying to tackle her sleep deficit.

🐦 @susanedmunds
f @susanedmundsauthor

Also by Author Name

Mummy Needs a Break

Mummy Needs Help

Susan Edmunds

OneMoreChapter

One More Chapter
a division of HarperCollins*Publishers*
The News Building
1 London Bridge Street
London SE1 9GF

www.harpercollins.co.uk

This paperback edition 2020

First published in Great Britain in ebook format by
HarperCollins*Publishers* 2020

EB ISBN: 9780008316105
PB ISBN: 9780008316112

This novel is entirely a work of fiction.
The names, characters and incidents portrayed in it are
the work of the author's imagination. Any resemblance
to actual persons, living or dead, events or localities is
entirely coincidental.

Set in Birka by
Palimpsest Book Production Limited, Falkirk,
Stirlingshire

Printed and bound in Great Britain by
CPI Group (UK) Ltd, Croydon CR0 4YY

For Liam and Livi

Chapter One

Maria Matthews, 10:30am: 'So the other day I taught my son how to put moisturiser on dry skin. Today I feel light, feathery touches on my calf. How nice, I think, darling son has noticed my legs could do with some cream. Look down and ARGH! He's taking snot from his nose and very gently rubbing it into my skin.'

Renee
Age: One day

It was a hospital midwife with hair dye stains on her fingernails who handed me my baby, freshly expelled from the warm, wet indoor spa pool of my uterus into the overly air-conditioned delivery suite. You'd think you wouldn't notice those details, but after thirty-six weeks of waiting, I'd developed some high expectations of what that particular moment should be like.

I'm one of life's organisers, even in the most mundane situations. The type who gives you a run-sheet alongside a birthday party invitation. So really, the just-go-with-it nature of childbirth was never going to be a comfortable fit for me.

My daughter's face was puffy and pink, like an old woman with a sinus-twisting case of hay fever. Her fingers were weirdly out of proportion, long and completely white. They looked like the hands of a waxwork witch who had terrified me at an amusement park when I was a child. Then, they had been curled around a purple crystal ball. This time they were forming angry fists as if the baby – *my baby*, I pulled myself up, this was *my* baby – had realised a bit too late that this was not where she had meant to be, and was trying to protest her way back to safety.

I leant back on the narrow hospital bed. It had been cranked into a seated position some time between when I summoned the energy to fire one last desperate push through my pelvis as the obstetrician peered into my nether regions, and when I'd been handed this little bundle of fury.

I could relate to her outrage. If I'd been picking a place to come into the world, it wouldn't have been this corner nook of a public hospital – sorry, 'world-class delivery suite' – where the lights above looked like the engines of an alien spacecraft and everything smelt of disinfectant.

'Mum'll know she's got this one around,' the midwife said and winked at me. The sound of my baby's cry cut through the air. I'd known there was a noise happening, and I vaguely knew she was distressed, but it had taken me a minute to make the connection that it was my daughter producing the wail. I forced a smile, but I seemed to be moving a beat behind the real world. It was like I was swimming in a fish tank while everyone else wandered around, peering in on me.

'I'm cold.' I looked for my partner, Nick, who was two steps away from the bed, his gaze locked on our baby in my arms. Was he trying to avoid looking at some other part of me? I was aware of a distant tugging from whatever tidy-up the obstetrician was still doing down below. Odd that she'd bothered to put a local anaesthetic on for that when everyone had been so keen to coach me, drug-free, through the baby's head creating the problem in the first place. I made a mental note to remind Nick of his 'your body knows what to do' chant next time he complained of a tricep twinge after a few too many reps at the gym.

Nick pointed at me, looking at one of the women for help.

'It's not cold, Renee.' She was brisk, whipping a blood-and-something-else-soaked sheet out from under me and replacing it with a crunchy plastic pad. 'Your body's in shock, it won't last.'

A nurse who had wandered in to collect some of the equipment from the corner of the room shot her a glance. 'We can turn the heat up a couple of degrees.'

Too right, I was in shock. Where I'd been used to a bump taking over my mid-section, there was now a wobbly pouch

3

of skin, being pulled down by gravity like a collapsing tent. It was shaking alarmingly as my body trembled. The child I'd grown used to as a foot poking into my ribs or a head doing lazy somersaults in my uterus was gone. I missed her even as she snuffled around at my chest.

The hospital midwife took hold of my left breast and angled it at my daughter's face. 'Let her have a go at latching. Does she have a name?'

I shot a look at Nick, who didn't seem to have heard.

The other woman winked. 'You've a few weeks before you have to decide but if she doesn't yet, you'll get a 'baby of' wristband for her ... not so great for the memory box.'

I shifted my gaze back to Holly. Nick and I had still been debating names in the car on the way to the hospital, although his arguments grew less strident as my contractions became more severe. 'Holly,' I said, settling on the most decisive tone I could muster. They didn't need to know he'd told me it sounded like something you'd name a dog.

***

Contractions had started to niggle at me at 6pm the previous day, while Nick and I were having dinner. We'd deflected his parents, who had got into the habit of expecting us to visit for dinner every Thursday. It was a ritual for almost all the three years we had been together but the half-hour drive from our Putney flat to their immaculate Georgian home in Blackheath became impossible in my last month of pregnancy when I could barely fit my bump behind the dashboard of our little Toyota.

By 8pm, I was no longer able to convince myself that the cramps hitting me like a punch to the uterus were practice Braxton Hicks, or just the complaints of worn-out ligaments. Nick frowned as I pushed him off towards the bedroom, anyway.

Since he quit his sensible, well-paying job (not that I was holding that against him) to follow his chaotic, nail-biting dream of starting a gym with his mate, Sam, and had to be up before the birds most mornings, he had been terrible at staying up late. Once, at his cousin's wedding, he fell asleep during the speeches and I'd had a huge job trying to convince his aunt and uncle that he was just tired, not drunk. I resisted the urge to tell them that it was their son they should be looking at if they wanted to know why the bar tab had run out more quickly than expected. I could just imagine having to tell our daughter that her father missed her birth because he'd been snoring in the corner.

My midwife, Karen, whom I'd been seeing virtually from the minute I emerged, bewildered, from my first-ever-in-my-life positive pregnancy test, had counselled me that the deliveries of first babies were hardly ever quick procedures, anyway.

'You can expect eight hours of active labour,' she had said as she thrust a birth planning worksheet at me. Usually I loved these things – a chance to fill in forms and make stuff happen. But it had contained such cheery questions as 'Would you prefer an episiotomy or for it to be allowed to occur naturally?' Nick had turned a deep grey when I'd explained what that term actually meant. Her clinic was around the corner from the offices of the events management firm I worked at and I dutifully trotted there on my lunch breaks. 'You'll need to rest at the start to ration your energy,' she had told me. 'Sleep, if you can.'

As if.

I reached for my phone and swiped to pull up the app to chat to my online mums' support group. Someone there would be around to coach me through an hour or two on my own. The responses started to flow almost immediately.

'No harm in checking in with the midwife,' Felicity, who ran the group, posted.

Another message popped up beneath it. 'Listen to your body. You'll know when it's the right time to take action. Have you any calming oils you could burn, pop in the bath for a bit?' I checked the name. Of course – Frankie. She and her three home-schooled children lived in a yurt on her parents' farm. She probably gave birth in a river or something.

An hour and a half later, I hauled myself up to turn over in the half-full bath, knocking a bottle of shampoo so it clattered across the bathroom floor. Half a minute later, Nick peered around the doorway, rubbing a hand over his face. 'All okay in here?'

I wiped the back of my hand across my forehead, which

6

was clammy with sweat. 'I was just trying to relax but it's not working very well.'

He gave me a look. It was one I knew well, deployed when I was mid-crisis at work and arguing that it was perfectly fine to exist on two and a half hours' sleep a night, or when I got upset over my mother not replying to an email I knew I shouldn't have bothered to send.

'Do you want me to call Karen? I think this is one situation you can't just power through on your own.'

I cringed and pulled myself up to my hands and knees. 'Yes. Okay. Not a time for DIY. Maybe just give her a call and see what she says.'

He nodded and disappeared. Another contraction hit. Frankie must have had some better oils than I did if she thought they were going to do anything.

There was muttering outside the door and the sound of Nick pacing the length of our poky flat.

Then he put his head around the door. 'She's gone away for the weekend.'

I struggled to sit up, bracing myself against the slippery plastic of the bath. 'What?'

'Something urgent. Apparently, the hospital has systems in place – we'll just head in there and there will be a duty midwife who will take care of us.' He was clearly parroting the lines she had given him. He caught my eye and must have seen the expression on my face. 'She says it'll be fine. They know what they're doing.'

'I'm sure they do.' I tried to slide down further into the

water. We'd discussed this as a possibility, and I had duly researched as best I could who might be on shift if that happened, but I had filed it away in the same best-not-thought-about category as the possibility of induction if I was still pregnant at forty-one weeks. 'Can I talk to her?'

He shook his head. 'She's just getting on a plane. She'll call you when she gets to the other end. Do you want to go now?'

Another contraction sucked at my cervix, sending a wave of heat up my body. I cringed. The steam from the bath was making me nauseous. 'I think I'll feel better if I'm out of the bath for a bit. She did say to stay home as long as possible. Can you help me out?'

We hobbled to the bedroom, his arm supporting me under my shoulders, a towel draped inadequately around me. I'd felt big before but now it was as if I needed my own moon. The distance between my hips seemed to have doubled in a matter of hours. I flopped into our bed, drawing my knees up to my chest. Nick crawled in beside me, tracing the bumps of my spine with his fingers. His movements became slower and less regular until they stopped entirely after about ninety seconds and his breathing deepened. I turned over. He'd fallen asleep again. How perfectly on-brand. Another contraction socked me in the stomach. There was no way I could stay in bed.

***

Nick appeared from the bedroom another hour later, wiping his eyes with the back of his hands, as I curled in a ball on the sofa. 'Should I be timing them or something?' He screwed up his face in the light of the living room.

'Could have started doing that five hours ago.' I looked up at him through my fingers. 'Half an hour more, then we'll go.'

He rolled his eyes and reached for the bunch of keys that he'd thrown on to the coffee table when he walked in the door the night before. 'Let's just go now.'

As I opened my mouth to disagree, another contraction rolled in. 'Okay.'

The hospital was less than ten minutes' drive from our home, but you could have told me that we were driving the length of the country and I would have believed it. We stopped at every red light and with each contraction I pulled myself up on the door handle, trying to scramble away from the pain. Nick had started to count down the time between them – one of the few practical domestic uses of his personal training skills I'd ever seen. I pushed out of my mind the thought that he could have the chance to use his first aid certificate for a roadside delivery.

'Another one in twenty seconds,' he intoned as we pulled into the hospital car park.

'No, no, no,' I moaned. 'I've changed my mind.'

'Sorry, hun, it's a bit late for that.' He hoisted me out of the car, and we stumbled through the doors of the maternity ward. 'You can do it, you're awesome.'

The midwife on duty took her time pulling on the blue latex glove she would use to examine me in the same manner that you might remove the giblets from a frozen chicken. Her blue-gloved hand buried in me up to the wrist, she nodded – almost impressed. 'Advanced labour,' she hissed at a passing nurse.

Half an hour later, the magic 10cm of dilation had been reached. The midwife whipped away the gas machine I'd been sucking desperately every minute. 'Now, you need to push. Like you're on the toilet.' Her voice was firm. 'It sometimes takes a few goes to get the pushing right. Next contraction, go for it.'

Nick was still counting the seconds. 'Get ready.' He squeezed my hand as it hit. I pushed as if I wanted to shove my intestines out through my urethra on to the bed. But at the end, the midwife was still looking at me. 'Try again next one.'

Nick patted my shoulder. Was this what he did to his clients? No wonder he wasn't earning as much as I thought he should. 'See if you can sort of push down more in the middle of your body?' He pointed to something he'd found on his phone. 'I see here it says ...'

The midwife caught his eye and he stopped. 'Maybe you could rub her back?'

I was stuck in an unending loop. Contraction. Try to push. Everyone watching. Everyone sighing. A monitor strapped to my stomach beeping. I'd lost track of time, either through pain or too much nitrous oxide. I became aware of the midwife staring at me more intently. I was fighting to keep my eyes open between each contraction. 'I think we should get an obstetrician in here, see if we can get you a bit of help getting this baby out, okay?'

An intervention. My antenatal class had spent an hour on the various methods that could be used to 'help' deliver a baby – forceps that looked like giant salad tongs and might cause irreparable damage to you or you baby. A ventouse that looked a bit like an electronic toilet plunger – and might cause irreparable damage to you or your baby. But I couldn't summon the energy to care. I just wanted it to be over. To go back home to my own bed and sleep. I would later see 'poor maternal effort' scrawled on my maternity notes. As if it were a lack of trying on my part that stopped a 3.5kg baby from gliding through my size eight pelvis.

After all that, I knew that Nick wouldn't put up too much of a fight over our baby's name.

***

I watched Holly snort and snuffle, trying to find her spot on my breast. Finally, her little mouth, which looked like one I'd seen on a newborn kitten when I was a child, connected with the tender, newly brown skin of my nipple. The suction was firm. Perhaps, in our search for a name, we should have considered Dyson.

'She's not on right.' The midwife who'd manhandled my

breast into position leant over, sliding the tip of her little finger into the edge of Holly's mouth, breaking the seal.

She gestured for me to try again. There had been a handout at the midwife's rooms with a photo of a small baby suckling at a voluminous, veiny breast. They'd said something about lining up the baby's nose to nipple. I waggled my breast at Holly who opened her mouth. The midwife watched, scribbling in my maternity notes book. 'That looks better, well done. Does it feel okay?'

'It feels pretty weird.'

I could see Holly's jaw moving as her eyelids fluttered shut. I reached out for Nick, who was hovering at the side of the bed. 'Do you want to hold her once she's finished?'

He nodded. I traced the line of her cheek tentatively. She was tiny. I had objectively known she was going to be small, of course. I'd told one friend the smaller the better. But she was more like a little doll than an actual human. Her skin was soft and so smooth it almost felt like it should have a scattering of marshmallow dust across its surface. The clock ticking on the wall tapped out the seconds in the silence. Someone had scrawled across its face that it was hospital property, as if you might try to sneak off home with it like some sort of low-rent souvenir. Clearly many people giving birth on this ward were not getting high-calibre baby gifts. Holly's sucking slowed into a butterfly tickle. I wiggled, trying to dislodge her. When she slipped off, still asleep, I tucked a hospital-issue blanket around her and passed her to her father, a bit like the Christmas ham my grandmother used to wrap in a trusty blue-and-white tea towel.

Nick grasped her in the crook of his arm, making her seem even tinier against his gym-honed bicep muscles and veiny forearms. He looked worried she would slip from his grasp. With a twitch of his body he turned her so she was stretched out down the length of his arms, her head in his hands. Her nose wiggled as if she were smelling something unpleasant. He was staring at her, transfixed. I watched them for a minute. While I was still feeling slightly bewildered and discombobulated, he seemed to have leapfrogged straight into the overwhelming rush-of-love stage.

I almost couldn't believe we'd ended up here. When we'd met, at my half-sister's thirtieth birthday party in the private function room of a Notting Hill restaurant, I'd just started in my job as an events manager – the first time I'd shaken off that 'assistant' title – and made a vow to stay single to focus on nothing more than getting as far up the chain of command as I could. Long-term, I wanted to buy the business from my boss, who terrified and inspired me in equal parts.

I had only wanted to stay at Natalie's party for half an hour to show my face. She was part of my dad's 'real family' – the one he had forgotten to tell my mother about before she fell pregnant with me. The party was totally Natalie. Big and loud and full of people who had lots of money and did very little to get it. I stayed in the corner, sipping a glass of champagne that would have normally cost half my wage, when Nick ambled over. He'd played rugby with Natalie's brother, Jonathan. 'Don't hold that against me,' he said with a grin as he leant against the brick of the wall. 'I'm not one of them.'

I raised an eyebrow. 'You're not?'

From the look of him, he was exactly one of them. His shirt and slim-cut jeans looked expensive. His haircut was definitely a three-figure one.

He seemed to realise I was appraising him and threw up his hands. 'Oh, I may look like them, but I promise I'm actually a real person.'

That had made me smile. You could spend all day with Natalie or Jonathan and feel like you were chatting the whole time but by the end of it you wouldn't be able to pinpoint a single thing that you'd actually talked about. Their mother, Veronica, had to tell them who I was just before my dad's funeral, when I was twelve. I guess he had been away enough during their lives that his visits to see me every year or two weren't even noticeable. Natalie, three years my senior, had treated me like some sort of exotic animal in a zoo at first, before finally accepting that I was actually quite boring when we ended up in some of the same classes at university together.

For my part, I'd instantly got over my gnawing jealousy of what I'd decided was Natalie's perfect life when I saw her mother tell her off at the funeral for her choice of shoes.

'Do you know' – Nick's voice had dropped to a near whisper so I had to lean closer to hear him – 'I think

Jonathan secretly listens to One Direction in those AirPods of his while he's out running with his mad dog.'

I had laughed champagne out of my nose.

'And Natalie, I reckon she writes out Nickelback lyrics in Valentine's Day cards for that weird boyfriend of hers.'

'Stop! I'm going to spill my wine everywhere.'

He had grinned at me. 'So how do you know her?'

I bit my lip. 'She's my sister.'

'Ah. Oops.'

We had ducked out and gone for coffee at a little café down the road that was a lot less glitzy. A year later, we were living together in our little flat.

I shifted my weight on to my left thigh and inched off the bed, finally swinging my legs around so the soles of my feet connected with the cold lino of the floor. I leant over to kiss his cheek and the top of Holly's head. 'I'm going to go and find a shower. I need a wash.'

Nick cocked his head to gesture to the gym bag he had thrown over his shoulder as we ran for the door of our flat. It was overflowing, one zip only half-closed, a nightie making a bid for freedom. Somewhere in there, there was an old smartphone loaded with rainforest sounds and soothing beauty spa melodies that I'd planned to have playing through the initial stages of labour. There might even have been a bottle of facial mist my mother sent after she missed my baby shower. I extracted the nightie, slid my feet into a pair of worn-in slippers, and placed one tentative step in front of the other towards the door.

. I looked back over my shoulder as I reached to pull it shut behind me. Nick was staring down at Holly, his entire body anchored completely still. I waved to get his attention. 'You two will be okay?'

He ducked his head in the tiniest fraction of a nod. In one of the rooms across the corridor, a woman was shrieking. Had I made that much noise? I felt like a lolloping hippopotamus, my midsection moving pendulously with each tentative step.

The communal bathroom was at the end of the corridor. I pushed open the heavy door and sidled in, still moving as if I was carrying a baby bump in front of me. The stalls were all empty.

***

I pulled out my phone as I entered the shower cubicle at the far end of the room, a sectioned-off space with a swinging half-door to shield it from the rest of the room. It was as if whoever designed it had decided that, having been laid out on the bed like a roast chicken mere minutes earlier, you'd be willing to give up most privacy from then on.

I pulled up the mothers' group online. Only a day or two before, there had been a message from someone about the pain of the first post-birth wee. What was I meant to do? I scanned through posts. Something about a car seat. A weird rash. There it was. 'Do it in the shower and try to lean forward a bit as you do,' Helen had advised. I wasn't totally sure but I had a feeling she was a doctor or a nurse. She seemed to have all the information any time anyone asked anything vaguely medical.

I stripped off my hospital gown and threw it in the metal-topped laundry bag in the corner, hanging my nightie on the hook on the back of the door. There were no mirrors in the room, which was probably fortunate.

I coaxed the tap on and slid under the lukewarm jet of water, trying to position myself according to Helen's instructions. I turned and let the water run over my face. The rhythm of the shower pressure melded with the pulse in the hospital air conditioning into a sort of hypnotic thump-thump. I crossed my arms in front of my chest.

I poked at my stomach. I didn't know what I expected, but it wasn't this. It looked as if I'd eaten a big dinner every day for the last six months. Where had my taut basketball of baby gone? Maybe I'd thought the bump would slowly descend until my body was ready to suck it all back in again. By the end of my nine months of pregnancy (which is actually ten if you think about it but who's counting?) I couldn't lie on my stomach, walk up steps, or fit in the car. But now I kind of missed that bump.

I turned the water off when the door to the bathroom opened and someone else traipsed into the room.

Pulling my nightie down over my hips, I shuffled out of the shower cubicle. The nightie was too tight – whoever had bought it for me had obviously not realised either that I wouldn't immediately be a size small again. The newcomer was brushing her hair, a toothbrush jammed between her teeth. She turned and grinned at me. 'Sorry, I didn't mean to disturb you.'

I waved it away. 'You didn't. I should be getting back to the baby, anyway.'

The other woman was a few years older than me but not many, perhaps in her late thirties, with a sensible bob haircut and kind eyes. 'How's baby doing?'

I opened my mouth and shut it again. Was leaving her behind the wrong thing to do? I gestured vaguely to the other end of the hospital. 'Good, I think. She's with her dad.'

The woman caught my eye in the mirror as she spread toothpaste on her brush. 'Mine too. Gotta take a break while you can. Who knows when there'll be another?' She smiled, brush in her mouth. 'You okay? First time?'

I nodded. I hadn't announced my pregnancy until fourteen weeks, reluctant to believe that the pregnancy was real. I'd been taking the pill but a course of antibiotics must have rendered it ineffective. Nick had almost fallen over when I had showed him the stick with its two lines. He'd open and shut his mouth like a fish before settling on: 'What do you want to do?'

What I'd really wanted was to push everything back a couple of years. To give myself time to build up a bit more of a career and for us to be a little bit more sorted – there were still months when there wasn't a lot of money left over for Nick and Sam to pay themselves once they'd paid their staff and their rent. But I knew there was no way I was going to do anything other than keep the baby. 'There's never the perfect time for a baby, right?'

His face had lit up. 'My mother is going to be over the moon.'

The pregnancy had been uneventful, although after the novelty wore off at about twelve weeks, I just wanted to get it over with. Nick's brother, Elliott, and his wife, Samantha, passed on half a house-load of baby gear. I'd quietly donated the onesie that declared 'supermodel in training'.

As predicted, Nick's mother, Ellen, had been intensely attentive, keeping track of my appointments and updates on Holly's growth. My own mother, however, disappeared at about the second month, after telling me she was certain that I would be mother of the year. 'You've been mothering me your whole life, you're a natural.'

I realised the woman with the toothbrush was still waiting for a response. 'Yes, first baby.' I forced a laugh. 'Don't know what I'm in for, right?'

'I'm sure you'll be great. They just need someone to love them, don't they? All the rest is just a bonus.'

She swished the water around in the sink, clearing out the smears of toothpaste, then retrieved a lip gloss tube from her pocket. 'Is your man any good?'

I paused. 'At what?'

'Does he help out around the house and stuff?'

He'd become a lot better over the course of my pregnancy. Beforehand, he left things until they physically became a problem for him before he dealt with them. His laundry pile would grow like a colour feature on our beige sofa until he ran out of work shirts and put it all away. He would leave a plastic container of leftovers on the kitchen bench until the contents were almost walking away before he'd deal with it. (I discovered this in an unfortunate battle of will he was unaware he was locked in with me while I tried to work out what his limit really was.)

But since one weekend when I'd tripped and nearly fallen on workout gear strewn all over the lounge floor, unable to see my feet due to my growing stomach, he'd snapped to attention.

'He's improving, I guess.'

She moved to hold the door open so we could both leave the room. A trolley rattled down the hallway somewhere in the distance.

She patted me on the shoulder as we prepared to set off in opposite directions across the ward. 'Hope it lasts. You married?'

I shrugged. 'He doesn't believe in it. Too many happy families in his life to see the appeal, I guess.'

She rolled her eyes. 'Whatever you do, don't break up in the first year. You're both basically officially crazy for the first twelve months.'

Waving back over her shoulder, she laughed. 'You think I'm being melodramatic, but you wait. You'll want to wring his neck in a month. But then somehow in a year's time it'll all be sort of okay again.'

20

I watched her wander off down the hallway, limping slightly. It had better not take a year to be 'sort of okay'.

***

Nick
Age: One day

Renee was propped up in bed, poking with one hand at a plate of food an orderly had placed in front of her. In the crook of her other arm she had balanced Holly, who had drifted off to sleep again. From the card on top of the meal, it seemed that she had received whatever the previous occupant of the bed had selected that morning. There was a lump of rice in one corner, a saucer of floppy cabbage, and some sort of meat with orange sauce.

She caught my eye. 'I'm not sure I'm that hungry.'

A nurse was leaning across her, making a note on a clipboard. She regarded the tray. 'I don't blame you.'

I caught her eye. 'She's been vegetarian for fifteen years.'

The nurse cringed and rummaged around in the pocket of her scrubs, producing a white swipe card. She lowered her voice and leant towards me. 'The cafeteria's closed but if you duck down the lift and pop out the staff entrance, just across the street is a good kebab place. This card will get you back in to the maternity ward. We're not meant to let visitors in at this time of night.'

'That would be amazing.' Renee's eyes seemed to go misty with the thought. 'Can you grab me—'

'A falafel, no problem,' I said, finishing her sentence.

'And maybe—'

'Chips?'

'Please.'

I winked at her and backed out through the curtain. 'Back in a bit.'

***

The man behind the counter in the kebab shop shot me a grin as he handed the bag of food over a quarter of an hour later. 'Rough day?'

I wiped my face with the back of my hand. I must have looked shocking. I'd been at the hospital for roughly eighteen hours straight. 'Actually a fantastic day, just a tiring one. I've got to take this back to my partner and daughter.'

The d-word felt odd in my mouth. He seemed to tally up the order in front of him. 'Got enough for two of them?'

I grinned. 'Oh yep. Only my girlfriend eats at the moment.'

He raised an eyebrow as I backed out of the shop.

***

Back on the ward, the nurse was still at Renee's bedside. Renee seemed to be firing questions at her. I smiled

22

– Renee's determination had been part of what hooked me in the first place. Once she decided something was going to happen, there was no other way about it. This kid would want for nothing.

Very-dull Natalie might have been her half-sister but she had grown up about as different from Renee as you could imagine. Natalie and Jonathan lived in their huge house in the country, where we used to have rugby practice on the front lawn at the weekends. But when Renee's mum, Marjorie, worked out that she wasn't going to get the live-in boyfriend out of Renee's dad that she expected, she packed the two of them up and they travelled around the country, with her taking work where she could. If it were now, she'd probably be an Instagram influencer or a digital nomad or something. Renee always told me I took far too romantic a view of it but it sounded pretty cool to me, as someone who holidayed once a year in the same place every year until I was fourteen.

The nurse tapped me on the arm. 'Now you're back you'll need to pass over your delivery and go. Visiting hours have ended.'

Renee struggled to sit up on the hospital bed, where she had positioned Holly across her chest, clutching her breast in one hand and the baby's head in the other. 'Even for fathers? You're sending him away?'

The nurse made an expansive gesture towards the other empty beds in the room. 'It's not fair on the other mothers to have people around all hours.'

'There's no one here.' Renee looked as if she might be going to cry.

'We could get a new one in at any minute. Sorry.' She shrugged. 'It's the rules.'

Renee watched her leave then turned to me, her eyes watery. 'I knew we should have paid the extra to have a private room. I can't believe they're sending you away.'

I squeezed her hand, shifting my weight on the single plastic chair placed next to the bed. I should want to stay. But after the night of labour then a day of visitors – my parents, a couple of Renee's friends – and a bit of wandering around with the baby while Renee tried to rest, the prospect of collapsing on my own bed at home was dancing in front of my eyes like a mirage. I couldn't even sit comfortably, let alone sleep, where I was.

'I'll come back first thing. Sam's taking all my clients for the next little while.' I brushed hair out of her eyes and landed a firm kiss on her forehead. I could hear her swallowing hard.

'What if something happens overnight? How am I meant to know what to do? How do I get her to feed when she's meant to?' Renee's voice was strangled. She gestured around the empty room.

I stroked her hair. 'The nurses said to call if you need them. They'll help you. Karen said she'd call you in the morning.'

Trust us to have a baby on the one weekend of the year the midwife gets called away.

I gestured to her phone, on which messages were pinging through. 'And you've got your mad group to chat to if you get bored. They're more use to you than I am, anyway.'

Renee turned her face away, focusing on the dark outside the window. 'You'll come back as soon as you're allowed in?'

I kissed her again. 'I will.'

The silence dragged out between us. She was waiting for me to say something meaningful, but my brain had checked out for the evening. What was I meant to say? 'Well done for expelling my baby from your body?' 'Thanks for suffering a third-degree tear for my kid?'

I leant over Holly, aiming to land a kiss on her cheek. Trying not to be too rough, I didn't put enough effort into the movement and came up short, executing an empty air kiss like the women Renee worked with would, while they looked over my shoulder at parties for someone more interesting to chat to.

I stuffed my phone and wallet into my pocket and, not breaking eye contact with Renee, walked backwards out of the room. She wasn't a big person, anyway, but she looked tiny in that hospital bed, shadows collecting under her wide eyes, her dark brown hair tied into a messy bun on the top of her head. As I made for the lift at the end of the ward, I flicked glances around the other rooms, looking for any of the nurses I recognised. Two were standing at their station, laughing over something on a piece of paper in front of them. They turned as I cleared my throat. 'I'm off. Will you keep an eye on her?'

The younger one gave me a withering look. 'That's what we're paid to do. They'll be fine. Go and get some sleep so you can be useful when she comes home.'

I stabbed at the lift button for the first of the car park levels. I had only the vaguest memory of where I had left the car. On the trip in, Renee had curled up into a ball every couple of minutes, shouting at me that she was going to lose control of her bladder all over the fabric car seats. Between contractions, she'd demanded to know why we had ever sold her car, with the leather seats that would have been easier to clean. It felt a lot longer than a day ago.

The car was parked halfway across two parking spots, near the lift door. I slid into the driver's seat and placed my hands on the steering wheel. Flashes of images of the night danced in front of my eyes. The midwives muttering about dropping heartbeats, me Googling for the right thing to say when Renee was struggling to push the baby out, the obstetrician's fixed smile. She'd got her wish of no major drugs, to my astonishment. When I broke my arm kickboxing it felt like I had morphine on tap. But they had given her roughly what you might get before you got around to the proper pain relief for a filling.

Then as soon as we'd started to recover from that, Renee and Holly had had to tackle breastfeeding. I was a useless third wheel for that, too, stroking her back while she tried to twist into the right position to get everything aligned. The tension in Renee's jaw and the way she tightly curled her toes when Holly tried to latch told me about as much as I could handle about the process.

I eased the car out of the parking spot and towards the main road, catching a glimpse of myself in the rear-view mirror. Everyone had been at pains to point out how much Holly looked like me, like some sort of weird reassurance that I was definitely the father.

Nosing the car out of the car park building and into the flow of evening traffic on the street, I watched the other drivers. They were all heading home, or out on a Saturday night date, or running to do some errand or other. Was I the only one whose life had changed completely over the last twenty-four hours? Maybe that was why people got those weird stick-figure stickers on their cars. If you didn't make a bit of noise about it, all the hard work you put into bringing a small person into the world might go unnoticed. Not that I'd done much yet, it had to be said.

At least at home I could chuck some clean sheets on the bed, sort out the heating so it was warm for Holly's arrival. It was late spring but the nights were still getting chilly.

I could still smell her babyness. People had talked about the smell of a newborn before but now I got it – there was a distinctive aroma that made you want to bury your nose in her fine downy hair, which weirdly was kind of all over her body. Although I had seen where that little head had been, mind you. When my mum kissed her cheek I'd wanted to say: Do you know where that's come from? She hasn't even had a bath yet. I didn't – even unwashed she still smelt more like a sweet biscuit than someone who had until recently been percolating in the bodily fluids of another person.

At last another driver indicated for me to merge into the right lane ahead of him so I could make my exit. I waved, still running through a checklist in my head of all the things that I needed to get sorted for their arrival.

Three years earlier, I'd been a single person, going through the motions at a crappy IT job for a broadband provider that couldn't provide a continuous connection under threat of death, living alone in my little flat. I'd assumed then that the closest I'd get to a family would be sitting at the table for my mother's overly elaborate Christmas dinners with my brother, Elliott, his wife and their horde of incredibly noisy children. Occasionally, my sister, Kat, would fly in from wherever in the world she happened to be.

Now, Renee and I had a mortgage on a marginally bigger flat, I had switched my job for a gym I owned where I had to keep other people employed, and I was somehow expected to keep a helpless infant alive for the next eighteen years, too. Some people seem to leave school all grown up, don't they? Others get it together at thirty. For me, growing up didn't happen until about 8.30pm in the evening of the March before my thirty-fifth birthday.

If only I'd known then what I was really in for, I might have tried to hasten the process a little.

***

Mummy Needs Help

Renee
Age: One day

Hey, have you heard the one about new mums and sleep? Apparently, we never get any of it, or something. Ha bloody ha. It's a pity I'm too tired to remember the punchline. Of course, everyone had told me we were going to be exhausted and look back wistfully on the days when we managed thirty minutes' sleep in twenty hours. I thought I'd understood. Babies aren't born with their circadian rhythms aligned. They wake randomly all day and all night, and you just have to go with that. Live your best life. Enjoy every minute because they grow so fast. Cherish the moments. #blessed

But I didn't really get it.

By the time Nick walked out the door to head home from the hospital that first day, I had been awake – apart from the odd five-minute snatch of sleep – for nearly thirty-seven hours. The labour had kept me up for one night of that, obviously. Then we'd had visitors to chat to and our baby to keep the energy fizzing. I slithered down in the bed as he shut the door behind him, tucking Holly in beside me. A nurse appeared in what felt like fifteen seconds. 'You can't have your baby in the bed with you.' She peered over us.

I cracked an eyelid open at her. 'What?'

'It's against hospital regulations. She needs to be in her

bassinette.' She gestured to the weird Perspex container next to the bed that looked more like something you might keep your lunch in.

I let my head rest more heavily on the unyielding pillow and looked down at Holly. 'I can't get her to move once she's asleep. She just wakes up.'

The nurse slid a hand under Holly and transferred her across. She screwed up her little nose as her face touched the cold sheet of the bassinette, but her eyes remained closed. The nurse gave me an 'I told you so' look and pulled the curtain shut behind her.

I closed my eyes. The room was spinning as if I'd just got off some sort of amusement park ride. My heartbeat was thumping in my eyelids. But just as the warm rush of sleep slid up my body, I was jolted back into the hospital room by a snuffling from the bassinette. I kept my eyes closed, willing her to stop. The noise became more insistent, with a grunt every other second. I rolled over and reached for the bassinette, patting Holly's back, my eyes still closed.

The grunting continued. I hauled myself up off the bed and over the bassinette, from which I retrieved her and propped her against my chest, swaying. She raised her little fists to her mouth. The universal baby signal for hunger. I groaned. My nipples were still smarting from our previous attempt. 'Are you sure?'

She started to push her hands further into her mouth. I wriggled back on the bed and unclipped my maternity top, trying to hold her head with one hand, position my breast with the other, and guide the two together. She snorted and contorted as she tried to make the connection. Just as she latched, her eyelids started to drift closed again. I stroked her cheek. Of all the personality traits she could pick up from her father, falling asleep mid-meal was not one I would have chosen.

'Don't fall asleep yet, little one,' I whispered. 'I cannot do this all again in another half-hour.'

My eyelids were so heavy. I could just shut them for a minute while Holly worked out what she was going to do.

'I have told you that you can't sleep with her in the bed with you.' The nurse was beside me, tapping my shoulder.

I squeezed my eyes shut before trying to open them. 'I'm not asleep.'

She clicked her tongue. 'Sure. Just snoring. Look, I know you're tired. But what if you dropped her off the bed or rolled on her in your sleep … you'd never forgive yourself.'

Chastened, I wriggled to unlatch her. Her eyelids snapped open. I bit my lip. 'I just want to go to sleep.' I was so tired that the air around me felt like water, but I did not have the strength in my muscles to swim against it. 'What time is it?'

The nurse looked at her watch. 'Almost one. You'll probably find she sleeps a lot better tomorrow. They go through a bit of a phase at first, wanting to feed lots. It gets the milk going. All that colostrum's brilliant for her.'

Tomorrow? First, I had to get through tonight.

When Holly's eyes floated shut again, I spotted my

chance. I pushed myself off the bed with my free hand, carefully supporting Holly's head with the other arm. Her lips were twitching.

Using only the muscles in my thighs – which until that minute I had suspected had disappeared some time around the third month of pregnancy – I rose to my feet, keeping Holly perfectly horizontal. I stretched out over the bassinette and lowered, half a millimetre at a time, towards the tightly stretched white sheet spread across the thin mattress.

As Holly's back slid closer and closer, I moved my grip so that she was at last lying flat on her back in the bassinette. I extricated my fingers one by one, my gaze fixed on Holly's face. As my last little finger pulled out from under Holly's back, I stood up. 'Please sleep well,' I whispered.

I crept back on to the bed, wincing as it complained at my weight. Perhaps it was going to be okay.

One step at a time, wasn't that what they said? I consciously relaxed the muscles in my legs, then my abdomen, chest, and arms. As I felt myself sink back into the respite of overdue sleep, Holly's arm hit the side of the bassinette. I held my breath. It took about two-and-a-half seconds before she cried.

I reached out to gather her up again and, cradling her against me, stumbled back to the bed and swiped open the screen of my phone. 'Keep me awake,' I posted to the mums' group. 'The hospital won't let me have Holly in bed with me and she won't sleep alone. I'm so tired.' I finished with a GIF of a sleeping child toppling off a chair.

I stared at my screen. Usually replies would flood in right away. But then, I didn't usually post in the middle of the night. Finally, one from someone called Mei Warburton. I didn't recognise her name. 'Maybe try playing some games on your phone or something,' she posted. 'They're right, to tell you not to bed share. So dangerous. You could fall asleep and smother her.'

I stared at the words. 'Thanks for the incredible insight. I hadn't thought of that,' I typed before deleting it.

Another message pinged up. Frankie. I wasn't even sure she had electricity in the yurt at night. 'Don't be ridiculous,' she tagged Mei in the post. That was a power move. 'She's literally been inside you for the last nine months. Of course she wants to be close to you. Just try to co-sleep safely, okay?'

I looked down at Holly in the crook of my left arm. Whatever Frankie's idea of safe sleep was, it probably didn't involve balancing above a two-metre drop to a hard linoleum floor. Maybe I could watch a movie.

***

At 3.30am, a nurse I did not recognise peered around the curtain and frowned when she saw my face. 'Everything okay in here?'

I opened my mouth but found I could not speak. Holly had latched back on, drifting in and out of sleep, but lying across me in such a way that I could not even reach my

33

phone any longer. I was counting creases in the curtains to keep myself awake.

The nurse was at my side, her hand on my shoulder. Her grip was firm and warm and I felt myself relax towards her.

'I'm so tired,' I spluttered. 'She just wants to feed. I can't put her down or she wakes up again. I haven't slept since Thursday. I can't work out how this "safe co-sleeping" stuff is meant to work.'

The nurse indicated for me to unlatch Holly and I rolled her on to my forearms.

'Let me take her for a little walk,' she said, watching my face for a reaction. 'You get a little rest before visiting starts again.'

'Are you allowed to do that?'

'I'll bring her back if I need to.' She grinned and winked. 'Don't tell anyone – but it looks like you could do with a break.'

I watched as she propped Holly against her shoulder, tucking my baby's head in under her chin, her body curled around as if she were still tucked up in my womb. The nurse – I realised I didn't even know her name – walked out of the room.

***

The breakfast trolley rumbled into the room what felt like thirty seconds later. I blinked – it took half a second to register where I was and that I was meant to have a baby somewhere near me. I whipped around. She was asleep in the bassinette, her arms thrown up as if in silent celebration, her fists clenched tightly. A hospital orderly pushed back the curtain.

'Breakfast?'

She looked chastened as I glared at her. 'Sorry. Baby sleeping?'

I nodded. 'The last thing I could cope with is her waking up right now.'

She grinned. 'You wait until you get back home, and you've got everything else to worry about, too. I had five kids and no one ever brought me breakfast in bed.'

I had to fight not to roll my eyes. 'Thanks for that.'

I watched Holly as I ate my limp cereal. She did look like Nick, with her almond-shaped eyes and heart-shaped face. Somehow his blond hair had won out so far, too. Her eyes were almost navy, a colour that I had been told would give way to bog-standard brown within a couple of months. Even in full sleep-thief mode, she was cute. Even if I wasn't her mother, I was sure I'd agree she was one of the handful of newborns who are actually objectively adorable. Not like a little old man at all.

It was only half past six. Who thought giving breakfast at that sort of time was appropriate? An hour and a half until Nick would be permitted back in.

There was a commotion on the other side of the curtain. A woman was complaining. 'Can I not just go home? I don't want to be stuck here by myself.'

Someone told her to get into the bed. 'You need to rest, Lauren. Have you anyone at home at the moment who could look after you even if you were discharged?'

The bed creaked and a bassinette wheel squeaked. I kept a wary eye on Holly. 'Mum will be back tonight, I guess. My sister's too busy at work to worry about me. But I don't need anyone, I'm fine.'

The other woman, who I assumed must have been her midwife, clicked her tongue. 'Well, I can't sign off on sending you off so soon after giving birth without anyone to keep an eye on you. You are barely even old enough to drive. Spend the day and we'll see how you're feeling at the end of it, when your mum's back here to help you again. This is a big deal, you know.'

The reply was belligerent. 'Of course I'm old enough to drive. I'm seventeen. I just can't afford a car yet.'

The door shut as the midwife left the room and the noises from the rest of the ward became more muted. It was like the recorded soundtrack of what someone might think a hospital should sound like in a movie. Shoes, the occasional shout, a lot of beeping. For a maternity ward, there were surprisingly few baby cries.

I took a sip of the overly diluted orange juice that had come with my breakfast. The only other time I had been in hospital in my life was getting my tonsils out when I was eight. Then, Mum had camped out on a chair next to the bed with me, passing me ice blocks to numb the pain. I'd been pleased to have her undivided attention for a whole forty-eight hours. What was the protocol for talking to someone else within the same room? Should I just strike up a conversation? Did she even know I was there?

I cleared my throat. 'You okay?'

She shifted her weight in the bed. The sheets made a static rustle. 'Are you talking to me?'

I grimaced. Maybe it wasn't the right thing to do after all. 'Yeah, just checking.'

The metal base of the bed groaned again. 'I'm okay. I'm over this place. Just want to get out.'

I felt the opposite. Once I was out into the car park, it would all be on me. Although no doubt Ellen would be on our doorstep as soon as she could get to the flat, wanting to shadow my every move and remind me that there was a better way to do it. When would my own mother show? Maybe it was best not to think about it.

'When was your baby born?' I tried to keep the conversation going.

'A few hours ago. I thought I only had to stay a couple and then I could go.'

There was the unmistakeable sound of a baby starting to snuffle. I could hear my roommate curse under her breath. A minute passed and the snuffling turned into a grumble, which threatened to turn into a full-blown cry.

A rustle indicated she had picked her baby up. Under the curtain, I could see she was on her feet, swaying from one foot to the other, muttering under her breath. 'I can't even remember any lullabies.'

I laughed, then cringed when Holly stirred. 'Neither can I, but I doubt they're going to judge you on the words. Just hum something that sounds a bit relaxing.'

I realised after a minute she was humming a version of a song I'd heard blaring from a car when I went to the supermarket a couple of days earlier. The lyrics were definitely not the type of thing you'd normally hear in a nursery.

Despite her best efforts, her baby was working herself into a frenzy.

Across the room, the curtain was yanked back and Lauren shuffled out. Through the gap in my cubicle curtain, which the orderly had left half open, I could see she was wearing a hoodie that bore a Disney logo. If I had passed her in the street, I would have unquestioningly accepted the idea that she was at least four years younger than seventeen.

Our eyes met as she shifted her baby on to her shoulder.

'I'm Lauren, by the way.'

I waved. 'Renee Campbell. Nice to meet you in this weird way.'

Lauren grinned. 'I'll walk up and down the hall for a bit. Annoy the nurses until they help me.'

I watched her. I was still working out how best to hold Holly but Lauren was slinging her baby around as if she had been attached to her for years.

'You've done that before.'

Lauren shook her head. 'I've spent time looking after my little cousins. They're all the same, pretty much.'

'You think?'

Lauren looked down at her baby, whose little legs were kicking at the air. Holly was somehow still asleep. 'It feels a bit different, I guess. Mackenzie's so tiny. But yeah, once you've dealt with a couple of them, there's not that many surprises.'

I lay back on the bed and tried to scrape a sliver of jam over the floppy piece of toast on my breakfast tray.

'Good luck.' I smiled at Lauren. 'I hope she settles for you soon.'

I watched as Lauren pushed open the door and ventured out on to the brightly lit corridor. The glare of a fluorescent tube bounced off her pink-tinged bleached-blonde hair, pulled up into a messy plait on the back of her head. I pushed my fringe back off my face. My skin was clammy from hours in the unnatural warmth of the maternity ward. When had I last brushed my teeth? I shut my eyes, willing my brain to shut off. Every time I relaxed, something unwelcome would ping in. Was Holly too hot? What was it Felicity had posted about them overheating? The nurses were determined to wrap her as if she was on an intrepid expedition to the Antarctic. Would I stumble on the stairs when we arrived home and drop her? Would we discover the apartment had a toxic mould problem? Helen had posted something in the group about the rate of respiratory diseases being caused by unhealthy old buildings. Our building probably hadn't been properly aired out since 1923. Would she be bullied at school?

I focused on my breaths, counting each inhalation. The room was quieter than it had been all night. I paused. What was missing? I flicked an eye open and watched Holly. After a minute, I jumped to my feet. Stabbing at the call button, I shouted for help. 'My daughter! She's not breathing!'

Chapter Two

Frankie Harbison, 7.33am: 'I told my mum I'm taking a few days away to get some time to myself. She goes, 'Oh, that's nice of Lachlan to babysit while you're gone.' I said, 'Yes, he's very excited to continue being their father.' Honestly!'

I stared at Holly's chest, then dropped to line my cheek up against her mouth to feel her breath. There was nothing. I patted her tummy. 'Holly!'

She started and took a shuddering sigh, then emitted a window-rattling wail. Lauren yanked back the curtain and stared at us. 'She's okay? Is she?'

I nodded. My heart thudding with relief, I collapsed on to the bed and scooped her up to hold her little writhing body against me. 'I think so.'

A nurse pushed past Lauren. 'All okay in here?'

I closed my eyes to push back my tears. 'My baby stopped breathing.'

She cocked her head to look at Holly for a minute.

Her screams had quietened to a whimper. 'Her lips aren't blue, so she's not been oxygen-deprived. Newborns do that sometimes, you know. Stop breathing for a little longer than you'd expect, then start again. It's quite normal.'

I rested my cheek against her little head. Her wails had eased to deep, shuddering gasps. 'It didn't feel normal.'

She nodded. 'I can imagine. We'll keep an eye on her for the next little while, okay? But most likely it's just weird newborn stuff. They keep us on our toes.'

Lauren grimaced at me and retreated to her bed across the room. I shut my eyes, trying to focus on the warmth of Holly's little body against me.

The nurse reached for my book of maternity notes, propped on the small cabinet next to the bed. 'While I'm here, is your bladder emptying normally?'

I stared at her, swaying Holly against me. 'I guess so? I've been a bit busy to keep track.'

'But you have gone to the loo since you had your baby.'

I nodded. My heart was still racing.

'And bowel movements?'

'Wait, mine or hers?'

Holly's had been a surprise. Deep black and sticky like something you might find underneath a car. It had taken a lot of baby wipes to get that off.

'Yours. We need to make sure that everything is functioning as it should before you leave.'

I sat up. Holly's eyes had drifted closed again. 'Wait, I'm leaving?'

'We'll keep you in for the next few hours at least, check out this breathing business, but you've been here the night you delivered and then last night – that's normally about the right amount of time for new mothers.'

'I was hoping to stay here until my milk came in – I've heard ...'

She cut me off. 'You're willing to wait another day or two here? It could take that long, you know. For some women it's a week before the milk really takes hold.'

I bit my lip. What did they expect me to do without it at home? The way she was looking at me indicated I was not meant to argue. 'I guess not.'

The nurse – I could see from her badge that her name was Liz – stared at me.

'Oh, sorry. No. No bowel ... whatever.'

When Liz left the room, I reached for my phone. Someone else had to have gone through this before. Balancing Holly against me, I tapped out a post to the group. Could it really be normal?

At this time of the morning, the responses were swift. Someone had had their child stop breathing for a full twenty seconds. Another had installed a sensor in her son's bassinette to ensure she knew the minute his movements stopped. She reckoned she hadn't had a full night's sleep in three years. Someone else cautioned against the type of monitor that clips on to a nappy. 'My son's kept falling off and every time the alarm would bleep and I'd convince myself he was a goner. But he was always just pissed off that this weird vibrating thing had woken him up.'

Felicity sent me a private message. 'Are you okay?'

I bit my lip. 'I guess so. It gave me a pretty massive fright.'

The icon indicated she was typing for several minutes before the reply finally showed up. 'Honestly, I think babies do these things to terrify you. Let me know if I can do anything to help.'

Lauren chortled from across the room. 'Want me to keep an eye on your baby while you go and perform your bathroom duties?'

I rolled my eyes. 'It can wait until my partner gets here. Honestly. I was warned there wasn't much dignity in child-birth but I didn't realise that would continue afterwards.'

'One of them pinched my nipple in the night.'

I had to bite back a giggle. 'What?'

'Mmm.' Her voice was surprisingly mature for someone so young. 'Trying to show me that there actually is some-thing in there to give Mackenzie if I try a bit harder. I am definitely going home even if I have to sneak out.'

'Wow.' I flicked through a magazine Nick's mother had left on the stand next to the bed. There was a film star who allegedly had 'bounced back' from the birth of her baby, rocking washboard abs at the beach six weeks after the birth. I eyed Holly. I couldn't imagine her letting me properly put her down for the next six weeks, let alone finding time to work out. Early on in my pregnancy, Nick had sent me some articles about how exercising while pregnant made for a better birth and healthier baby and various other magic post-pregnancy outcomes. I'd started off humouring him but after the fourth or fifth message I fired back a few home remedies to avert hair loss and he'd taken the hint and kept quiet. Not that he was a good trainer for me, anyway. A good yoga class was more my style, though he claimed it didn't really count. Nick was a fan of things that you could do 'to failure'. I resisted the temptation to tell him that our relationship shouldn't be one of them.

Holly snorted in her sleep. I reached out for the bassinette. Her eyelids were still puffy and her nose was slightly squashed. Despite the smattering of blonde hair on the top and sides of her head, and disappearing down her back, she had no eyebrows at all. I hadn't been prepared for that. I had to stop myself reaching out to stroke her.

I picked up my phone to take a photo to send to the mums' group. They had become my online squad through the pregnancy when my friends found it hard to relate to my angst over which bassinette would be the best bet and what I would want to wear in labour (pretty much nothing, as it turned out). They understood my despair when, in the first flight of pregnancy hormones, I had sobbed for hours when I discovered the batteries in the TV remote had run out. I'd even become an admin more recently, approving membership requests and turning off comments on posts that became a bit too heated.

A few of the women lived near enough to me that we

could form our own real-life coffee group and sign up for antenatal classes together. My friends from work would look at a picture of Holly and see just another newborn baby. The women online would know exactly what went into getting her into the world.

As expected, Felicity commented almost immediately. 'What a gorgeous little one! Those eyelashes!'

I stared at Holly's face. She was right, they looked like something you might pay a week's wages to have stuck on to your eyelids. She definitely didn't get those from me.

I switched over to my messages to Nick. 'Are you bringing me a coffee?'

***

Nick
Age: One day

I transferred all my clients to Sam but that didn't stop me waking before dawn the next day. A rubbish truck clattered down the street, as good as any alarm clock. I reached out in bed for Renee, feeling for the familiar curve of her thigh. It took me a couple of seconds before I remembered that she wasn't there – and why. She was in hospital with my baby. I was a dad. How bizarre.

I rolled out of bed and reached for my iPad on the bedside table. I might now be a father but I wasn't going to have a 'dad bod' if I could help it. I flicked on a high-intensity interval training workout video and recovered one of the dumbbells I'd stashed behind the bedroom door.

Half an hour later, workout complete, I emerged from the shower to the sound of my phone vibrating across the bathroom vanity. Four new messages were propelling it. I stabbed at the button to open them. Renee. Holly had stopped breathing. I spat my mouthful of Listerine. What? I swiped through to the next message. She had started again. Then 'bring coffee'. I pressed her name to call her, trying to keep my voice calm. 'What is going on? How did she stop breathing? Why?'

She was whispering. 'She's asleep now. It's okay. I'll fill you in when you get here. Apparently it's normal.'

'Normal? How?'

She sighed. 'Just a baby thing. I've got it under control. Get here soon?'

I left my phone in my lap once we had hung up. It was only ten kilometres to the hospital but the two of them seemed very far away. Where was that daydream about me riding in to rescue my little girl from any crisis? Her first health scare and I'd been in the bloody shower.

***

I paced the linoleum outside the maternity ward, waiting for the doors to click open at 8am. I leant against one wall, scrolled through my phone. Walked to the other, browsed the pointless pamphlets on the wall. As if we didn't know that we needed to give our kids fruit and vegetables. The coffee in my hand was going cold. I had tried to find a bagel with buffalo mozzarella and tomato to bring her to mark the end of her nine months of soft-cheese-abstinence, but the best I could come up with was a melted camembert mess from the supermarket. As it cooled it was starting to look a lot less appetising and more like stodgy plastic wrapped in carbohydrate.

My phone buzzed in my pocket. I clocked the caller ID. Frank, one of my longest-serving personal training clients. We would normally catch up every other morning.

I sent him a text message to remind him. 'Sam's got you today. See you in a couple of weeks, okay?'

He replied a minute later. 'Righto – keen to run a couple of ideas I spotted online past you.'

Whatever blog he'd been scanning, it could wait. Owning my own business had been such a huge dream that it felt ungrateful now to resent the work that came with it. But it would have been nice to be able to take the odd day off – you know, for things like having a new baby – without having a work call to worry about.

At last the intercom buzzed and the automatic doors made a subtle click. I took a hesitant step towards them and they slid open. A woman in scrubs nodded in what I assumed to be welcome as I half-jogged past the nurse's station.

Renee was lying flat on her back, staring at the ceiling,

when I arrived. Pulling a chair out a fraction from the window, I squeezed between her bed and the wall, kissing her cheek as I sat. Holly was asleep in her bassinette, her little face serene in repose. Renee shot me a warning glare as I approached, ready to drop a kiss on to her round cheek. 'Let her sleep.'

Renee seemed to tense every muscle in her body as I sank into the chair, only relaxing when the plastic legs stopped squeaking against the ground under my weight. Her smile looked forced as she wriggled to sit up. 'You're here.'

I handed her the coffee and bagel. 'Told you I would be. Here as soon as they let me in. What happened? She stopped breathing?'

She put her hand over her face. 'Don't ask. It was terrifying. It felt like she didn't sleep at all until then and then after that I was too scared to take my eyes off her. I'm so freaking exhausted.'

I twisted her fingers between mine. 'Why do they think she stopped?'

She spread her hands. 'Apparently they do these things to freak out their mothers. But they want to keep an eye on her this morning, anyway. Make sure no repeat performances. Then they kick us out and it's all on you and me. Did they warn us this might happen? I don't think they did.'

I shook my head. We'd had a terrifying prenatal first aid session where a couple of ambulance officers had taught us how to help a choking baby with an over-the-leg-back-whacking manoeuvre that looked almost worse than the alternative. But no one had said anything about babies deciding breathing might be optional.

'Can you get some sleep now? I'll keep an eye on her. Promise. I can manage.'

She stared at me as if I'd suggested she pop out for a quick cross-country ski. 'You'll wake me up if she needs me? She might be hungry soon.'

I nodded. Her eyes were too wide. It reminded me of when she would stay up all night for days before a big event, running through seating plans and drinks lists. Except back then, no one was expecting her to keep it up for eighteen years.

'I promise. You have nothing to worry about.'

She turned on her side, first one way, then the other. I pulled out my phone and scanned a news site, in case my gaze on her was somehow karmically keeping her awake. Ten minutes later a trolley clattered by just as the humming air conditioning seemed to change gears. Renee sat up. 'This is ridiculous.'

A doctor poked her head into the cubicle. 'All okay here?'

Renee squeezed her eyes shut. 'It's too hard to sleep here. I'm shattered.'

The doctor nodded. 'I know.' She edged over to the bassinette, where Holly was still asleep. 'No more breathing episodes?'

Renee shook her head.

'Okay. We can probably go ahead and start the process to discharge you. Probably just baby apnoea. There's no evidence that those sorts of episodes are any sort of precursor to anything more serious, so you don't need to worry about that. Are you two confident that you could get back here if need be, you have access to a car?'

Renee frowned. 'But what do we do if it does happen again at home?'

The doctor clicked a pen. 'I expect you'll find you just wait a couple of seconds and she'll probably click back into the normal rhythm herself. But you know if you're worried at any stage, you can call for help.'

I took Renee's hand when the doctor had gone and massaged her palm with my thumbs. 'We'll look after her together. We can do it. Take turns sitting with her if we need to.'

My phone buzzed. I swiped at it to turn it off. Whatever Frank had discovered about his quadriceps or his metabolism, it could wait. Renee's gaze travelled over my shoulder and out the window.

I rubbed her forearm. 'Sorry. I'll turn the phone off so we're not hassled with my work stress.'

It took her a second to realise I'd spoken. 'Oh no, it's fine. I didn't really notice. It all just seems a bit like another world right now. I'm in my baby bubble.'

Holly was starting to stir, raising her tiny hands to her face. The way she frowned was just like her mother. 'It's a beautiful bubble to be in.' I squeezed Renee's arm again, hoping to prompt a smile.

She switched her gaze to Holly. After a pause that was a little too long, she sighed. 'Yes. It is.'

***

I'd always thought I was a pretty careful driver. I wasn't one of those teenagers with a modified car, racing other drivers at the lights. I had had one speeding fine my entire life, when I didn't realise that an open road had narrowed to a residential speed restriction.

But it turned out that driving my baby daughter home in the car was another thing, entirely. I'd never driven so slowly, paused for quite so long at stop signs or railed so hard at stupid, reckless overtaking manoeuvres as I did on the drive home from the hospital.

It took until early afternoon for the nurses to sign off the paperwork to let us out. By then, Renee was beside herself with tiredness, refusing lunch and drifting off as she held Holly to feed.

She sat in the back of the car next to the baby capsule we had laboured over installing a week earlier. As we pulled out of the car park, Renee threaded her arm through the car seat's handle as if Holly might fly out the window if she was not physically restrained by her mother. I caught her eye in the rear-view mirror as an elderly woman in an ageing hatchback cut us off at the last roundabout before the turn off to our street. 'Has it always been this bad? Elderly hooligans?'

Renee smiled slowly. 'Maybe you're usually one of them.'

***

I pulled the car in to our designated parking spot in the semi-underground car park that went with our block of flats. There were six in the building but somehow the ones on the top two floors got two spots each while Renee and I had to squeeze our little car into a spot in the corner next to the rubbish bins.

'This feels a bit weird.' I reached for Renee's hand to help her out of the car.

She looked back over her shoulder as she unclipped Holly's seat from the base and carefully extracted her from the car. 'What do you mean?'

'It's not just our place now, is it? It's our "family home".' I made little air quotes with my fingers.

She rolled her eyes. 'It's still our flat. There's still that red wine stain in the lounge and the shower that only sometimes has decent water pressure. Have you even washed the towels?'

Damn. I knew there was something I'd forgotten. I'd bought a couple of bunches of white tulips from the shop on the corner and popped them on the dining table but I'd forgotten about the laundry. I scuffed the toe of my sneaker on the ground. 'I've made sure the dodgy radiator in our bedroom's working properly. The Moses basket is all set up in there if that's where you want her to sleep.'

Renee hoisted the capsule on to her hip. 'Yes. She needs to be in with us for at least the first six months.'

I stepped aside to let her go ahead of me up to the flat. 'I bought her a night light that can go on half strength.

Elliott told me it's easier to get them back to sleep if it's not too bright when you're changing them or whatever.'

Renee rocked Holly as she waited for me to unlock the door to the staircase to our flat. 'What colour is it?'

'Oh ... kind of yellow? Orange?'

She nodded. 'Just as long as it's not blue.'

'Blue?'

'Bad for sleep habits, I think.'

***

Renee
Age: Two days

Somehow, Holly was still asleep when we got home. Then she continued to sleep as I transferred her to the Moses basket, which Nick pulled through from the bedroom to the lounge so that we could watch her little chest rise and fall as we sat on either side of the room, trying not to stare at each other.

I shot Nick a look as he leant over to look at her serene little face. Was he doubting my stories of a night of sleeplessness? She'd only woken for a couple of feeds then dropped straight off again.

Frankie had sent a message before we left the hospital. 'Don't worry about the schedules or anything they try to tell you to do,' she'd written. 'You just listen to your baby.

Go with the flow and fit in with her. Luna didn't have any
sort of recognisable routine for twelve weeks.'

I'd closed that message quickly. Twelve weeks! Did all
the daytime sleep mean she would be up all night?

I leant back against the sofa cushions and tried to
switch my mind on to anything else. There was a waft
of something unusual in the air. A bit like a hotel swimming pool when the person on the lounger next to you
was wearing too much cheap perfume. I looked up at
Nick, who was halfway to the kitchen. 'Have you been
cleaning?'

He smiled at me over his shoulder. 'I wanted it to be
nice for you and Holly.'

'Oh. What cleaning product did you use?'

He frowned. 'Just the usual, I guess? Whatever was in
the cupboard.'

I heaved myself up off the couch, gingerly shifting
my weight from my arms to my legs. 'Better open some
windows. Who knows what's in the fumes of that stuff?
I meant to buy some of the environmentally friendly one
before I went into hospital, but I totally forgot. Can you
put it on the shopping list?'

Nick watched as I pushed open two windows above
Holly's head. 'I've just turned the heating on again.'

'I'm just concerned about her breathing. You know
asthma runs in my family. Anything could aggravate it.'

Nick ducked his head and concentrated on switching
the kettle on. 'Okay. Sorry. Want anything to eat?'

'Actually, I might take you up on that offer of taking turns watching her if that's okay. I need some sleep myself.'

I pushed open the bedroom door. The bed was unmade, a basket of clean washing still waiting to be put away at the end of it. And he'd worried about cleaning the kitchen.

'Do you want your tea?' He appeared behind me, cup in hand.

I took it from him, placing it on the bedside table. 'I might have it later. Wake me if Holly is upset?'

***

The afternoon was giving way to evening gloom when I jolted awake. Nick was sitting on the end of the bed, holding Holly in the crook of one arm. She was flailing at the air, getting ready to scream. I reached for her. 'What time is it?'

'Almost half five. You slept a good couple of hours.'

I cringed. 'I feel worse.' I wrestled off the clasp of my bra so that Holly could find her way in.

'It's better if we try to feed her before she gets so worked up. Makes it easier.'

He nodded. 'Want something to eat?'

'I guess. What have we got?'

'Casseroles, mainly. Your friends have been dropping off all sorts of your weird vegetarian things while you've been sleeping. Your internet friend Ruth dropped off about six frozen things.'

I frowned at him. He put up with the time I spent chatting to the group but didn't yet seem to accept any of them were quite as good as 'real' friends – basically, anyone I'd met anywhere apart from online. Even he would have to be impressed by Ruth, though. She was wrangling her own baby and a teenage stepson. How she found time to cook for anyone else was beyond me. 'She's a good sort. When's your mum coming around?'

Holly pulled off and I shifted her over on to my shoulder, jiggling her awkwardly.

'I told her to give us a couple of days. That's what you want, right?'

'Yeah, I guess.'

I could feel he was watching me. Usually any mention of his mother was enough to provoke a fit of eye-rolling. She meant well. My ex, Jordan, had a mother who made no secret of the fact that she thought I wasn't good enough for her precious (flaky, unreliable, dishonest) son. Ellen, by comparison, was so overly nice that she made me feel guilty and irresponsible.

She would start cleaning the stove while she chatted in the kitchen. Putting dishes away when she came for lunch. Nick claimed that she was trying to be helpful but I always felt it was as if it was a silent judgment that I should have got to it first.

'What about your mum?'

I grimaced. 'Who knows. I don't even know if she got my message.'

Nick's eyes widened. 'You haven't heard from her?'

I wriggled on the bed, trying to find a comfortable way to balance Holly against my body. Surely my mother's unreliability could not still be a surprise to Nick. 'Not yet.'

He stared at me. 'Wouldn't she want to know?'

'She's busy. Off on a cruise with that guy—'

'Henry.' We finished the sentence in unison.

'Yeah, him. He's taken her to Alaska or something.'

'But her first grandchild ...'

I looked at my hands. 'Holly will still be here when the cruise finishes, right? Those whales or whatever it is they're looking for might not be.'

'Can I get you a cushion or something?' Nick gestured at the bed. 'I don't know what to do to help.'

'I'm not sure there's much you can do unless you can grow some of these.' I gestured at my chest. 'It's all kind of a one-woman job.'

I stared down at Holly, pulling my mind back from a vision of my mother. What must it have been like for her to have her dream of a little family come crashing down when I was barely older than Holly? I could imagine the fierce protectiveness she must have felt, bundling me into her little campervan and telling Dad where to stick his money. It was just the two of us for so long – it took more than twenty years for her to even consider another relationship and I only had one boyfriend before Nick, always sure that the world was either going to desert me like my dad or prove to be lovable but flaky, like Mum.

I realised I was crying, though I couldn't work out why. Holly was the most beautiful baby in the world. I'd already looked online to find out what the requirements were to get her into television commercials. She seemed a sure bet for a contract for a nappies ad by the time she was six months old, provided she could master staying awake at the appropriate time of day. Nick reached for my arm. 'Hey.'

I pulled it back. 'Just baby blues.'

'Really?'

I sniffed the kind of unattractive snort that you no longer care about once you've given birth in front of a room full of strangers. 'It's okay. I really just need to take it easy for a little while.'

He kissed the top of my head like a TV sitcom dad. 'I'll go and get us something to eat.'

I watched as he shut the door of the bedroom behind him. My cup of herbal tea still sat on the bedside table, now completely cold. It smelt like dish soap and leaves. Was it the one that was meant to help with breast milk? I took a tentative sip. That stuff was expensive. Holly sighed and snuffled as she dozed off again.

***

'Hey, Ren.' Nick stuck his head around the door twenty minutes later. 'Sorry to bother you. Half an hour for that casserole, you reckon?'

How was I to know? I did not even know what type of casserole he was looking at. 'I guess?'

He nodded and ducked out. There was a clattering from the kitchen. A drawer slammed shut. 'Where are the oven trays?'

I eased Holly off and into the crook of my elbow and stood up. 'In the oven.'

I padded out towards the kitchen. Nick was pulling cling wrap from tin foil, sliding the wobbly casserole on to a silicone tray that I had kept under the sink for baking. 'Not that one, use one of the metal ones.'

He ducked his head. 'Sorry.'

I pointed to a notepad on the end of the kitchen bench. 'I was thinking we could note down Holly's feeds and nappies and things? So we know what's going on. No doubt Karen will ask me when she comes round to check on us.'

Nick slammed the oven shut.

'I'm aiming to feed her every two hours for at least fifteen minutes.' I jotted down the numbers down one side of the paper, Holly against my shoulder on the other side. 'Then she is meant to have half an hour or so of playing, then back to bed. As she gets older, we just extend her play time. I don't think she had a proper feed just now.'

Nick traced the numbers down the page. 'Okay. That looks fine. But what does she ... do?'

'What do you mean?'

'What's play time when you're a day or two old?'

I paused. The book with the shiny woman on the front

hadn't covered that bit. 'I guess just like lying on her mat or whatever. Play her music, show her stuff. They are meant to hear 15,000 words a day to build their vocabulary and get all the brain stuff going. Lots of eye contact.'

Nick stroked the back of Holly's head. 'I saw a workout online, where you use your baby instead of a weight ...'

I stiffened, an image of Nick throwing his weights to the floor when he had finished a set at the gym dancing in front of my eyes. 'Maybe when she's a bit older?'

I followed him through to the lounge, where he sat on the couch and reached out for Holly. Her eyes flicked open as she was passed into her father's arms and she made a noise that sounded a bit like a put-out cat. He jiggled her.

'Let me.' I reached for her. As I scooped Holly up, the mewling turned into a roar. Her little scrunched up face was growing rapidly pinker.

'What's upsetting her? Was it me?' Nick wiggled back on the couch as if to get out of her line of vision.

'I don't know. She shouldn't be hungry again so soon.'

I started to pace the floor, humming the one lullaby I could remember. Could she be cold? Reacting to something I'd eaten? Worse – allergic?

Nick watched. 'What can I do? I feel kind of useless.'

'How am I meant to know? I haven't done this before either.'

***

The midwife rapped on the glass pane of the front door early the next morning.

Nick answered the door, throwing an old hoodie over a pair of rugby shorts. 'She's in the bedroom,' I heard him say as he ushered her through.

I was sitting on the bed, pillows piled behind me, Holly balanced on my arm, which was propped up by a TV table.

'How's everything going?' Karen lowered her bag on to the floor. 'I'm so sorry I couldn't be there. Did the hospital team take good care of you?'

I turned to face her. I could see in the dressing table mirror over her shoulder that my skin was pale and dark shadows were pooling under my eyes. 'It was fine. But this is the only way I can get her to sleep longer than half an hour or so, and it kills my shoulder.'

Karen reached for my maternity notes book. 'Not sleeping well?'

'I'm so tired I put my empty bread bag in the fridge and threw my phone in the bin after I made my toast this morning.'

Karen bit her lip as though she was trying not to laugh. 'Is there anyone who can give you a break, take her for a bit so you can get a nap?'

Nick coughed. 'My mum's really excited to help where she can. You just say the word, Ren.'

Karen nodded. 'Good idea. I won't weigh Holly today because she's asleep and it would be a shame to wake her. Babies do tend to lose a bit of weight after the birth, anyway. How are you recovering, Mum?'

So now I'd lost my name, too? I made a helpless gesture with her free hand. 'I'm having the most ridiculous hot flushes in the night.'

She grimaced sympathetically. 'Night sweats. It's a hormonal thing. Won't last.'

'They'd better not! I'm waking up absolutely drenched. It's horrible. Then I get so cold. And the afterpains ... no one told me about those.'

Karen grimaced. 'Sorry. Not much you can do but ride it out, I'm afraid. You might be able to get a herbal supplement to help a little bit but, like all this baby stuff, it's just time that sorts it.'

***

Renee
Age: Three months

When we first got home from hospital, it had almost felt like we needed a roster to keep all the people in line who wanted to visit. There was awkward Mona from work who had to come over and pretend that we didn't remember she'd once said she couldn't stand babies. Nick's parents. His brother. Natalie, who brought a tiny, expensive and completely impractical pair of possum-fur slippers. But by the time Nick was back to work and I could actually do with some help holding Holly while I attempted a shower, only a hardy handful kept turning up.

Ellen was the only one who remained completely reliable. She had started coming over for two hours every morning and I'd begun to look forward to the clatter of her sensible-heeled court shoes on the steps outside the door, and the chance to pass Holly off to waiting, competent arms and slink back to bed to shut my eyes. Unlike Nick, who always looked slightly possum-in-the-headlights when I tried to get him to take over, Ellen had a comfortably capable way of folding Holly into her body.

She still wasn't really sleeping. Longer stretches, definitely, but we were up four times a night at least. I'd asked the group for advice after an appointment at the doctor's where my mind had gone completely blank when I'd been asked for my date of birth.

'Is it possible that lack of sleep is actually eating my brain?' I typed out. 'I'm sure I get more stupid by the day.'

Frankie replied almost immediately. 'Have you thought about a cranial osteopath? They can honestly work wonders.'

Helen responded next. 'Not sure there's any evidence to prove that osteopaths can help babies. In fact, I think there's some dangers.'

Someone else added another message: 'Have you checked for tongue ties?'

Ruth replied next: 'No advice. Just solidarity. I remember

when Xavier was first born I was barely sleeping and one night I launched myself across Simon and kind of slapped him back into bed because I thought he was the baby falling out. He was not impressed.'

From the bedroom, I could hear Ellen whispering to Holly in the next room, then humming. There was a rustling sound – she must have been transferring Holly to her portacot. I tensed, waiting for the grumble, but there was only silence. There was more rustling, then the sound of the hallway cupboard opening.

I leant half out of bed and pulled open the bedroom door. 'What are you doing?'

Ellen shot me a look over her shoulder. 'Just thought I'd mop the kitchen floor, love. You get some rest.'

I shut my eyes. 'I'll do it when I wake up, promise.'

She frowned. 'Get some rest. You've a chance while Holly's out to it.'

Her mouth dropped open in horror when I brushed away a tear. 'Please leave it?'

Ellen scurried over to me and pulled me towards her.

We had probably only hugged twice before in our lives but I let myself sink into her, my head resting almost on top of hers. 'Sorry. Probably just hormones.'

She looked at me. 'What's the matter?'

I looked away. 'It's silly.'

She put her arm around my shoulders. 'I bet it's not.'

I took a deep breath, focusing on pulling my breathing into a regular rhythm. 'It's just that it feels like I can't get anything right at the moment. Now even my floor's not good enough.'

She bit her lip and leant back to look in my eyes. 'Renee. Sweetheart. You're doing a wonderful, wonderful job. I'm just trying to help.'

She watched me as I pulled my face into place. 'It's hard for everyone else to know what to do because Holly needs you so much. So we just do what we can. It's no judgment on you. I promise.'

I swallowed a lump of guilt in my throat. 'Sorry,' I croaked. 'I'm just super tired. I'll lie down.'

She patted my shoulder. 'I'll come and get you if Holly is upset. Let me do some chores. I promise you won't even notice. It'll make me happy.'

I raised an eyebrow. 'Happy?'

She grinned. 'Not the chores themselves but, you know ... helping. Promise.'

***

I'd wondered what I'd do to pass the time when I was finally on maternity leave. Would I read books in the sunshine with my dreamily sleepy baby beside me? Or go for walks with her in the extremely expensive pram, wearing my suck-it-all-in leggings?

But I still hadn't worked out how to move Holly once she was asleep. She'd become heavier and heavier lying on my chest. Counting her breaths, I'd get to fifty before

I poked at her a bit like an unexploded bomb. But invariably as soon as I slid one arm under her to try to shift her across to the portacot, she'd bite her lip and scrunch up her nose, pushing herself up on her arms to peer at me like I was some form of alien life. It was only when I lay very still again and allowed her to slump back across my chest that she'd give me a dreamy, gooey grin and settle back to sleep. So at least half of the day's naps were still spent with her on me, her body weight pinning one arm down. The free arm went a bit numb if I tried to hold my book or phone in any one position for too long. As for walking, I was still recovering trust in my body. It's a notable day the first time you sneeze and have to change your pants. For the first three days after Holly was born I was also completely incapable of reining in any flatulence. That was nice when we had visitors. Even three months on I still wouldn't want to laugh too hard while standing upright.

After twenty-five minutes of staring at the ceiling, trying to force myself to sleep, I gave up. The house was empty – Ellen and Holly had disappeared off out on a trip around the block.

I flicked on the TV at low volume. Nick and I had been watching some sort of police drama. I couldn't get into it. It used to be our thing, curling up on the couch together and chatting while we watched Netflix. I tried, because I could tell he was getting twitchy about the lack of time we were spending together. But my lack of short-term memory meant I could barely remember the names of the people I had worked with 14 weeks earlier, let alone keep up with which character was which and who might have murdered the beautiful woman in the TV programme. It was always the woman who came to some sort of brutal end, wasn't it? Nick offered to take back every negative thing he'd said about *Grey's Anatomy* so we could binge watch it together but the first episode we'd tried had revolved around a sick kid and I'd stayed up all night Googling the chances of Holly having the same disorder.

If I was at work I'd be going into a Monday morning meeting with my iPad calendar open on year-view. I'd wanted to be an event manager since I took over organising my own birthday parties from my mother the year I turned eleven and she wrote invitations but then forgot to post them. I'd got my first full-time event planning gig the same year love-of-my-life-turned-ghoster Jordan had shuffled out and it had been the most constant thing ever since.

I'd just finished a big product launch for a whiteware company before I took leave. It had gone flawlessly, down to the waiters in matching white-and-gold outfits and the goodie bags shaped like washing machines. But by the end of the evening my feet were aching, and conversing with drunk salespeople was becoming less and less bearable. Now I couldn't imagine how I'd ever go back.

***

I was halfway through loading the dishwasher when I heard Holly and Ellen clatter through the front door. Ellen was shhing valiantly but Holly was grumbling in a way I knew was guaranteed to become a meltdown. I slammed the stainless steel door shut. 'Coming, darling.'

By the time I was beside them, approximately two metres away, she was turning pink with rage. I scooped her up from Ellen. The back of her onesie felt warm and slightly gritty. The smell was unmistakeable. 'Let me do that,' Ellen said and reached out for her.

I brushed her away. 'It's fine, honestly.'

As I took her through to the bathroom to change her nappy, I sent Nick a text: 'Changing a super-sized poonami! Want a pic?'

I stuck one finger between her ankles as instructed in the baby books, and wrestled a wipe under her. She screwed up her face and arched her back. As I reached over for another wipe, she wriggled clockwise, smearing more of the yellow gloop over the change table and up her back.

I'd almost exhausted the packet of wipes by the time I'd got her changed. Her clothes lay in a pile on the floor. Holding her to my shoulder, I squatted, using one hand to roll them into a ball. Soiled leggings in one hand, Holly in the other, I paused. No one told you that this was why prenatal exercise was important. You needed good muscles to get up from a very deep squat. I heaved myself up. There was that familiar leak again.

There was a knock at the door. 'Just me.' Ellen peered around the bathroom door. 'All okay here? I didn't mean to pass her over to you like that.'

I exhaled. 'I know. It's fine. Could you hold her for me? I need to get her into a fresh change of clothes. But I need to sort myself out first ...'

She reached for Holly and bounced her on her hip as they followed me towards the bedroom.

I looked back over my shoulder. Clad only in a nappy, Holly's little pink body was so deliciously squishy that I actually understood why some people talked about wanting to eat a particularly cute baby. I usually settled for blowing raspberries on her back. Ellen's face was lit up with an ear-to-ear smile as she bumped Holly from one hip to the other, singing some sort of nursery rhyme. Holly had forgotten her outrage and was reaching across Ellen's face for her dangling earring. She ducked her head away just as the chubby little fingers made contact.

'She's barely had a feed this morning but I don't know what I'm meant to do to get her to take an interest. I can't force her to eat, can I?'

Ellen kissed her on the top of the head. 'Try again in a bit. She doesn't seem too stressed about it at the moment. Not that long until she can try solids?'

I wriggled a fresh top over my head. 'A couple of months maybe. I can't wait. It still feels like I've been keeping sandpaper in my bra for the past year.'

Ellen grimaced in sympathy and checked her watch. 'You can still make it if you go now?'

I stared at her. 'What? Go where?'

Ellen smiled again at Holly's upturned face. 'You mentioned that your coffee group was meeting up.'

I felt my shoulders slump. Leaving the house. It still wasn't one of my favourite things to do.

Ellen patted my arm. 'You should go, it'll be good for you to see your friends. I'll get some more housework done for you while you're out, the noisy stuff.'

***

I squeezed into a pair of jeans I had not worn for seven months and pulled a breastfeeding top over my head – one complete with a weird opening that was meant for easy access but always just reminded me of the puppet Zippy from a programme I'd watched growing up. I was sometimes tempted to manipulate it to make my top 'talk' when I got sick of people getting too close to Holly when we were trying to do the supermarket shopping. Someone at my baby shower had given me one of those covers that you're meant to take out with you to breastfeed discreetly in public but I'd not even bothered to try it. Even Nick agreed it was only fair that we start putting a blanket over our own heads when we had dinner, if we were going to expect it for Holly.

I regarded myself in the mirror. There was no avoiding the tiredness. How long was that going to go on for? People kept promising me an end in sight. When she was six weeks old everything would change. When she was twelve weeks.

Now, the line I was being given was that she would start to sleep better when she was moving around a bit more on her own. It was only a pity I had to wait until she was about seven months for any of that to happen.

Ellen was sitting on the bed when I emerged from the bathroom, holding Holly on her lap so that she could push down with her sturdy little legs, as if she were on some sort of soft trampoline.

'Doesn't Mummy look pretty?'

She turned Holly so she could face me. Her wide face stretched into a gummy grin.

'Shall we go, sweet pea?'

If I'd had the choice, I would have suggested some sort of pyjama party where people could turn up in their bath-robes if they wanted. I'd been virtually living in mine and it was starting to smell decidedly questionable, a mix of sweat and old breastmilk.

***

The group was already assembled around a big table in the middle of the café when I arrived. The four women all looked as if they came from a different country to the one I was stranded in. And theirs had hair dryers and makeup. I forced a smile as I slid into a seat next to Ruth, who was expertly downing a coffee while she fed her son.

She kissed my cheek. 'Lovely to see you. How's Holly?'

I gestured to her. 'Still as cute as ever.'

She grinned. 'Morning, darling.' She leant over and peered into the stroller that I had parked inexpertly next to the long table. Holly kicked a leg in response. It was clad in a bright pink sock. Where had the cute little furry Ugg boot gone that was meant to be covering it? I would never have purchased such a ridiculous item for her myself – not when she seemed to be going up a shoe size every other week – but it had arrived in the post from Natalie and it would be just my luck that she'd turn up for an impromptu visit and want to see them on.

Ruth was still staring at Holly. 'Isn't she just the most perfect little baby? Look at her gorgeous little mouth. She's so serene in there, taking it all in. If it was Xavier, he'd have started bellowing by now.'

'Actually, I think she hates me.' I pulled the blanket up to Holly's chin. She was awake, staring at the toys dangling from the hood. 'Give it three minutes and she'll be complaining.'

Ruth laughed. 'Pardon?'

'I'm joking ... partly.' I forced a smile. 'It just feels like she doesn't want anything to do with me sometimes.'

Ruth put her hand on my arm. 'Oh, honey. She loves you. She really does, I promise you. You just have to see how her little face lights up when she sees you.'

I shifted in my seat. The other women at the table had fallen silent.

'Don't even worry about it. You're doing great and you'll grow up tight as anything. Promise.' Ruth shifted Xavier so

73

that he was sitting on her lap, facing the rest of us at the table. He reached out for a sachet of sugar and stuck one end in his mouth. 'No one really has it sorted at this stage.'

There was a murmuring of agreement around the table.

'I told my husband that I had diarrhoea when I didn't so that I had an excuse to shut myself in the bathroom for twenty minutes and leave him with Max,' Helen offered at last, from the other end. She stared at me over a huge iced coffee with a swirl of cream on top.

The other women giggled.

'I told mine that the doctor said I wasn't allowed to carry my baby for three months after the caesarean,' Melanie whispered. 'I'm just desperately hoping that no one tells him it's really six weeks. But it's the only way to get him to actually consider how much I have to do in a day.'

A waiter appeared at my elbow and handed me a coffee that I was sure I had not ordered. Fiona smiled from across the table. 'We made an educated guess.'

I mouthed my thanks. Even the smell sent my taste buds into a flutter. But when Holly had been up all night, one of the things everyone seemed to agree on was that a breastfeeding mum drinking caffeine could make it worse. I took a tiny sip before replacing my cup, rolling it around on my tongue.

'It just seems like everyone else is a lot more sorted than I am.'

'Honestly, the group is a bit of a mixed blessing like that,' Ruth said. 'People make out like they've got this most perfect life, don't they? I bet even that Mei woman finds her baby doesn't do what she wants him to sometimes.'

Helen nodded. 'Yeah, there should be an honesty rule. You can't come in until you tell us one brutal truth about your life.'

'Like how my biggest fear was constipation after the birth, not the having the baby bit?' Melanie laughed.

'And how my mother-in-law has these memories of how perfectly behaved all her kids were, sleeping through the night from day one without a peep – the only thing she doesn't add to those stories is that she's almost totally deaf so if my father-in-law didn't hear the kids and wake her she wouldn't have had a chance,' Helen offered.

'And we all know how likely that is,' Ruth said, giggling.

Helen pursed her lips. 'Yep. No wonder my husband's so emotionally stunted.'

The table fell quiet. 'Joking,' she added. 'Mostly.'

I gestured at Ruth to look at Xavier. He'd been gumming the end of the paper sachet and had detached it, allowing half a teaspoon's worth of sugar to transfer to his mouth.

Ruth gasped. 'I promised Simon he wouldn't have any sugar in his first year. This is like a week's worth in one hour.'

'Here.' I passed her a napkin. 'I'm pretty sure you can extract most of that before he swallows it.'

She tilted her son back over her arm and swished at his mouth. He wriggled away from her, licking his lips, his pupils dilating.

I winked at him. 'Maybe I should just start inhaling sugar, Xavi? Might help get my energy levels up.'

***

Nick
Age: Three months

I watched the clock as I guided my last client of the afternoon through her cooldown stretches. She was what Sam and I referred to as one of our RABs – rich and bored. These women were not coming into the gym to achieve any physical results. They turned up so that they could drop into conversation with their friends that they had a personal trainer. They put way more effort into drinking chai lattes at the café next door.

Renee would be beginning the afternoon naptime routine at home. She had been introduced to someone who purported to have all the answers for baby sleep. What to do and when to get that elusive twelve hours through the night. If you asked me, all she had the answers for was how to convince a whole lot of sleep-deprived parents to part with some of their cash.

She had scheduled in our joint calendar the times of each nap during the day. We were meant to have Holly up for an hour and a half, first eating and then playing. Then we'd swaddle her and put her into her bed, patting her bum until she slept. It was down to a science – a pat every other second while 'shhing' at about the level of a loud shower. She looked like a little caterpillar with her arms and legs pinned in place. So far, success had been limited at best. Renee usually managed to get her to sleep within about ten minutes but it was fraught. She'd often emerge from the room covered in tears – most of them from her own eyes. I wasn't even allowed to attempt it on my own yet.

At least I felt useful at work. At home, everything I tried to do was wrong. Even when I tried to make Renee her favourite dinner – a super garlicky pasta bake that I used to roll out whenever she was having a bad day, even though it's totally terrible for my carb count – she turned up her nose. Something about it transferring to the milk and upsetting Holly.

When the gym doors closed behind me on that first morning back, I'd felt like I'd crossed some sort of invisible line and was back on safe ground. It's hard to summon the right response to a photo of projectile vomit when you are in the middle of trying to convince someone whose jeans cost more than your car that they really need to sign their membership over to you. That guy who wanted twice-daily strength sessions would never have been anywhere near a baby, let alone something that came firing out of the baby's body.

It was not until Moira coughed that I realised I had left her in a lunge position a little too long. The over-zealous air conditioning had fired up goose bumps over the exposed

skin of her forearms. 'Okay, shake it out.' I forced a smile.
'Good work today.'

Moira pulled on her cardigan. 'How's your baby?'

I pulled out my phone and showed her the photo I'd
added as my backdrop, feeling a little rush of warmth up
the back of my neck at the sight of her little, squashed face.
'So cute. I can't believe I used to say I didn't want kids.'

She patted my arm. 'I knew you'd love it. How's Renee
holding up?'

I shrugged. 'Fine, I guess? She's a good mum.'

'You tell her that?' She was looking at me hard.

'I think she knows.'

She ran a hand through her hair. 'Make sure. It's hard
for her.'

I frowned. 'It's all a bit new for me, too.'

She shrugged and patted my shoulder. 'I'm sure you're
doing a great job.'

I watched her collect her stuff and shuffle to the
changing rooms, then jogged to the reception desk, where
I retrieved my keys from underneath the overhang of the
desk.

'I'll be back in an hour or so,' I half-barked at the new
woman, Maia, who was minding it. Sam and I had hired
her a month or two earlier but she'd only started the day
before I went on leave. She looked as though she was barely
out of school but she had come well recommended as a
sort of administrative genius. Sam informed me that she
also wanted to train to be a personal trainer. There was

something about her face that looked familiar but I could not place it.

She nodded. 'All okay? Anything I can do to help?'

I paused. It had been a long time since anyone on the front desk had offered any assistance. We'd been through a run of people who thought they were doing us a favour by turning up to work and sitting on their phones all day. 'I don't think so. Thanks though. Can you flick me a text if Sam comes in?'

She smiled. 'For sure. You've got a lot to worry about at the moment. How's it all going?'

I stared at her, unsure how to answer. 'It's ... kind of mad?'

She giggled. 'Yeah, I can imagine. I'm sure you're a great dad.'

***

A taxi had stopped outside our flat when I reached home. A woman was huddled over a bag, extracting money for the driver. She looked up as I approached. 'Nick,' she said with a grin. 'It's lovely to see you.'

I nodded slowly, my brain struggling to keep up with what I was seeing. Had Renee told her to come and visit? Was she expecting this? 'Marjorie. Let me help you with your bag.'

Our steps fell into time as we plodded to the front door, up the stairs to our flat. Bass was thumping from the neighbours across the hall, shaking the ageing brick walls. I pushed open the door.

Renee was sitting on the floor, her laptop on her knees, Holly cradled in my mum's arms on the sofa next to her.

'Hi, honey, I'm just moderating a couple of comments, trying to get some honest discussion going in the group for a change.' She did not look up as I entered the room. 'Holly's refused a nap this afternoon, so I figure we'll just go for bedtime and hope for a fresh start tomorrow.'

I cleared my throat.

Renee looked up and locked eyes with the woman beside me. 'Mum! What are you doing here?'

Chapter Three

Felicity Compton, 11.24pm: 'Whoever came up with that phrase 'sleeps like a baby' was just totally mad, weren't they? Should be 'sleeps like a husband'. I don't know how Scott managed to sleep through both our girls coming down with a tummy bug overnight.'

Renee
Age: Three months

I felt my jaw go slack as my mother strolled into the room and set her bag down against a wall.

'I wanted to come and meet your baby.' She seemed to force a laugh as she took a hesitant step towards me. 'That's allowed, isn't it?'

I blinked. 'I thought you were off on a cruise with ...'

Mum waved her hand at me. 'Henry. No. That wasn't

going to work out. I left the boat in Alaska and popped straight on to a flight here to see you.'

My mother had brought the world's most enormous bag, a huge tattered old suitcase that she had picked up from a charity shop when I was child. It took up most of the space between our apartment's front door and the entrance to our tiny kitchen.

She beamed at me and I smiled despite myself, letting her pull me in for a squish-your-breath-out hug. 'How is everything going? How's my beautiful granddaughter?'

Her hair was still shoulder-length and springingly curly, although it was now a sort of pastel-pink-tinged grey. She'd tried to pull it under control with a colourful scarf.

'We're doing okay.' I exhaled into her shoulder. 'She's gorgeous. And demanding.'

'I couldn't imagine your daughter being anything else.' She stroked my cheek. I frowned. Did she mean my childhood attempts to schedule a dinner time? Or to make sure I had what I needed for whichever school I'd ended up enrolled in for any given year?

'Where shall I put my bag?'

I pointed to our cupboard of a third bedroom. There was only room for a bedside table on one side of the bed and you could virtually reach from one wall to the other while standing in the middle of the room. The walls were still papered with an unsettling faded lime green that I had meant to paint over when we were doing the nursery but had run out of time. But it had a nice view out over the street and you could see the sun set across the city in the evening. The bed sheets were passably fresh.

'How long are you planning to stay?'

She shrugged, her arms spread wide. 'However long I can be useful for, my darling.'

Nick gathered up her bag and disappeared from the room. I avoided his eyes.

She leant over Holly, who stared up at her, scowling, turning a board book over in her hands.

'She's very little,' Marjorie offered, running her finger under Holly's chin. 'They're not exactly cute at this age, are they? But she's definitely got character. Just like you when you were a baby.'

I coughed in surprise. Cute was exactly the word I would have used to describe her – middle-aged-man hairline and all. I picked her up and pulled her to my chest.

Ellen cleared her throat and shuffled to her feet, collecting her sensible handbag from beside the couch. 'I think she's very sweet. I'll be going and let you two catch up. It's nice to see you, Marjorie.'

My mother nodded.

Ellen peered around her to look at me as she made for the door. 'Just let me know if you need anything, Renee. You're doing a great job.' She shot me a pointed look.

Nick returned a few minutes later, his gym shorts swapped for a pair of jeans, a box of teabags in hand. 'Fancy one? I'm just making myself a green tea.'

Mum smiled. 'That would be lovely.'

As he returned to the kitchen I scuttled in behind him, Holly still in my arms.

'You're okay with this?'

He turned, ducking a kiss on my cheek and Holly's. 'What can we do? She's your mother. She wants to see her granddaughter, I guess. Not my place to object.'

'She's only my mother when it suits her.'

He grinned, rifling through a drawer for what was left of the clean crockery. 'Give it a chance. Maybe she'll be helpful to you.'

***

There was splashing through the paper-thin wall from the bathroom as I tapped out another post to the mums' group a couple of hours later.

There were some guaranteed ways to get people talking – in order: sleep, feeding, and fitness. I stayed away from minefields like vaccinations or the merits of breast milk versus formula. I had discovered there was a tightrope to walk between being controversial enough to boost engagement and being so inflammatory that the conversation would turn into an all-out war that led to members quitting in droves.

Mum had offered to wash Holly to give me 'a few minutes to myself' before I attempted Holly's bedtime. It had seemed a reasonable offer – surely even she could manage to hold a child in warm water and apply one of the fourteen different types of baby bath that I was given at my baby shower. She could even skip the lotion afterwards if Holly was in full-on flailing octopus mode.

I turned back to my laptop. In my pre-baby life, running a social media account was something I could do before I even had my first coffee of the morning. We once had a million engagements in a week for a video promoting a comedy festival when a comedian had rolled out a particularly crude joke about a politician who'd been caught having an affair. But dealing with the sleep-deprived mother market was quite a different proposition. I tapped out a couple of lines then deleted them. What would the equivalent of Barney Henderson and his sex-on-the-job gag be for the mum market? Someone who'd joke about bedtime bad habits, maybe. Some tips for better breastfeeding. Felicity had mentioned something about some nipple cream possibly being offered for review. That actually would probably be pretty helpful. My nipples were still a sight to behold.

Something personal would have to be the way to engage them on an otherwise uneventful Tuesday evening.

'Why do I feel like I'm failing already?' I typed.

I sat back and stared at the screen. It was jarring to see the words there in black and white, even from someone who had recently shared intimate details about post-birth bleeding with these women. 'I wanted her so much. I love her so much. But now she's here I just can't feel anything but worry about the world I've brought her into. Does anyone else feel like this? It's normal, right? Other people expected their babies were going to veer from one disaster to another but had them turn out to be pretty normal adults?'

Mum and Holly appeared in the doorway. Holly was wrapped haphazardly in a towel that was meant to be the shape of a baby dinosaur. It had been turned sideways so that one of her arms was stuck in the hood. Mum grimaced and held her out to me. 'Sorry, sorry.' She dusted herself off. 'I forgot I'd promised I'd be at a pottery workshop tonight.'

'What, now?' I scooped the towel around Holly's midriff. 'You can't even dress your granddaughter?'

She shrugged. 'Sorry. Out of time. See you in the morning probably.'

***

Forty-five hours later, I was bent over the cot at a ninety-degree angle, covering as much of Holly's body with mine as I could, shhing in her ear and patting her on her bottom, trying to remember the way the baby whisperer had shown to cup my hand just so around her behind. My lower back had passed through the discomfort stage and was now half-numb. I counted the pats in my head. Ten. Twenty. Thirty. Her grumbles had given way to snuffles before finally quieting to slow, deep breaths. I paused, holding my body a fraction of a centimetre above hers. Every time she took another breath, I allowed myself to straighten a little bit more until I was finally on my feet, clutching my hips like someone three times my age.

I inched backwards out of the room, holding my breath for fear of waking her.

When I opened the bedroom door, Nick was waiting in the hallway. 'What are you doing?' I hissed. He shrugged. 'Moral support?'

I scowled at him and pointed to the lounge. 'Do not wake her up. She's barely napped today and everyone says lack of sleep is terrible for their development.'

We settled on to the sofa, my feet in his lap.

'Do you think she's down for the night?' He rubbed the ball of my foot between his thumbs.

'Not answering that.'

He looked up at me. 'Why not?'

'Might jinx it. One day she'll sleep through but I cannot focus on that. It's like planning to pay off your mortgage by winning the lottery.'

He smiled and worked his fingers across my foot, rubbing the spot on the side where my high heels used to squeeze my toes.

One thing no one tells you about having a baby who doesn't really sleep is that you become obsessed. It's like the worst hobby in the word. I made a list of all the things that people suggested might help: Me cutting out dairy. Me cutting out strawberries. Lavender essential oil. White noise. Sleeping bag with feet. Sleeping bag without feet. Swaddle. The heating turned down a bit. The heating turned up.

I kept a running tally in my phone where I would compare the dismal results of one trial with the worse attempts at another. When we had a better night, I checked which of the things on the list I had deployed.

So far, it seemed that a combination of white noise, swaddle, rain on the roof and an ambient temperature of nineteen degrees Celsius was the optimum. This was not easy to achieve in a block of flats built in the late 1800s where 'ventilation' came in the form of wind whistling through dodgy brickwork and gaps in the window framing.

I'd turned to the baby whisperer when I'd admitted to the group that I still hadn't had more than a couple of hours' uninterrupted sleep.

'Your baby's old enough to sleep train,' Mei had asserted. 'It'll be a couple of days of hard work but then everything will get so much easier.'

'Like crying it out?' I only vaguely knew what was involved in sleep training but just the sound of it was enough to put me off.

'You don't have to just leave her to cry,' another woman replied. 'You can try the verbal reassurance method, where you go in after five minutes, tell her to go to sleep, then after another six, then seven and so on.'

'Isn't that worse? Does telling them to go to sleep actually make them feel any better? I'm pretty sure she doesn't do what I say yet.'

'Honestly, there's no evidence that crying is at all bad

for babies,' Mei replied. 'Some people even say it's good for developing their lungs. It's totally normal and you'll be really grateful you did it.'

Frankie had jumped into the conversation at that point. 'Hold up, it's basically child abuse, leaving your baby to cry. Would you leave your husband sobbing in another room and just stick your head around the corner every few minutes, telling him to shut up?'

'Child abuse? You don't know what you're talking about.'

The conversation had become so heated I'd had to turn comments off and post some funny memes to try to break the tension.

But Felicity followed up with a link to a woman's website who offered a gentler version of sleep training. Sleep hygiene, she'd called it.

The house was so quiet that I could hear the walls creaking with the wind. A truck rumbled along the street outside. 'Was that Holly?' I cocked my head to listen.

Nick gestured to the baby monitor propped in the corner of the room. 'Have a look.'

We huddled over the screen as it powered up. The image of her cot was grainy, black and white.

'What's she doing?'

Nick leaned closer. 'I'm not sure ...'

Her eyes flicked open and she seemed to look directly at the baby monitor camera. She screwed up her nose, then beamed.

I leant back against the sofa cushions. 'That girl is never going to sleep.'

Nick looked at me out of the corner of his eye. 'You're not going to go and try to pat her again, are you?'

I bit my lip. An irresistible urge to giggle pushed up through my chest. I buried my face in my hands, my whole body shaking with laughter.

Nick put his hand around my shoulder, his face horrified. 'Ren, it's okay.'

I looked up at him, wiping a tear from my eyes. 'It's okay, I'm not crying.' I gasped for breath. 'It's funny. Isn't it? Spending all this time worrying and stressing about getting her to sleep. Then she's out for five minutes. It's ridiculous.'

He was still watching me as if unsure what I expected him to do.

'I'm just going to give up.'

He made to get up, then hesitated. 'On what?'

'This whole sleep thing. She can come into bed with me tonight.'

He looked at me. The only time we'd tried to have her sleep with us, I'd fallen out halfway through the night as he starfished further and further across the bed and Holly drifted closer to me.

'Your mum's in the spare room ...'

'Yep.'

'Couch it is, then.'

***

Mummy Needs Help

Renee
Age: Four months

I flicked through my group feed on my phone with one hand as I paced the room, rubbing Holly's back with the other. There was another influx of new members. Sometimes it was hard to tell if they were real people or bots trying to scam us. I pressed the button to let the least suspicious in.

Having Holly in bed with me was helping. But when she woke in the night she would no longer cuddle up and go back to sleep after a feed but would instead latch on and off for what felt like hours every time, or – worse – refuse completely and become inconsolable unless I was walking around the room or offered her the jolly jumper. I decided I had to give the latter up when my eyes drifted shut while I watched her at stupid o'clock one morning. The next thing I knew, she was shrieking, toppling forward like an amateur trampolinist trying to perfect a double flip.

The biggest problem was that even when Holly was asleep, I couldn't stop.

I couldn't leave her side, checking that her temperature was right, her breathing was regular, she hadn't developed some weird rash. If I managed to sit down, I ended up scanning blogs for art projects I could put together for us to tackle when she woke. I had assembled a whole box of pipe cleaners that Holly was meant to run her fingers over to experience new textures, and big black and white boards to prop alongside her when she had tummy time on her hypoallergenic play mat. I enrolled her in a music class. I spent far too long using my index finger to measure the separation of my abdominal muscles, trying to work out whether I was strong enough for a 'baby and me' dance class. Mum would just roll her eyes and hide behind a book when I tried to set up each new Pinterest-inspired educational opportunity. Nick just looked put out that I wasn't putting as much effort into catering to his needs. I'd told him to give Ellen a ring if he needed a mother.

One trick Holly had mastered was doing tiny little semi push-ups. From behind, with her little bald head and chubby arms she looked a bit like one of Nick's clients at the gym.

What Mum hadn't told me when she arrived promising grandmotherly assistance was that she had rented out her house for the remaining time she was meant to be away with Henry and now had nowhere to live. Nick was counting down the days until she could shift back – he'd had to go and buy an air bed to sleep on the floor of the nursery because our couch was about as comfortable as a slab of concrete wrapped in candy floss.

Nick's surge of helpfulness had lost all momentum. He did not seem to realise that if I had to give him a full rundown of how everything should be done, I might as well just do it myself. At the weekend, he told me he was going to take Holly out so that I could have a nap or a bath in peace ... or whatever I would want to do if I uncovered a spare minute in this new life where none of my time was ever my own. But it took me about half an hour to show him where all the supplies were that he would need and then they were only out forty-five minutes.

He scheduled a few hours off work to take a surprise picnic on the afternoon of her first round of vaccinations. Then he looked bereft when I said it wasn't going to work out.

He'd even stopped joining in on my photo sessions with Holly. From the first week, every Saturday, I'd lie with her on the bed and make faces into the camera. Initially, it had been just luck to get a photo where she was pulling a face that didn't make her look like a Cabbage Patch doll. But lately she'd started to try to copy my expressions. One morning, I'd be midway through a very serious monologue about how she was going to grow up to be clever, smart, rich, and successful – you know, no pressure – snapping away, and she started opening and shutting her mouth like a goldfish. So now I know what my daughter thinks I really look like when I'm passing on the secrets of life.

She'd also perfected a deep frown she would produce any time I had the camera on her for too long. Baby modelling plans were put on the back burner but not completely forgotten.

All the things I used to love about Nick were suddenly driving me up the wall. The way he would spring surprises on me to cheer me up when I was becoming overwhelmed with work or other worries. The way his easygoing the-universe-will-deliver approach to life goals was a perfect antidote to my meticulous-but-sometimes-boring planning. Now, I just needed to know what was going on so I could have some chance of feeling a tiny bit in control.

I stomped my way around another circuit of the bedroom. Mum wandered out of the spare bedroom just as Holly's eyes were drifting shut at last.

'You want me to hold her so you can get a few things done around the place?'

I stared at her. 'No!'

She took a step back in surprise. 'Sorry, I was just offering, darling.'

'If I pass you to her, she will wake up. Honestly, Mum.'

Mum's face fell. 'I'll go and tidy up the kitchen a bit then, shall I?' As she turned away, her shoulders shook as if she was trying not to cry.

I followed her through to the next room. She hadn't tidied the kitchen in the whole time she had been staying, not that I was going to bother to point that out. 'Mum, I'm sorry. I didn't mean to upset you. I'm just so tired. If she doesn't get a good nap this time I think I will actually lose my mind.'

She wiped her eye with a tissue that she had stuck in her bra. 'Why don't you let me help you a bit more, so you can get some rest? You let Ellen spend more time with Holly than me.'

I sighed. 'Let's not get into this now.'

She looked at me, her eyes wide. 'Get into what?'

I took a deep breath, trying to keep my voice as quiet as possible for Holly. 'You really want me to say it?'

She nodded.

'Fine. I can't start leaning on you because who knows when you're going to bail? You do know that's what you've been doing for fifteen years? Turn up when it suits then disappear when it doesn't?'

Her mouth hung open. 'Do you really think that? That I'd just leave you and Holly?'

'Yes! It's what you have literally always done. You do what you need to do and who cares about the rest of us. I'm used to it but I don't want it for her.'

Mum stared hard at the countertop. 'I don't know what to say to that. I gave you everything when you were little. I was always there for you.'

'Yeah, in your way, I guess you were. But I wasn't very old before I realised most mothers aren't ditching their lives and running off to a new town every six months and serving baked beans for dinner for a week, are they? What was I, twelve, when I decided to take over all the looking after myself? I don't want that for Holly – having to grow up and have adult worries before she's even a teenager. It's like I've been a mother for twenty years, not a few months.'

'We were best friends!'

'Yeah, we were.' I took a deep breath. 'But I needed a mum. I had enough friends.'

She pushed past me, headed back to the bedroom. 'I'll go out for a bit, get out of your hair.'

***

I settled on the couch, inching Holly down on to my lap, and pulled out my iPad. My heart was still racing. It had been years since I had given my mother a serve like that. My instinct was to race after her and console her but I pushed it down. The group would take my mind off it. My posts about our lack of sleep were generating a steady stream of private messages in my inbox from women who were convinced they were utter failures because they couldn't get their kids to behave like the routines in the books told them they should.

One of them was Lauren, the teenager who'd shared the room with me at the hospital. She said she'd recognised me from the group at the time, though I couldn't have looked more unlike the hair-straightened, perfectly made-up maternity photoshoot picture I was still using for my online profile. I stared at it. What did it say about my current state that I still preferred to present myself to the world in full eight-months-pregnant waddle mode?

She complained that all her friends were going out to a new bar opening but she couldn't join them because no one else could get her baby to sleep. Even she never knew when she would finally be able to get Mackenzie down. I started to tap out a reply. 'There are some benefits to having a baby at thirty. It's been years since I've been to a party like that ...'

I deleted it. Would she think I was telling her that having had a baby as a teenager was a bad thing to do? Instead, I sent her a cheery message reminding her that even by the time her baby was twenty-one, she'd only be a few years older than I already was, and she'd have loads of time to go out. And surely they go to sleep without you well before they're twenty-one. Right?

I followed it up with another message, in case she thought I was brushing her concerns away.

'Don't think the older mothers have it sorted, either. I really have no idea what I'm doing. Every day I get to the evening and think, 'Thank goodness we made it through another one.' Then it takes me an hour and a half to sing and rock her off to sleep. But then about an hour later I wake up in bed next to her and think I've squashed her and have to wake her up to check she's breathing. I honestly think we're all just muddling through as best we can.'

I was sending my iPad to sleep again as my mother clattered through the door, her arms laden with paper bags.

'I've been shopping for Holly,' she whispered, our earlier fight seemingly forgotten.

She emptied the contents of one bag on to the couch. An old hair roller fell out and rolled on to the floor, followed by a dish brush, and one glove with no pair immediately obvious.

'From the rubbish dump?'

She frowned. 'Haven't you heard of heuristic play? I thought this would be right up your alley, with all the stuff you've been doing for her lately. It's wonderful for their brains, playing with everyday objects like this. I knew she'd want me to choose these things.'

She nodded so firmly that her ringlets wobbled.

'Right.'

'It'll be our thing.' She smiled at me tentatively. 'I'll set aside time every day for her and we'll do this together. From what I've read, she'll be a little genius by the time she's three. I bet Mozart was always playing with hair rollers and whatnot.'

'Okay.'

The smile turned into a megawatt beam. 'Wonderful. Wonderful. And I was wondering maybe if you'd like her to come and stay a night at my place when I'm back home? Give you a proper break.'

No way that was happening until Holly was at least six. Mum would probably forget Holly was there and head off on a three-week road trip or something. 'Let's just do one step at a time, okay?'

Mum's play project lasted longer than I expected. When Holly woke from her nap, she was presented with a wooden spoon and an old metal colander. She tentatively reached for them.

'Try banging them together,' my mum chirped, guiding Holly's hands.

I caught her eye. 'Really?'

She grinned as Holly started waving them in the air, sometimes connecting the kitchen implements and sometimes wildly off course. 'I'll have moved out before she has enough co-ordination to reach peak volume.'

***

That evening, when I traipsed into the kitchen after settling Holly for her 'bedtime', Nick was sitting at the little trestle table in the corner, the colander, wooden spoon, sieve and whisk spread out around him. He was staring at a piece of paper. I had that disarming jolt of otherness. Sometimes I looked at him and was shocked at how attractive he was. He was still almost completely wrinkle-free and hadn't a grey hair in sight. Meanwhile, I looked to have added a decade. The unfairness of it bewildered me. He had a kind of movie star grin that would make people do anything for him and a cute blond faux hawk that would have looked silly on any other adult but suited him perfectly.

He was sitting next to my prized new possession, a state-of-the-art electric breast pump I had picked up at a bargain price online. I'd methodically sterilised all the parts, and carefully fitted the pieces together. It was far too complicated for a sleep-deprived brain but Helen had dug up a YouTube video explaining it all. Assembled, it looked a bit like one of those horns a circus clown might hoot at you with.

I slid into the chair opposite Nick and plugged the

machine into the wall, attaching the suction cup under my top. I flicked it on and it started a rhythmic grunting sound. The suction started like a flickering tapping, before switching over to long, groaning inhalations.

Nick's head snapped up. 'What in God's name is that?'

I gestured at the pump. 'A breast pump. State-of-the-art, apparently. Lots of great reviews online. I thought I'd start storing some milk so that someone else might be able to do the odd feed instead of me.'

He frowned, watching me adjust the cup of the pump. 'You know how I told you I worked on that farm for a while when I was at school? That looks and sounds pretty much exactly like when we put the cups on the cows.'

I threw a pen at him. 'Don't be horrible! I'm not a cow.' The machine made a revving sound as it switched back to butterfly tapping.

'That's not what I meant.' He gestured at my chest. 'But you know, it might take me a while to think of those in the same way again.'

I shrugged. 'It'll take a while for them to be available to be thought of that way again. I feel like you just have to look at them and they'll spurt milk in your eye.'

He sighed and pushed the paper he had been staring at towards me. 'We need to get some more clients coming through the gym. I don't know what's going on with Sam. He's even less interested than usual lately.'

'That's odd. Needs a holiday maybe.'

He shook his head. 'He's out of luck there. Next

one to take time off is me when we get to take Holly somewhere.'

'That would be nice.'

He looked at me. 'When do you think we can do that?'

I leant back on the chair, creaking on to the two back legs, then was pulled back by the tug of the breast pump. 'Who knows. Maybe by the time she's three?'

He was half-smiling and didn't break eye contact with me.

'Maybe we can try a long weekend away before that.' I was suddenly self-conscious. 'What's going on? Is it the pump? Almost finished.'

He was still looking at me. Did I have a smear of dinner left on my face? I had fallen back on reheating a brilliant orange frozen curry I had found in the freezer, so it was quite likely. I dabbed at my face. 'What?'

He shook his head and looked back at his notes. I grabbed his hand. 'What?'

He looked up and rested his chin on his hand. 'Do you know what day it is?'

I frowned. 'Not off the top of my head. Tuesday?'

'Monday. But that's not what I meant. The date?'

I reached for my phone and flicked open the calendar. 'It's – oh, crap.'

He smiled thinly. 'Thought I might crack a beer.'

I reached for his leg as he walked past to the fridge. 'Babe, I'm so sorry. Your birthday. It's just with the lack of sleep ...'

He bent to kiss my head as he left the kitchen. 'It's okay, Ren. You've got lots of your plate. I have one every year, remember? You can make it up to me next time.'

***

I reached for my phone on the bedside table as soon as I heard Nick plod out the front door for work and gallop down the stairs to the bus stop out the front of the building the next morning. I'd pretended to be asleep when he looked in on us to avoid the weird cheek-kiss goodbye thing we now had going on, where we made empty promises about getting back into our bed together some time soon. Holly was nestled in next to me, my mother still asleep in the spare room.

It was amazing what I could share online with the women in our group that you'd never talk about in person.

I'd been struggling with the whole post-birth constipation thing. Something about the combination of dehydration from breastfeeding and having no muscle tone in the lower half of my body since the birth had made even that most normal of processes a bit of a trial. I wrote about it in detail in the group – down to my tip of using a step stool to prop your feet on. And it got thousands of comments. I'd never tell Nick. He'd be mortified. Where had the girl gone who wouldn't use the bathroom if there wasn't a scented candle waiting?

It was such a relief to talk to a whole group of women

who had the same concerns I did. Is my baby eating enough? Is X grams enough weight to put on in three months? Why do all the girls' clothes talk about kids as if they were something you'd buy from the bakery, but the boys get T-shirts saying they're superheroes?

Nick suggested I go and do a weekend yoga class at Yoga Junction, where I always used to practise before I had Holly. They had a mum-and-baby class that I had planned to take her to but he reckoned I wouldn't be able to relax and do anything if she was with me. He was probably right. I had tried to do a few sun salutations at home with her by my face but she'd just grabbed my ponytail when I dropped into downward dog.

The sun was starting to come up. There were five new messages in my email inbox, as well as a lot of spam. Two were from Lauren. One was a picture – her baby looked exactly like her. The other was a dump of sentences that seemed to have been written in the dark with autocorrect on. The only coherent one was: 'I'm so tired, why won't she sleep?'

I bit my lip. I didn't have the answers. 'I find Holly sleeps better when she's in with me. Can you safely co-sleep?'

The icon fluttered to indicate she was typing a reply. 'Maybe. My mum took her in the end so I got a couple of hours. But now she's going to be in any minute on my case about getting up and doing chores or whatever. I never get a bloody break.'

'Can you tell her how you're feeling?'

She didn't reply for a few minutes. Then, finally: 'No point. She'd never understand.'

***

Nick
Age: Four months

Sam strutted into work just after nine. That might be something that wouldn't be worth remarking on in an office but we were running a gym and half of our clients have been and gone by half past eight.

I fell into step beside him as he wandered towards the office, presumably ready to sling his bag under his desk and head out to the floor.

He grinned at me. 'Morning, mate. How's the dad life going?'

I smiled despite myself, feeling the imprint of the grooves in the air bed where they dug into my back all night and meant I could only lie in one position for hours on end. 'Still great, thanks. Didn't you have any clients this morning?

He stopped at the water cooler and turned away from me, filling a cup slowly. 'Nope. Maia took over the only one I had today.'

'Maia?'

'Yeah, good chance for her to upskill and all that. You've been going on about succession planning, right?'

I stared at him. Maia still had no qualification beyond a basic first aid certificate.

'Okay ...'

He raised his cup in a 'cheers' gesture and turned away.

'Is something going on?'

He punched me on the shoulder. 'What are you talking about? I'm just taking a step back. Like you said. Start working on the business, not in it.'

I followed him as he ducked away and around the corner towards the main room, where rows of machines were stacked up alongside each other. There was a person at about every second one – not bad for mid-morning in the middle of the week. And a lot better than when we started training people in the granny flat attached to my mother's house while I was studying to become a trainer. I muttered a silent thanks to whichever grandparent had taken out an old-fashioned endowment life insurance policy that paid out when Sam hit thirty. Until Holly came along, the day we opened the gym had been one of the proudest in my life, with a big party organised by Renee down to the range of signature smoothies and tiny protein cookies. She'd been in her element, wearing a bright blue mini dress and fierce heels, ordering waiters – and me – around. I'd stopped her in the corner for a kiss. 'You really do love your job.'

She had kissed me back. 'I do. And I love you.'

When had been the last time she'd said those words to me? Months, I reckoned.

I put a hand on Sam's shoulder. 'I reckon we probably

need to amp things up a bit, right? Make sure we don't get a winter lull this year?'

He raised his hand in a mock salute. 'I'm on it, captain.'

I watched him as he strolled across the floor, dropping to check the oil on the hinges of a pec deck machine that a blonde woman in her early twenties was using. He muttered something to her as he straightened up again and she laughed.

I pulled out my phone to send Renee a message. 'All okay at home?'

I already knew it would be a waste of time. She barely responded to my messages – or if she did, it was hours later. Meanwhile, she was able to have thirty-five simultaneous conversations with the mad members of her mothers' group. There was no point calling because any time I tried she was just putting Holly to sleep or had just got into the shower for the first time in a decade. Usually I would just end up speaking to Marjorie and there was only so much of my day that I could spend doing that.

I wandered back to the reception desk. Maia looked up from her work. 'Sorry, I meant to tell you about filling in this morning but I didn't get a chance. I just took his client for some interval training in the park and bodyweight stuff. He sent me notes.'

She tucked a piece of smooth, glossy hair behind her ear. She looked younger than her twenty-eight years.

'Has he been asking you to do that much?'

She bit her lip. 'No, just today. He had something he had to do.'

I paused. 'Okay. But let's get you some proper training if you're going to step up.'

She blushed and grinned. 'That would be great.'

Chapter Four

Priti Bashar, 1.34pm: 'Okay, emergency. I was in the lunch-room at work, wiping down the bench after I made a coffee. My boss came in eating a sandwich and had some mayo on his cheek … AND I REACHED UP WITH THE CLOTH AND WIPED IT OFF! What is happening to meeee! I've only been back at work a week. He's going to think I've completely lost it.'

Nick
Age: Four months

Who would have thought going to a yoga class could be so difficult? When I first suggested it, Renee looked at me as if I had told her to go and climb Mt Kilimanjaro a couple of times in the half-hour between Holly's bath and bed. But she had been friends with the yoga teacher, Rachel, for ages so it wasn't as if she couldn't just pick up and leave if something went wrong at home, anyway.

I almost thought I was never going to get her out of the door.

As the time to leave grew closer, she started pacing the floor, writing lists, asking me whether I was sure I would be okay for an hour alone with Holly. It was like watching her prepare for the time she flew to Kenya on her own to bring her mother home from a hospital stay. Then, she was worried about what condition her mum would be in. Now she was just going around the corner to the yoga studio.

With five minutes left to spare, I almost pushed her out to the car. Holly was almost asleep in the carrier against me. Renee settled her lips on the top of her slowly spreading mop of hair and inhaled as if she wasn't sure when they would ever be reunited again. 'You call me ...'

'If we need you. Yep, I will. Promise.'

'There's milk in the fridge if you need it. Test it on your wrist. But I should be back before she needs a feed.'

'I know. Go.'

I could hear my mother emptying the dishwasher in the kitchen, and her mother flicking the television on in the lounge.

It was kind of humiliating that they seemed to think I needed two babysitters to help me look after my own child.

Holly still asleep resting against my chest, I wandered back into the flat. Mum had moved through to the lounge and was tidying magazines on to the rack in the corner.

Marjorie had settled on something with a shrill laugh track. One more week until she could move back to her own place. Not that I was counting.

Our bedroom was in front of me. How long had it been since I'd slept in my own bed? I tentatively took a step, as if I was walking into someone else's house. It smelt strongly of Renee – her perfume, a bit of her shampoo and that breast milk scent that she was embarrassed about but which was weirdly endearing.

Holly started to stir, reaching her head back to look up at me. I cupped the back of her head in my palm. 'Hello, sweetheart.'

My stomach somersaulted as she grinned.

'Mummy's out but I thought we could hang out for a bit.'

I wandered into our tiny living room, gazing down at her perfect little face – the fine dusting of white dots Renee told me the doctor had called milia still on her tiny little upturned nose, perfectly pursed little red lips and the flush in her cheeks from pressing her face against me in her sleep. She had started to develop a habit of staring hard at me then giggling when I caught her eye. With the tiniest suggestion of a frown on her face, she looked so much like her mother. I shot Marjorie a look but she was focused on the screen.

I transferred Holly to the mat on the floor, lowering her down in my arms as if I was landing a hovercraft, and making the noises to match. Lying down beside her, I tried to direct her gaze to the toys assembled on what looked like a woodworking horse across the mat. 'That's a zebra.' I pointed to one. 'And that's meant to be a cat, I think. It's a bit wonky. Did Mum make this?'

Holly looked at me and chortled. I caught her eye as she kicked her legs in the air. 'Mum may have a crafty side we never knew about.'

We lay, side by side on the mat, contemplating the room. I reached for her chubby little hand and let her wrap her fingers around mine. She was wriggling from one side to the other, trying to roll over.

'Don't you manage that without your mother here or I'll never hear the end of it.' I gave her a faux-stern look. 'Now, will I tell you what noise those animals make? That's what parents do, right? Or sing you a song?'

The sunlight was reflecting off the glass cabinet under the TV. I could see Holly watching the lights dance across the ceiling.

I tested a few warbles of 'Twinkle Twinkle Little Star'. 'Are there really only four lines? There must be more than that?'

Holly snorted and grinned at me again. I reached over and blew a raspberry on her merino-onesie-clad stomach. She shrieked.

I could hear my mother clattering through from the kitchen. 'Everything all right in there, Nicholas?'

I looked up. 'Yep, Mum. We're having a great time, aren't we, Hol?'

Mum settled on to the couch in front of us and looked

at me. It was the kind of stare she used to use when I was a teenager and she suspected I'd been up to something I shouldn't have. Marjorie raised an eyebrow. 'I'll put the kettle on.'

Mum waited until she was out of the room. 'Have you talked to Renee properly lately?'

I tickled Holly under the chin. 'Sure, you know, just the usual stuff. Bit busy at the moment.'

She cleared her throat. 'I'm worried about her. She seems quite down. Have you noticed?'

I opened my mouth to respond but she cut me off.

'More than just tired. You might encourage her to go to the doctor, maybe. Hormones can do funny things. My cousin Louise's daughter was quite depressed ...'

I brushed it away. 'They'll just stick her straight on drugs at the first mention of it. Honestly, you have no idea how quick they are with that stuff these days.'

Mum raised an eyebrow. 'But if she needs it?'

I shook my head. 'She doesn't need that rubbish in her body. She just needs a proper sleep and maybe some more exercise and better food. She seems to live on toast and cashew nuts.'

Mum stared at me and made a show of smoothing her skirt. 'Well, I've told you what I think. I'll leave you to it.'

She was still looking at me hard. 'Just keep it in mind. See you soon, my darling.'

I raised my face for a kiss but she moved past me and landed one on Holly. She laughed when she saw my face.

'Sorry, other darling. Give me a call and let me know how she's doing.'

She reached for her handbag, which was resting on the arm of the oversized breastfeeding chair that now dominated the room.

My phone bleeped. A text message from Sam. I pushed the button to open it. 'Okay, I'll do it. I'll drop off the stuff first thing Monday morning.'

I raised an eyebrow. Stuff?

Another text bleeped through. 'Wrong person, sorry, mate. Just trying to hook up the cleaners.'

I frowned. Our cleaners had been organised for years. 'What stuff do they need?'

He replied straightaway. 'Tell you about it later.'

I looked at Holly. 'What is going on?'

***

Renee
Age: Four months

I slunk into the back of the yoga class, positioning myself on the mat closest to the door. We weren't meant to have our mobiles on but I turned mine to silent and propped it up in my bag, where I could just make out the screen. Rachel mouthed a welcome to me. She'd pulled her hair up into a loose ponytail and was wearing some tropical-print leggings and a long T-shirt with a fitted singlet showing through the arty cut-outs. I loved her because she didn't look like what you'd expect from a yoga teacher. She had split with her husband while she was pregnant with her second baby but then got together with a new guy and had virtually shone with happiness ever since. She was joking about testing her luck by trying for a third child when I pushed through the door to the warm, ylang-ylang-scented studio.

I concentrated on sinking into a 'comfortable' seated position, trying to keep my mind in the room.

The yoga session had been suggested because, the Sunday previous, Nick asked me whether I really minded that he was going to a movie with a friend. It wasn't even something he really wanted to see but he was taking any offer that would keep him out of the flat for a couple of hours and away from my mother's performance of 'Marjorie Turns Over A New Leaf'.

I had to avoid his eyes. 'Of course not.'

'I'll stay if you want me to.'

'It's fine.'

When he left, I had to lean against the door and coach myself through some breathing to stop the tears. What about me? When did I get to go for a walk by myself? When did I get to have lunch with a friend? He was off filling his cup or whatever and I couldn't even find mine.

He ducked back to pick up his forgotten wallet and found me lying on the floor. I'd sort of slumped down and found I couldn't get up. There wasn't anything wrong with me physically but I just felt like there was a huge weight pinning my muscles to the floor and there was no way I could hope to move them. I just lay there imagining what it would be like if I had to stay there for ever. What would happen to Holly? She was happily trying to stick a high-heeled shoe up her nose but how long would that last? Would my mum come home from the shops or wherever she'd gone and think I'd finally lost the plot? I could feel my heart beating in my neck and the lump that was forming on one side of my breast from where Holly had favoured the other all night. If I concentrated on it too long I could feel the prickle then drip of milk starting to trickle down my side. Every breath was like working against an enormous weight.

As soon as he opened the door and, slack-jawed, asked me what was wrong, I was in tears.

I felt guilty for even suggesting I wanted a break. I love Holly.

But I missed what it was like to live my life before, too. Sometimes I just wanted to be Renee. Not Renee, Nick's partner. Not Renee, Holly's mum. Definitely not Renee, Marjorie's daughter. Everything I used to think defined me was slipping away. We hadn't even decided whether I'd go back to full-time work – that dream of becoming a shareholder in the business before I was forty was looking about as likely as learning to fly. And the one thing I knew I was pretty good at – being organised and making sure everything happened exactly as it was meant to – was a pretty useless skill when you had become a servant to a tiny dictator.

So he suggested the yoga session – almost a full hour just for me. But then I didn't want to go and leave her. What if she missed me? What if we both cried the whole time?

Easing into a warrior sequence, I feared that was going to be the case. Rachel shot me a concerned look. I tried to turn my lips up into a smile. It was forty-five minutes. Surely anyone could make it through that. By the time we were into a series of sun salutations, I wasn't having to force the smile. It had always been my favourite move, if I swooped my foot through in just the right way, I would almost feel graceful. Rachel caught my eye and winked. 'Can that pelvic floor of yours handle taking the lunge a bit lower?'

I transferred a fraction more weight into my front foot, then quickly retreated. 'Definitely not.'

She smiled. 'Don't worry, we'll get there.'

***

Nick
Age: Five months

It wasn't that long ago that every Saturday would start with a run in the park and then pancakes and coffee with Renee.

But this one began when, trying to find a comfortable spot in the spare bed, I rolled on to something hard under the duvet. Reaching for it, I discovered it was a small can of baked beans. I put it down then picked it up again. It made no more sense the second time than it had the first.

Renee was still tucked up in bed with Holly but she opened an eye when I stuck my head around the bedroom door, and gestured for me to come in.

I held up the tin. 'Do I want to know why this was in the spare bed?'

She winced. 'Sorry. Holly picked it out of a shopping bag the other day and I must have stuck it there while I was putting the laundry away. That was days ago though?'

I sat on the end of the bed. 'I guess I sleep more deeply than I realised.'

'What are you up to today? Saturday off for a change?'

She moved Holly on to her stomach on the bed next to her. Holly lifted her head and grinned at us before using one pudgy arm to propel herself on to her back. Renee tickled her under the armpit and rolled her on to her front. 'Clever girl. Show us again.'

I kissed the top of each of their heads. 'Wondered if you wanted to go for a walk in the park this morning? It's looking like it'll be a nice day.'

Renee reached for a hair tie to pull her hair off her face. There was a fine dusting of dry shampoo around her hairline.

She nodded. 'Yeah, okay. Let's find that cute hat your

mum bought, though. She's not allowed sunscreen till she's six months.'

I hoisted myself on to the bed and edged under the duvet on the other side of Holly. 'How did you sleep?'

She shrugged. 'Bit better actually, only woke maybe three times. And she settled again pretty quickly.'

I squeezed her hand. 'Maybe we're getting there. Mum was a bit worried about you the other week but I told her that you'll be totally fine.'

She looked down at Holly, who was sucking intently on her index finger.

'Yeah.'

'Maybe I could shift back into our bed soon.' I tried to keep my voice light.

She looked up quickly. 'Let's talk about that later on.'

***

Renee and Holly were on the sofa taking selfies while I squished blueberries on to the top of pancakes in the kitchen. Holly was chortling wetly and even Renee giggled a couple of times. I almost didn't want to interrupt them by taking the plates through. I'd made Saturday pancakes for years. At first, I made them with coconut flour, to keep up with my paleo diet. But after about three months of that, Renee told me she thought it tasted like eating corrugated cardboard and it had been refined carbohydrates every week from then on. But when was the last time we had done it? I couldn't remember.

As I carried the plate over to Renee, she twisted a tiny curl of Holly's fluffy, nearly white hair around her finger and smoothed it back from her face. It still hadn't properly grown back on the ridge of her skull where her mattress had rubbed it off when she was first born. Renee's cheekbone protruded so much as she bent to rest her head against Holly's that it caught the light. When had she lost so much weight?

I slid on to the couch beside them and put my arm around Renee's shoulders. She shifted slightly so she was leaning against my legs.

'This is nice.' She looked up at me.

From the kitchen, I could hear my phone buzzing. Who would be calling at 9am on a Saturday?

I extracted myself and trudged through to find it. I flipped it over, dusting off some flour from the screen. It was Sam.

He sounded like he'd run across the room to call. 'Can you come in to work?'

'What? Why? Don't you have a thing with Rachelle today?'

I could hear the pulse of workout music thudding in the background. 'I just realised we've got our inspection today.'

I exhaled hard. We had a licence to run group fitness classes that came prepared and choreographed – but it meant random inspections every other month to ensure we were delivering them to the instructions. It needed to be flawless, right down to the timing of our shouted encouragement to the class, and the woman we had filling in on weekends was ... not.

'I'm meant to be going to the park with Renee and Holly. Can you handle it?'

'Sorry, mate. You know I barely know my left foot from my right. If I try to remember to tell them to feel the burn every fourth rep or whatever, I'll just fall off the stage. We could chance it with Lorraine, but ...'

Last time we'd been assessed, the instructor had forgotten to form-check the squats and one newbie had hurt her leg. The assessor had warned us we had to improve if we wanted to keep the licence. Having Lorraine swearing to herself when she started off a set on the wrong leg would not be a good look.

'Yeah, okay. I'll do it. Let me just talk to Renee.'

When I turned around, Renee was standing in the doorway, rocking Holly on her hip. They were wearing matching pink pyjama tops and staring at me with the same frowns on their faces. 'Talk to me about what?'

'It looks like I'll have to go into work today. It's just one class then I can come straight home.'

Her shoulders sagged. 'Okay.'

Holly reached across Renee's face and thrust a finger firmly up her mother's nose as she turned back towards the living room.

I put an arm out to stop her. 'We could go tomorrow?'
She shrugged me off. 'Yeah, maybe.'

I followed her. 'I'm sorry, Ren.'

She shook her head. 'Whatever, it's fine. You've got your life outside us.'

It hung unspoken between us – that she didn't. But wasn't this all what she had wanted?

***

When I got to the gym, the main floor was packed. All it took was a couple of warm days and everyone seemed to remember that they might one day need to wear a swimsuit again. Sam was peering through the internal window from our office and waved for me to come in.

I shut the door behind me. 'Class is at 10am, right? What's the easiest version for me to run through?'

Sam gestured helplessly. 'It's all Greek to me.'

I flicked through my stack of handouts that came with every new routine release. 'Think I'll just stick with one of the old favourites. Enough of the class should know it to carry me through.'

He clapped me on the shoulder. 'Lifesaver. I'll meet her at the front desk and schmooze a bit, then send her in just in time for you to do your thing. I've let Lorraine know she'll be second-in-command today.'

I nodded. 'Sounds like a plan.'

I manoeuvred so I was blocking his path to the door. 'Hey – is there something else going on you need to tell me about?'

He stared at me.

'What's this stuff you were texting about dropping off last week?'

He blushed and focused intently on stabbing at something on the carpet with the toe of his trainer. 'Don't tell anyone.'

'Okay ...'

'We're trying to have a baby. Rachelle and me. It's not going so well and she's been pushing me to do a sample so the doctor can work out whether it's a problem at my end. With my end, so to speak. We're not at that lunch right now because she's not in the mood to see people with kids at the moment.'

I laughed with relief. 'Is that all?'

He threw a stress ball at me. 'What do you mean, is that all? It's frickin' embarrassing is what it is. I've put it off as long as I can.'

'I thought you were going to tell me you're selling drugs or something. Mate, that's fantastic. Is that why you've been arriving late? Trying to time it or whatever?'

He nodded, avoiding my eyes. 'It's pretty awkward, right? Not very sexy.'

I gave him an awkward sort of one-arm hug. 'Any kid would be lucky to have you as a dad.'

He nodded. 'Thanks, Nick. Don't tell anyone I'm wanking in a cup or I'll kill you.'

***

Renee

Age: Five months

We didn't go to the park. We didn't get to have the afternoon picnic we were meant to have to make up for not going to the beach, either, because Sam-the-business-partner takes precedence over Renee-the-life-partner and Holly-the-daughter, apparently.

Once Nick got to work and did the class there turned out to be innumerable crises and problems to deal to and he didn't even think about getting home until after 4pm. It's so predictable.

I'm sure he thinks that I've got this amazingly cruisy existence where I just roll around on the floor with Holly all day taking cute pictures for Instagram and trying to turn her into a brand rep for the clothes I can't afford to buy. Meanwhile, he's slaving away overseeing the workouts of his array of well-off middle-aged ladies who'd probably prop his photo on their bedside tables if they could get away with it.

He doesn't even realise I spend a good part of my life playing the 'is that peanut butter or poo?' guessing game and discovering little pools of vomit and old breast milk that somehow remain on my body even after my admittedly short showers. When I get a break from that, I sneak in a bit of extreme Googling. Things like 'how statistically likely is my child to die before she's 10?' or 'what are the symptoms of [some obscure, horrific disease]?'

He can't understand why I fantasise about getting out when I simultaneously feel like my lungs are being pulled out of my chest when I'm away from Holly. I suppose that's fair enough when I can't even really explain it myself.

When he finally arrived home, I was cold with anger.

He tried to put his hand on my arm while I was changing Holly's nappy but I snatched it away. 'Can you not?'

He sighed as if he could not believe that I was being so unreasonable, wanting to be able to use two hands to balance wipes, child and nappy. 'Do you want me to take Holly? You can go and lie down.'

I rolled my eyes at him. 'So easy, isn't it?'

'I don't know what you mean.'

'I'll just go and have a rest, shall I? Except that everything that needs to be done now will still need to be done when I get up and it'll just be later in the day with less time left to do it.'

He put his hands up, his palms facing me. 'Okay. Tell me what you'd like me to do.'

Tears were streaming down my face, and once I felt them start to drip off my chin, it was too late stop them. 'Why do I have to be in charge of everything that needs doing? Can't you see what needs to happen?' I tried to sniff the words out in between heaving sobs.

He was staring at me. 'I didn't realise you were so upset. Babe, I thought you wanted to be in charge with Holly. I thought that you like that I just roll with it.'

I hadn't realised I was so upset, either. But my body

was shaking with a mixture of anger and what felt like soul-ravaging despair.

He held out his arms for me but I found I couldn't move. Holly nestled into my shoulder.

'I'm just going to take Holly to bed in our bed for a bit, okay?' I brushed past him.

I pulled back the duvet of the bed, curled around my daughter, and pull the covers up around us. In our cocoon, I reached for my phone. The group was having a bit of an early Saturday evening lull. I opened the box to make a new post. 'Help,' I began. 'I don't know what's going on. I'm so sad and angry all the time and I'm not even completely sure why. I mean it's partly my partner. But maybe not all him. Has anyone else been in this position?'

I lay back on the pillow and waited for the replies. A private message flicked up from Felicity. 'You okay?'

I stared at it. 'Not really.'

'When Harlow was born, I had a period where I was really down. The doctor gave me something for it and it came right super-fast. Maybe you should look into it?'

I screwed up my forehead. 'I don't think it's anything I need the doctor for. Just feeling a bit low. I'm sure Nick would tell me I just need some fresh air and Omega-3, or something.'

She replied immediately. 'Okay but, you know, keep it in mind.'

Someone else replied on my post. 'If you've got a good GP you could go for a chat and check your hormone levels and everything. I was throwing dishes at the wall twice a week until I did some blood tests that showed I was massively deficient in all sorts of things.'

Frankie added another comment: 'Think about everything your body's been through in the last year. It's not surprising you're out of sorts. Do you have someone you can chat to? My sister-in-law got great results with reiki.'

Helen replied: 'Yeah, you're amazing! Don't forget it. If you have to do something for you, you've totally earnt it. Book in a massage or something.'

I had to check her name twice. Helen was usually the one with bossy medical advice. Where was her instruction to get eight hours' sleep and five servings of cruciferous vegetables now?

Swallowing, I tapped out a reply. 'Thanks all, that makes me feel better. Will see how I go.'

***

Renee
Age: Six months

I tried to expand our calendar of activities a little bit every week, so that no one (cough, Nick, cough) could suggest that my melancholy was because I was stuck moping around the house.

Ruth had talked me into signing up for a physio class

for new mums, which I had to admit held markedly less appeal than the cake-decorating tutorial or cheese-making demonstration I'd wanted her to come to.

The car park was full of people carriers and minivans when I arrived. It still made me giggle that you could be a couple and a little Suzuki Swift was just fine. You might even squeeze into a little two-door if you were really economical about what you carted around. But then suddenly you added a baby to the mix and you had to have at least a large sedan, preferably a station wagon but even better one of those things that looked a bit like a space shuttle on wheels, complete with a sliding door. These vehicles are so ridiculously unsexy that most of these women probably didn't even know what they were called before they had a baby but now it's 'so practical'. You don't get a wet back when you're leaning in to put your baby into her car seat on a rainy day. There's room for a stroller. You can stash a huge nappy bag on one of the seats and still have room to pick up your mum or your friend or even – maybe one day, not that I was thinking about it at all – have another baby.

The advertising had promised the physiotherapist would have us run through checks to ensure everything had gone back to where it was meant to be, whether we could jump on a trampoline without waterworks (I'm paraphrasing), and whether we sometimes lost our T-shirts in the gaping hole between our abdominal muscles.

The woman taking the class looked as if she'd never

even looked at a child. She was tall and lean with shiny wet-look leggings stretched over her lean thigh muscles.

I studied the ceiling while she took us through a series of exercises where we lay on our backs with our babies on top of us, lifting one leg tentatively off the floor, then the other. Holly lay on my chest at first before rolling off and thrusting her arms shoulder-deep into the handbag I'd propped next to us.

I tried to relax into it. I was focused on trying to hover one leg off the ground at forty-five degrees while pointing the other at the sky when we were interrupted by a screech. 'What is that?' Ruth sat up.

I stretched up to look through the window. 'I think it's my car alarm.'

One of the babies started to whimper. I sat up, looking for Holly, who had managed to develop a sort of roll-wriggle that could get her surprisingly far quite quickly. She stuck her head out from under a coat hanging on a bookcase near my feet. My keys were clasped in her hand, which was opening and closing on the panic alarm buttons on the car remote.

'Holly!' I swooped for them. Her lower lip jutted as I stabbed at the button to stop the wailing.

The teacher was watching us. 'All okay?'

I nodded. 'Sorry. I'll keep better watch on this one.'

Holly looked up at me and grinned, her bottom front teeth almost oversized in her mouth. I tucked the keys back into the zip pocket of my bag and moved it a little further from Holly.

'Okay, let's move on to our pelvic floors. Think of it like a big muscle sling.' The teacher beamed at us. 'It's holding all your internal organs in place there.'

Sitting next to me, Ruth shifted uncomfortably. 'I don't think I could even find a little muscle bandage much less a big sling. I'm not sure everything will ever go back in place.'

I caught her eye. 'Imagine what it would be like if we had another one.'

She snorted. 'I'd probably have to wear some sort of control pants permanently to stop it all falling out.' Ruth took a deep breath in and out, as instructed by our perky teacher. 'But there's more chance of that woman eating a pie than there is of me having another baby.'

'Not keen?'

'I'd have to actually let Simon touch me for that to happen. Can't imagine anything worse right now.'

The woman to her right, whom I didn't recognise but who had clearly been pretending not to listen to us, smiled ruefully. 'Neither can I. When you have a baby hanging on to you for half the day, the last thing you want is anyone else touching you. Especially when he tries to touch my breasts.'

I shuddered. 'Yuck.'

Fiona's toddler, Luka, wriggled and pushed off her lap while her baby, Finn, watched from the floor.

'Honestly I'd be happy never to have to think about it ever again. Two is more than enough for me,' Fiona said, watching her daughter scurry across the floor towards another table. She turned back to us. 'I can't believe anyone wants to do anything other than go to sleep when they get into bed. We could go away for a weekend and I'd just spend the entire time in bed. Alone. Imagine what it would be like to have the bed to yourself.'

We shut our eyes in shared bliss. 'That's never going to happen to me again,' Fiona moaned.

Ruth put her face in her hands. 'Maybe we could all go and live somewhere together and raise our kids as a coven of single women.' She was joking but I realised it didn't sound like an awful idea. 'I'd never have to get out of my comfy maternity singlet again.'

Holly and Ruth's son, Xavier, seems to be passing an old pen back and forth, taking turns to stick it in their mouths.

'Maybe we should go and buy some nice stuff,' Fiona hissed. 'Help get some of that back again. Or at least look the part.'

I frowned. 'What do you mean?'

'Like some proper, nice, pretty underwear, even if they're breastfeeding bras. I didn't want to spend any money on them to begin with because I thought it was only going to be for such a short time but now I'm thinking it's probably going to be worth it. The hand-me-downs I got the first time around are pretty grim now ...'

Ruth grinned. 'Good idea. Might be fun.' She elbowed me. 'Good to keep you out of the house a bit longer.'

There was a shout from across the room. Fiona scrambled to her feet. 'Luka!'

Luka had pulled her sparkly tulle tutu over her head so that only her face was showing and was in the process of removing her nappy, all while doing what looked like some version of the macarena by the huge incandescent-lamp-lit fish tank in the corner of the room.

'Luka, come back here right now!'

***

An hour later we were in the dressing room of the lingerie department down the road from my flat. I had always been vaguely intimidated by the staff, who I assumed would look down their noses at anyone who did not know the difference between a cut-and-sew and a three-part bra. I could just imagine what they would think of my selection at home, of should-have-been-white bras and might-once-have-been-black pants. Holly was sitting on the floor in one cubicle with me, bashing a plastic coat hanger against the floor, while Ruth and Xavier were bustling around in the next. Fiona, for all her effort to get us there, had vanished.

I slid a wide bra strap on to my shoulder. It was cushioned in the way I was used to with sports bras, but with delicate lace across the cup and a discreet little flap that you could pop open for easy feeding access. It was actually surprisingly attractive. But even if it was the perfect undergarment, it was so expensive I could never justify it.

'Can I help you with sizes?' The assistant was hovering outside the curtain.

'No, thank you, I'm fine.'

Holly's head snapped up. I tried to stretch my face into the most reassuring smile I could manage. 'Won't be long, sweet. Want another rusk?' Half a sticky teething rusk had adhered to the inside of my jeans pocket. I peeled it off.

She held her hands up. Holding the bra together with one hand at the back, I leant forward to pick her up.

Her breath started to catch in her throat with a mewling whimper. I rocked and bounced from one foot to the other, singing under my breath. Then she stopped. I looked down. Her eyes were shut and her stomach seemed to be tensing. What was going on? She hadn't struggled with gas for months. She swallowed hard and grimaced. Then it happened.

What felt like a relentless stream of vomit erupted from her mouth and all over me. It kept coming, dripping down my legs and coating us both. It seemed impossible that so small a body could spew forth so much liquid.

I was used to the milky smell of the little spits she did after a big feed but this was something else. It hit next-level parmesan-cheese-vomit smell, something that I had never been able to cope with. Suddenly I was back in the bar I had worked in while I was at university, cleaning up after patrons who'd had four too many Tequila Sunrises. I felt my stomach heave. Before I could stop it, a rush of vomit flew out of my mouth, too, and covered the front of her onesie, my jeans and the beautiful bra.

Ruth's mouth dropped open as she pulled back the curtain. 'What the hell?'

Something was pooling in the left cup of the bra. 'Get me out of here.'

Ruth grabbed her coat, which had been hanging on the back of her cubicle door and wrapped it around me and Holly. She pushed me towards the door. 'Go, get yourselves home. I'll deal with it.'

Head down, I ran for the door of the changing rooms and then across the main floor of the shop. I could feel something warm oozing down my stomach. 'Please don't let that drip on the floor,' I whispered to Holly, keeping my gaze down as we scurried past the shop attendants.

I was almost there when I noticed an elderly man had stopped to admire a display in the middle of the aisle, stretching his walking stick out behind him like a hurdle across the floor. As I planted my heels on the floor, I felt something squelch beneath my feet. My right foot slid as vomit hit shiny tiles and I felt my body move forward towards him, as if in slow-motion. I collided with his right hip and he turned to look at me. As he straightened, his right arm brushed across my soaked torso and Holly's drenched hair. He looked at me in horror.

'I'm so sorry,' I had nothing. I couldn't even offer a wipe.

A woman appeared behind me. 'Excuse me, madam? Are you going to pay for that?'

I looked over her shoulder desperately to where Ruth

was waving. 'My friend – over there? She's going to cover it. I'm sorry, I have to go.'

I stuck my head down again and ran out into the sunshine on the street.

***

I plunged us both into the shower when we got home twenty minutes later. As the water splashed over us, I caught her eye. For someone who'd been so exaggeratedly sick, she looked very cheery. 'Those poor women,' I bit back a giggle as I rubbed at the folds of her ear with a facecloth. 'I bet they'd never seen anything like it.'

She frowned as if cross with me for laughing. 'I'm sorry, honey, it's just ... her face.'

My body shook with laughter. The woman who had tried to stop me as I rushed for the door had taken a step back, her mouth dropping open, when she realised what she was looking at. And we must have been a sight. I'd stripped Holly in the boot as soon as we got back to the car, and put her in a fresh nappy and change of clothes that I had stashed in our nappy bag. I had never considered that I might need a change of clothes for myself so drove home hoping desperately that I wouldn't be stopped in some sort of random licence check.

With Holly nestling into my chest ten minutes later – perhaps fuelling up for round two? – I reached for my phone and pulled up a search engine. What were these supposed symptoms of postnatal depression, anyway? Google provided a bullet-point list of answers. Crying. Well, yes. All the time. Both of us. Fear. Who didn't fear pretty much everything in the world when you've just brought a small person into it? Fatigue. That just seemed unfair to include. Loss of interest or pleasure ... I put my phone down on my lap, then picked it up again. Maybe it was worth at least running it past the doctor.

As I swiped through my phone to find the clinic number, it rang.

I stabbed at the button to answer it.

'Yep?'

'Oh, sorry.' The voice at the other end sounded contrite. 'Is this a bad time?'

'No, it's fine. What can I do?'

'You'll think this is weird ...' She trailed off.

'Oh?'

'It's Lauren. From online? I found your number from your work website. I was hoping you might have a minute to talk.'

'Is everything okay?' The last messages we had traded were inane banter about our babies' distaste for sleep.

'I just need to see someone. Can Mackenzie and I come and see you? Is that all right?'

I paused. Online conversations I could cope with. But meeting someone in person? Cringe. My previously pristine house was strewn with baby paraphernalia – swaddles over the back of the couch, nipple cream on the coffee table. I'd actually done the 'sniff test' to determine whether a camisole I wanted to wear had been through the wash or not. You never quite knew what you might find if you stuck your hand down the back of the sofa cushions – half a biscuit if you were lucky. But on the other hand, I had no plans. Nick would no doubt be working late again. This girl was only seventeen. What harm could there be in having a stressed-out teenager and her baby come and visit? She was hardly going to do me any damage. She must have been more scared of me than I was of her.

'Come over for a coffee. I'll text you with the directions.'

'Oh, thank you.' She sounded as if she might cry. 'I'll be there soon.'

***

Nick
Age: Six months

I was in the staff kitchen – it was really more of a cupboard off the back of the main gym floor – making my lunch, when Maia came in, bearing bags of whatever it is you bought at those expensive delis that now lined most of the streets around us.

'Everything okay?' She gave me a searching look as I tried to shake a protein shake with one hand and scull a glass of water with the other.

'Just tired.'

She nodded. 'Can't be easy, having your business and a baby ...'

I avoided her eyes. 'I can't complain, I'm a lucky guy, right?'

I found I couldn't smile. I *was* a lucky guy – I had everything I wanted, a lovely partner, beautiful baby, and a semi-decent flat. I even had the work thing sorted at last. So why did it feel like it had all gone a bit wrong? From somewhere beyond the door we heard the clang of someone dropping weights too heavily on the floor. I winced.

Maia was still looking at me.

I sighed. 'It takes a bit of adjustment, I guess, to get used to. Just kind of fitting in at home.'

'Not your wife's number one anymore?'

I nodded. 'She's not actually my wife, but yep. Selfish, huh?'

It was like I was the third wheel of my family. I'd never been madly keen on the idea of a baby because I thought it would be so restrictive, having to worry about someone else all the time, like that.

Growing up, I'd always tried to push back against the conventions of what was expected or what I 'should' do. This was not always easy with my parents' friends circle being what it was. One of their closest friends' children was literally an Olympic athlete who married a top-level lawyer.

Whatever teenage rebellion I'd planned never quite worked out, though, and I went off to university and did the IT degree my parents were expecting – and which, fortunately, they paid for. It wasn't until I'd been working for almost ten years that I got the chance to chuck it in and follow my gym dream.

It was a rare moment of doing something purely for me. Usually I figured I should cause as little disruption as possible for Renee so she could catapult towards the greatness that was so obviously coming for her. But with the gym, I just jumped at it. I figured it was the start of a whole new stage of life for me and Renee, who was still the coolest person I'd ever met, even with her desire to alphabetise the spices in the kitchen cupboard.

Now we were Mum, Dad, and the kid, after all, and the things I'd worried about – having to keep to a schedule or plan things months or years in advance – didn't seem to be the biggest problem at all. I was more than ever Robin to her Batman – but it was beginning to feel a lot like this was a movie where the sidekick was decidedly optional.

Maia shook her head. 'Hang in there. It won't last, I'm sure.'

'You are?'

She tried not to laugh. 'Well, no. But you know, I don't think it will. I don't know. I've never even met your partner. But you seem lovely. I'm sure you'll be back on track in no time. People deal with this stuff every day.'

She watched me flop a sachet of tuna into a bowl then passed me a salad from her bag. 'I thought you might have forgotten your lunch again.'

I met her eyes. 'It's hard, this bringing your lunch thing. But babies and budgets aren't a great mix.'

She held my eyes as I used the too-small spork to scoop up a mouthful of some weird combination of watermelon and seeds.

'This is amazing.'

She smiled. 'And totally within your carb count. I checked.'

I still had not even told Renee about Maia. I was not sure why – she was the perfect person for the job. Overqualified if anything, really, for our business. And it wasn't like there was anything suspicious going on; every interaction we had was totally professional. Although I did have to admit that I got on better with her than with random Lauren, the teenager who had suddenly appeared in my house.

I didn't even get any warning that she was coming to stay. I arrived home and there she was. She and Renee had Holly and another baby sitting on the floor between them, kind of batting at each other. Renee introduced me to the teenager, dressed in a pair of tight sparkly jeans and a camisole top, her extremely blonde hair like an ironed curtain on each side of her face. She said her name was Lauren and she was apparently desperate for somewhere to stay. This was presented to me as if it was totally normal for someone Renee had met online and briefly shared a hospital ward with to have a crisis and need to come over.

I pulled her into our bedroom. 'What are you doing?'

She shrugged. 'She doesn't really have a lot of support. She and her mum are having an argument – I know what mum drama is like. I thought this was a way I might be able to help.'

I frowned. 'But why here? How do you even know her, really?'

Renee had looked as if she might cry. 'Just from the mums' group. She needs someone.'

I rolled my eyes. 'The bloody mums' group. It's taking over your life.'

She turned away from me. 'Can you not? I'm just trying to do the right thing. Her mum's basically chucked her out. She's harmless.'

I followed her back into the lounge and pulled out my phone while they discussed sleeping bags or teething or bedtimes or something. Lauren seemed to be scrambling to agree with everything Renee said.

I had learnt not to join in on any baby conversation – when I told her that I had read that breaking the habit of feeding to sleep might help babies sleep better she didn't speak to me for an entire evening.

When it became clear that they weren't going to wind up the baby chat in a hurry, I picked up my iPad and went into the spare room. My desk was still set up there from when I used to do all the gym admin at home in the evenings. There were bags all over the bed and underwear strewn across the pillows. Had we not just recently cleaned Marjorie's stuff out of this room?

I retreated and headed for the bathroom instead. Settling on the toilet, I opened my iPad.

A message bounced up on my emails. I clicked on it. Maia. What was she doing working at this time of night? She was on an hourly wage – we couldn't afford to have her on all hours.

'Just wanted to let you know that I've signed up for a PT course starting in a couple of weeks. It's mostly online but I'll have to take off early one evening a week,' the message blinked at me.

'That's fine, thanks for letting me know,' I tapped back. 'Now log off. Work can wait until the morning.'

I switched over to the file I had been working on, a revamped programme for Aiyad, one of my longest-standing clients. I had a suspicion that he did very little exercise whatsoever between his weekly sessions with me, though he claimed to be working out daily. Soon another message notification blipped up.

'It's fine, I'm waiting to go out with some friends, so I'm killing time anyway.'

I sent her a GIF of a baby hurling her bottle on to the floor. 'Another raging night here.'

She sent a smile emoticon. 'You're lucky to have such a cute family.'

I realised I was smiling, too. 'See you tomorrow.'

Renee knocked on the door.

'Coming.'

She was waiting in the hallway when I emerged. 'What are you up to?'

142

I shook my head. 'Just checking in on work.'

She paused. 'Okay. Holly's down for the night. I'm going to order some pizza for me and Lauren. Want some? I can get that weird cauliflower base you like.'

I brushed imaginary fluff off my trackpants. 'Sure.'

'You haven't got work to do?'

I pulled the door shut behind us. 'It can wait.'

I settled onto the sofa next to Renee, who was cradling a mug of tea. Lauren lay on the floor by her feet, flicking through a magazine.

She looked up at us, pointing at a glossy page. 'It says here the average married couple only has sex twice a month. That's crazy.'

Renee raised an eyebrow. We still hadn't managed it at all since Holly emerged into the world. 'I wouldn't believe everything you read.'

There was a squawk from the spare bedroom. Lauren cursed and clambered up from the floor. 'Why will she not just go to sleep?'

Renee patted her leg as she went past. 'Try not to stress about it. The more uptight you get, the harder it is to get them to sleep. Bring her out if you need to. I don't know many babies who'll settle themselves at this age.'

I looked at Renee out the corner of my eye once Lauren was out of the room. 'Twice a month, eh?'

She flinched away from me. 'Don't get any ideas. I still don't even feel human.'

I rested my hand on her thigh. 'Sorry. It's okay.'

She put her hand over mine. 'I'll get back to myself eventually.'

I pulled her hand to my mouth and kissed her fingers. She smelt of baby lotion and soap. 'Why don't you book in one of those beauty treatments you used to get? Try for another hour to yourself this weekend.' Before she fell pregnant, she'd had a standing monthly appointment with a beauty therapist and always seemed to come back a little more willing to walk around the flat without much on.

Her head snapped up. 'Are you serious?'

I bit my lip. 'I ... think so? Might be relaxing?'

She pushed herself up off the couch. 'I don't know about you, but I don't think a stranger pouring hot wax on my bits and ripping out my pubic hair by the roots is that relaxing, really.'

She took a gulp of tea and clattered the mug down on to the coffee table. 'I'm going to check on Lauren.'

***

Nick
Age: Six months

Maia and Sam were on the tiny balcony outside the staff kitchen when I finished with my second client of the morning, each nursing huge cups of coffee. The gym is in a converted warehouse and the brick wall along the

144

balcony is so high that you can't see over it when you sit outside. Sam hadn't given any update on his baby-making exploits and I'd not wanted to ask. He was laughing at something Maia was telling him like it was the funniest thing he'd ever heard.

Her face was tilted towards the sliver of sunlight that forced its way between two office blocks across the road. I raised my hand in greeting but neither noticed.

I pulled a tin of protein powder out of the cupboard and chucked a spoonful into the blender with some coconut milk. I could still see their movements in my peripheral vision.

Finally, there was a burst of road noise as they slid open the door and stumbled back inside, still laughing.

'Oi, you two.' I tried to keep my voice light. 'What time do you call this? Haven't you got a ten-thirty?'

Sam rolled his eyes at me. 'Sorry, Dad.'

Maia caught my eye and smiled. She was wearing bright pink lipstick that made her teeth look extra white.

I turned to my emails. There was one at the top of my inbox promising a new menu at Renee's favourite restaurant, by the river in the middle of town. There was a time when we went there every week. It was the scene of her twenty-ninth birthday – a night where we started with cocktails, drank bottles of champagne for dinner, and somehow ended up at a very suspicious karaoke bar well after midnight. I could still remember her word-perfect but pitch-awful rendition of a Madonna song. It was when her hair was shorter and a bit fried from an attempt at bleach, so it would have been a passable impression if the sound had been off. The next year – her thirtieth – she'd been pregnant and in bed by 9pm.

I looked at the clock. 10.25am. If I got organised, I could get my mum to babysit. Lauren would be there, no doubt, but the idea of leaving her in charge of the babies made my stomach constrict.

I sent Renee a text. 'Fancy a dinner date?'

The reply was almost instant. 'What? With you?'

I rolled my eyes. 'Yes, me. Tonight? Mint has a new menu – lots of veggie stuff as per ...'

I flicked over to the website. If I made our booking for 8pm that should give enough time to get the little person off to bed. After I'd sent the message, I leant back in my chair.

Somehow Sam was back again and he and Maia were giggling about something else, as she tried to pull a file from a shelf above our computers. I put my head down, focusing on my keyboard. 'Is anyone on reception?'

Maia ducked her head and scuttled out of the room.

***

Renee

Age: Six months

It took me days to make the doctor's appointment. Every time I pulled up the number on my phone, Holly would cry and I'd have to cuddle her, or they wouldn't answer within three rings and I'd remember there was some piece of housework that needed to be done urgently. Basically anything to avoid actually putting a time in my diary.

When it finally happened, the appointment was scheduled for first thing in the morning. Even though my doctor had never shown any ability to run to time, I made sure that Holly and I were outside the clinic doors twenty minutes early. One thing I had discovered in my short stint of motherhood was that whenever you were running late, something would go wrong. The later you were, the more dramatic the wrong thing would be. We stopped on the step outside and I jiggled her on my hip, pointing out trucks passing on the road.

Lauren was still asleep in the spare room when we left, Mackenzie tucked in a portacot next to the bed. From what I'd heard, they'd been up half the night. I slid a note into the room. 'Catch up with you when I get back. You're doing great.'

Nick was not happy that she was still around – he'd only just managed to switch from the air bed in the nursery to the spare bed and now he had transferred back again. He hadn't even bothered to bring up the idea of moving back into our bed again.

But what was I to do? She was like a little lost puppy. The longer she stayed, the less likely it felt she was going to move back with her mother. I had at least convinced her to let her sister know that she was okay, in case they were worried. But the way she talked about her mother, it wasn't looking good.

'She just sits on the couch drinking wine all night and expects me to keep the household going all day,' she'd said one evening, sniffing and brushing away tears that tracked her heavy mascara down her face. 'It's like since I became a mother they expect me to run the whole house while they just skive off. Then the minute I don't do absolutely everything, they tell me that I'm neglecting my baby.'

She pulled the hood of her sweatshirt up over her head despite the warmth of the flat, like a protective shell.

I'd reached out to rub her leg. 'It's okay. We'll get it sorted.'

'When does life go back to normal?'

I watched her face, searching for the right words. 'I'm not sure that it ever goes back to "normal", if you mean like it was before.'

She looked up. 'I guess not.'

She stared off into the distance, twisting a piece of hair around her fingers. 'I wish it was a bit harder on the guys.'

I laughed and the sound seemed to surprise us both. 'I totally agree.'

***

Just as the clinic doors were due to open I felt Holly tense, then a familiar smell. My shoulders slumped. I looked down at her, in the carrier on my chest. 'Really?'

She grinned back at me. I kissed her cheek. 'This won't be cute for too many years.'

By the time I had retreated to the car and changed her nappy in the boot, then scurried back to the surgery, we were late.

We huddled into the corner of the waiting room, pretending that the flimsy material of my blouse would be enough to protect her from the germs being propelled across the room by a large man power-coughing. I should have just booked her in for a doctor's appointment while we were there – there was no way she was leaving without some sort of bugs on board.

Eventually, the doctor ushered us through to what looked like a cupboard converted into a tiny treatment room. She was a short woman with bright red, shoulder-length hair. She must only have been a couple of years older than I was. She smiled at Holly as we sat down. 'What brings you here today?'

I stared at her. I'd rehearsed the words in my head in the car trip over but now I couldn't get them to flow in order. Holly stretched out in my arms, trying to grab for the cup full of pens that was far too near the edge of the doctor's desk.

'Um ...' I ventured at last, 'I think I might need some help with my mood. I'm feeling a bit low. Still.'

The doctor nodded. 'Okay. How long have you been feeling this way?'

I tried to think. 'Probably ever since Holly was born.

At first it was just tiredness. But I can't shake it. I cry at everything. I cried because Holly has this cute little teddy in the cot but one day she's going to grow up and she won't want it any more. Then what will become of it?'

Tears threatened to start again. I stared at the doctor. 'I don't feel like it's normal.'

'Okay,' she said after what felt like minutes. 'It sounds like you might have a bit of postnatal depression. Do you think you've been feeling generally low and sad like this for more than a fortnight?'

I nodded. 'More like three months.'

'Are you struggling with appetite? Sleep?'

'I think everyone with a baby struggles with sleep.'

She smiled. 'That's true. But when you are in a position to sleep, are you able to?'

I shrugged. 'Not really. There's a lot going on in my head.'

'Do you have people you can talk to? Lean on?'

I nodded. 'I have friends. My mum's around at the moment, surprisingly. My mother-in-law's been really great. But ...'

'But it's not enough?' I ducked my head. She nodded. 'You might be surprised at how many women feel like this when they have a new baby. It's not something a lot of people like to talk about but it really is quite common. There are things I can prescribe you that will get everything back to something like normal ...'

'Like drugs?'

'Yes.' She patted my leg. 'But don't worry, I'm not suggesting you go on to medication for ever. We'll start you off on a short course, then see how you're feeling. Okay? Being a mum is tough. Think of it as just a way to help you get back on track.'

I rested my head against Holly's cheek. 'What about feeding Holly? I thought I couldn't have much medication. I've not even been taking cold and flu.'

'There are a few antidepressants that seem to be fine with breastfeeding. Very little actually gets through to your milk, you might be surprised. I'll prescribe the most common. We have lots of options, Renee.'

'Are you sure? My partner doesn't believe in medicating for this sort of thing.'

She snorted. 'If I told you how many people are taking something ... I promise it's totally normal.'

***

As I got back to the car and clipped Holly into her seat, my phone buzzed. Nick wanted to go out for dinner. I paused. Like *out* out? Alone?

I couldn't very well say no. It felt like I'd be slapping down any suggestion he made about spending time together for months – although, to be fair, he didn't make it particularly easy for me.' What time? Who'll look after Holly?'

He replied almost instantly. 'My mum's happy to. Let's go out once she's asleep. You've got Lauren there too, right? She can help. Cover her board this week.'

I sighed. 'She's not paying board.'

'I know. I wasn't serious. Wouldn't leave her in charge. Come on. I miss you.'

At least dinner out had an end time. If it was just the two of us, we could come home after an hour or two. Going out. It was what people did, right?

I looked at Holly, who was sitting in her car seat, chewing the plastic ring of a rattle shaped like a giraffe.

'Mummy might go out for a bit tonight with Daddy.'

She gazed at me solemnly and almost seemed to shake her head.

'Not for long. You'll be fine.'

She withdrew her sticky fingers from her mouth and stuck one in her ear.

'I'll tell Gran she can call me if she needs me and I'll come right home.'

Holly moved her finger from her ear into her mouth.

'I bet it won't even be that fun.'

My phone bleeped. A text from my mother. She had disappeared back to her house as soon as the house sitters moved out but now seemed to be regretting it. She had a pottery class and then an appointment at an art gallery with half an hour in between – would that be a good time for her to come and visit? I dropped my phone back on the seat. I did not have the energy to manage her schedule. I was still trying to get rid of the sheen of body oil she had left on the bath after luxuriating in it every night of her stay.

***

'What should I wear?' I cocked my head to look at Holly a few hours later. 'Want to come and check out my wardrobe with me?'

I was pretty much back to the size I had been before Holly was born, though I was a little squishier around the middle. It was like whatever had been in there previously generally supporting the outer layers had disappeared. You could stick a finger into my abdomen and it felt like it might just keep on going in for ever. Abdominal muscles, I supposed. That's what was missing.

Unless I moved or wore anything tight-fitting, though, you couldn't really tell that I wasn't my normal self. I positioned Holly on the floor under some of my long maxi dresses, so the floaty material would waft over her face. She giggled and batted some of it away.

'What do you reckon?' I pulled out a couple of dresses. One was short and tailored charcoal matte satin with a cute tucked-in waist that had been my go-to for any last-minute work events. The other was one I'd never worn, picked up on sale when I was pregnant, to remind myself that one day I'd get back into my normal sizes again. It was a knee-length sheath with cut-outs of sheer fabric. I had imagined wearing it with my big clumpy knee boots and some dramatic makeup. I regarded it warily. It was a bit of a change from my harem pants, camisole and cardigan uniform. I held the dress up against me. Maybe it was worth a shot.

Holly made a strange gurgling sound. I pulled the clothes back and found her rolling towards the back of the wardrobe, her arms wrapped in the tassels of a kimono.

I wriggled down to lie beside her. It was cool and dark under the rack of clothes, which all smelt vaguely of floral washing powder. Some of the longer bits of fabric rubbed against my face. 'This is weirdly relaxing.' I looked at Holly, who was kicking her legs in a maxi skirt I hadn't worn for years. 'Maybe we stay under here for a bit.'

Lauren peered around the door. 'What are you doing?'

I shuffled over so that there was a space beside me. 'Hiding. Do you want to join us?'

She frowned but dropped to her knees and, holding Mackenzie to her chest, wiggled in next to me. 'This is a bit weird.'

Holly stuck a tie from a wrap dress in her mouth.

'Totally, but Holly seemed to be having a good time so I just thought I'd join her. How are you doing?'

Lauren shut her eyes. 'I'll get there. My friends are all going out to the pub tonight. Like every one of them.'

I exhaled. 'That sucks.'

'Do you reckon Nick's mum would look after Mackenzie, too?' Her voice was small.

I turned to face her. 'Sweetheart, I don't think ...'

She sat up, brushing a pair of silk pants off her face. 'Yeah, sorry. She'd probably freak out anyway. Seems to be her thing.'

I watched her as she hauled herself to her feet. 'It won't last.'

She nodded. 'Sure.'

***

Nick
Age: Six months

I arrived home from work early, to find Renee and my mother trying to convince Holly to drink from a bottle. Renee was wandering around the room with it, singing to Holly and thrusting the teat towards her mouth.

Holly would screw up her face and turn away each time.

'Try rubbing it on your skin, maybe, see if it's easier if it smells like you,' my mother suggested.

Renee gave it a quick wipe in her cleavage and tried again. Holly threw herself back in her arms.

Renee shot a look at Mum. 'What are we going to do?'

Mum shrugged. 'It's okay. If she won't do it, she won't do it. Give her a good feed and put her down before you go and we'll be fine. I can give her a bit of banana or something if she looks hungry.'

She looked up at me. 'Nick will understand if you can't be out as long as you normally would.'

Renee looked up, seemingly astonished to see me. 'Oh, hi.'

'You changing your mind?' I realised I still wasn't completely convinced it was ever going to happen.

She shook her head. 'No, of course not. I'll just go and switch out of these clothes.'

My mother took the bottle from her hand. 'I'll carry on here for a bit, see if I have any luck. You go.'

Holly was craning her head around her grandmother, trying to catch my eye. I winked at her. 'How's my beautiful girl?'

My mother stroked her cheek. 'She's such a sweetheart. So engaged with the world. Interested in everything. It won't be long before she's crawling, then you'll have trouble.'

I smiled. 'Easily bored.'

My mum nodded. 'Yes, but that's a good thing, isn't it? You wouldn't want one of those babies that just kind of sits around and lets the world happen to them.'

I shrugged. 'I feel like that might be a bit easier.'

'You don't mean that. How's work?'

'Really good.' I found my energy level spiking at the thought of it. 'We seem to be signing up new members all the time at the moment, lots of PT clients. And we hired a new woman a while back who seems to be working miracles.'

My mum raised an eyebrow. 'Where did you find her?'

I frowned. 'Sam hired her. I'm not sure actually.'

'And what does Renee think of her?'

I felt a flush in my cheeks, which I willed away. 'They've not actually met yet. Renee hasn't been into work recently.'

My mother turned back to Holly. 'Oh well, perhaps you could have everyone around here one day for lunch or something. Renee's a bit isolated here, you know.'

I turned to a magazine that was lying open on the bench. Renee might not have been out socialising a lot but she wasn't exactly isolated. Her phone was constantly bleeping with messages from her mum friends and she worked for hours at night on her group, answering messages online.

Then there was Lauren, whom I could hear in the bathroom with her baby. She looked like something off one of those terrible reality television programmes about mad pregnant teenagers, with her heavy eyeliner and too-strong perfume. Our basin was absolutely covered in tubes and sprays and things I couldn't even identify. Clothes were spilling out of the spare room – and only a few of them her baby's. How long was she expecting to stay?

A noise in the doorway made me look up. Renee had returned. She was breathtaking, her hair arranged in the soft wavy curls she used to do every morning for work and wearing a dress I'd never seen before with a big see-through patch down one side. She was wearing the boots she'd bought on a trip to Italy.

'You look amazing.'

She looked at her feet. 'Thanks.'

She'd done her eyes with dark eyeshadow stuff and had put gloss on her lips. She produced a piece of paper and handed it to my mother. 'This is just a list of things that I thought you might need to know about bedtime. She needs to have the heater on because she can't handle any sleeping bag and she's too little for any covers. It helps to have the white noise on at about half-volume. Wait until she's showing some tired signs before you try to get her to sleep but if you wait until she's too tired it's even harder. If cuddling her to sleep doesn't work, just wait for me to come home or give me a call and I'll come.'

My mother put her hand on Renee's arm. 'I remember. We'll be fine. If there are any problems I will ring you.'

'You promise?'

My mum kissed her cheek. 'I promise. Go and have fun, you two. You both deserve a break.'

Renee flicked a look at me. 'I'll just go and give her a quick feed, then we can go.'

***

Renee
Age: Six months

When we walked into the restaurant I had to will myself to keep putting one foot in front of the other. It was packed. A table in the middle was surrounded by women who looked like they had come from one of those advertising agencies where you had to have your hair a certain length and style before they'd let you in the door and you had to buy your clothes from one particular place. They were all tiny, blemish- and wrinkle-free and laughing in that slightly-tipsy-but-not-unattractive drunk way that some women seem to pull off. Me, if I'm in a group I'm just super awkward until I've had too many drinks and then I'm a bit loud and obnoxious.

The waiter showed us to a table that was tucked away in the corner, like they wouldn't actually normally have sat anyone there but Nick must have been persuasive when he made the booking.

He clasped my hand as we walked across the room as if he thought I might turn and bolt at any minute.

A family group was leaving the table next to us. One of the men was stooped over, holding the hands of a toddler who teetered on tiptoes, pushing through the crowd towards the door.

I watched them. 'How old do you think he is?'

Nick turned to look as if he hadn't noticed they were there. 'Not sure – one?'

'Probably. I'm sure Holly will be walking by then. She's so advanced.'

I gave the menu a cursory look and placed it back down.

Nick smiled. 'You know what you're going to have?'

Usually I would complain about only having a caramelised red onion tart or bowl of chips to choose from when we went out. Here, I could have chosen a pasta, some sort of Japanese thing, or a multi-course vegetarian degustation 'chef's special'.

I bit my lip. 'It all looks lovely.'

He stared at me as if trying to will me into eye contact. 'Do you want to try the degustation?'

I frowned. 'Doesn't that usually take something like a week and cost about as much as a small car?'

He grinned. 'We haven't been out for months so I think we can afford a little bit extra. And I can ask if they can make it speedy?'

I shifted in my seat. This was meant to be fun. Why couldn't I relax?

'Okay, let's give it a go, if it won't take too long.'

'And a drink?'

'Soda and lime.'

He paused and raised an eyebrow. This was the home of the passion fruit mojito. 'Not feeling well?'

I stared at the crease running down the middle of the white tablecloth. 'I've just started taking some drugs. They're not meant to go with alcohol.'

He'd turned to try to get the waiter's attention but paused. 'What kind of drugs?'

I took a breath. 'Antidepressants. I might have a bit of that postnatal misery.'

I shrugged. He could judge me if he wanted to. All I could think about was Holly at home. Was she crying? Did Ellen remember that she needed her snuggly? Were my notes about the heater clear enough?

Nick opened his mouth to say something but a waiter appeared beside him.

As the man walked back towards the kitchen after taking our orders, Nick folded his arms and leant back in his chair. I braced myself for the story of how he'd run his way out of depression when he'd been stuck behind a desk for years ruing his capitulation to his IT degree.

'You don't want to see if you can use a more natural method first to help your mood? I could start work a bit later and you could work out first thing. That endorphin rush ...'

I shook my head so hard my dangly earring hit me in the cheek. 'Getting up earlier is literally the last thing I need. You've just got to trust me on this one, okay?'

There was a shout at the next table. One of the women had knocked over a bottle of red wine and it had fallen towards us, its contents dripping off the side of the table on to the floor. I looked down. And into my bag, it appeared. I quickly nudged it away with my foot.

'I'm so sorry.' The woman sitting nearest us started to dab frantically at the mushroom suede leather. 'We're clumsy at the best of times ...'

I had to bite my tongue. I hadn't brought my favourite bag out since Holly was born because it wasn't big enough to hold nappies, wipes and all the other things I had to cart around when she was with me. Now it had a large red blotch in the middle of one side. There was no way that was moving.

'It was an accident,' I mustered at last and turned back to Nick.

He was answering a message on his phone. I waited.

He looked up. 'You okay?'

I studied the tabletop. 'That's why I don't have expensive things, I guess.'

'Sorry, Ren. We can get you another one if it doesn't come out.'

I shook my head and took a deep sip of my sparkling water. Why had I started my antidepressants on probably the only day this year that I was going to go out? 'Why do I need an expensive handbag, anyway, these days?'

The waiter appeared at my arm again, sliding a small plate in front of me. What was it with vegetarian options and pumpkin?

'Pumpkin parfait with ginger marmalade,' he muttered. Nick was handed something that looked like slices of raw meat. He slid a bit on to his fork where it drooped like soggy ribbon.

'Maybe we could go for a walk after dinner? It's been ages since we went and tried on samples.'

It used to be my favourite thing, popping into a department store after dinner to try on makeup I would probably never be able to afford to buy.

I tried to look enthusiastic. 'That sounds fun.'

Our plates were cleared and the next course appeared. I could see Nick trying not to laugh.

'A caramelised onion tart,' the waiter announced.

We ate in silence. I scanned the room for inspiration for something to say that didn't involve Holly. My mind was stubbornly blank.

'I'm just going to go to the bathroom, be right back.'

Nick nodded.

***

When I returned to the table, Nick was staring at his plate. His smile had vanished, his face stony.

'All okay?'

'Uh huh.' He shovelled a forkful of food into his mouth and shifted his gaze out the window behind me.

'Nick. What's going on?'

His eyes were cold when he finally made eye contact with me. He could have been a stranger. 'You got a lot of messages on your phone while you were gone. From your *group*.' He said the word as if it was something distasteful.

'Okay ...'

'I thought I should check it wasn't an emergency.'

'You looked at my messages?'

'Good job I did, too. "Nick seems to think that being a dad is something he can do when he gets a free minute."' He fired the words at me. I'd never seen him so angry. '"I don't get any support. He just cruises around and does what he likes and I have to keep everyone alive."'

He lowered his voice when a woman at the next table shot him a look. 'Is that actually what you think, Renee? Do you think it's easy for me? Trying to run a business and be a good dad ... meanwhile you let random strangers live in our house, spend like every spare minute on your phone, and now, I find, have some sort of depression you just haven't bothered to talk to me about? Bet you told them all about that.'

I shut my eyes. 'It's just letting off steam.'

'Yeah, maybe ... but how many members have you got on there? Sixty thousand, you said the other night? What if my clients, my friends, see it? I am not a bad father.'

163

'Sure, you're not. But it damn well feels like you need a mother, too, half the time.'

My phone started to hum across the table, vibrating with a phone call. Nick reached out to stop me answering it. I flipped it over. It was Ellen. Standing, I swiped to speak to her.

Nick waved for me to sit down but I shrugged him off, scuttling in my stompy heels to the door.

Outside, the night air was cool and it had started to spit with rain. 'Is everything okay?'

I could hear Holly wailing before Ellen spoke. My nipples prickled with breast milk.

'I'm having some trouble getting Holly to settle.' Ellen sounded apologetic. 'I'm actually wondering if she's coming down with something. I tried banana and one of those custard things she usually likes. I wondered if hearing her mum's voice might help.'

I gulped. 'I'm happy to try.'

Ellen must have held the phone out. 'Hi, honey.' I tried to make my voice light and soothing. 'Daddy and I will be home soon.'

A couple walking past caught my eye and smiled.

'Can you cuddle up with Gran, sweetheart?'

The crying got louder. There was rustling and Ellen spoke again. 'Never mind. You two have fun, I'm sure we'll come right any minute. Maybe we'll go for a walk. Fresh air usually helps.'

I hung up the phone reluctantly. Nick was watching through the window.

A taxi pulled up in front of me, the driver looking at me expectantly. I hadn't even realised I was standing in the taxi rank. I held up my hand for him to wait and pushed back into the restaurant to collect my handbag.

'Sorry.' I gestured to Nick. 'I've got to go.'

He pushed back his chair. 'Now?'

'Your mum can't settle Holly. I can't sit here thinking about her being upset at home.'

'I'm sure she'll get her sorted. This is important.'

I sighed. 'Really?'

He turned away from me. 'Fine, whatever. Just go. Maybe chat about it with your group on the way home.'

I stared at him. 'Aren't you coming, too?'

He put his head in his hands. 'No, Renee. I've ordered this meal and I'm going to pay for it. I might as well enjoy it. You do what you need to do. I think we both know you're doing that anyway.'

***

I raced up the stairs as soon as the taxi stopped outside our block of flats. All was quiet as I flung myself through the front door. Ellen looked up. 'She's asleep.' She stood, brushing something off the front of her skirt. 'I hope you didn't come back on my account.'

I turned away. 'It's okay. It wasn't going that well, anyway, to be honest. Where's Lauren, was she any help?'

She paused. 'I've not seen her all evening, actually.'

The door to the spare room was ajar. I pushed it open. The room was empty.

'Lauren?' I looked in the bathroom. Empty again.

I pulled out my phone. 'Where are you?' I tapped out a message. 'Terrible night out. I was hoping we could debrief.'

I returned to the room where she had been sleeping. Tucked under the edge of the duvet was a piece of crumpled paper. 'Had to go – Mum trying to get me to hand over Mackenzie. I'll message you.'

Chapter Five

Megan Campbell, 5.40pm: 'Having twins will be fun, they said. They'll keep each other entertained, they said. Well, guess what?! My twins have been having a competitive round of Heads Shoulders Knees and Toes for the past 20 minutes while I've been trying to cook dinner. They're each trying to be louder than the other and I just want to hide in the cupboard and drink all the wine in the house.'

Renee
Age: Six months

The house was quiet when I woke the next morning. I reached for my phone as Holly snuffled around for her morning milk. It was just after 7.30am. I'd gone to bed before Nick arrived home and by now he would be at work. My phone screen was blank. Not a single message from him. My stomach gurgled with something that felt a bit like guilt. It was normal to vent, wasn't it? I wasn't doing anything that unusual. It's not like I had many people to talk to anywhere else.

What had woken me? Holly could usually virtually cartwheel across me in bed without disturbing me. There was an urgent rap on the front door.

I wriggled to the side of the bed and hoisted myself to my feet, shifting Holly's weight on to my left hip. It had to be Lauren. I'd been sending her messages every time I woke in the night but so far they had not even shown as having been received, let alone replied to. I was more worried about her baby than Lauren herself – no doubt she would find a couch to collapse on no matter what she'd been up to all night. But Mackenzie was still so little for her age and seemed permanently slightly terrified. The idea of her camping out in someone else's lounge made me feel slightly ill.

Maybe I should phone her mother. Lauren was disorganised and floundering a little as she tried to work out her new routine with her baby, but weren't we all? It was hardly cause to expect her to give up her child. But then she did not sound as if she was the most reasonable of women.

Whoever was at the door knocked again, even louder. Holly protested as I heaved us out of the bed, stumbling the few steps to the doorway to swing it open. A man who could have been no older than twenty stood on the doorstep, a clipboard in his hand. 'Good morning, how are you today?' He was firing off the sort of energy that I had not felt in a long time.

I regarded him warily. 'Fine, thanks.'

'I just wanted to talk to you about your power bill. Do you want to save a bit of money?'

I sighed. 'I'm sure I do but now isn't really a good time. Isn't it a bit early?' I adjusted Holly's weight against my shoulder.

'We try to get people before they head to work for the day. It'll only take a minute.'

'I'm sure, but babies don't really understand that concept ...' I gestured at Holly.

'Can I just leave you some information to read? Pop back a bit later at a time that's more convenient?'

I took a step backwards. Holly wriggled against my shoulder so that she was turned half to face him, as if wanting to appraise the man who'd caused her to be wrenched from bed.

As he held out a pamphlet, she drew herself back and sneezed enthusiastically over the paper in his hand. A fine spray of mucus extended to the pad he carried in the other. His mouth curled with distaste as I handed the pamphlet back.

I shrugged as he backed away, wiping his hands on the sides of his jacket. 'I think she's coming down with something. We might go back to bed.'

We watched as he disappeared towards the neighbour's door. I gave Holly a high five as we turned back towards the house. 'That's a skill that could come in handy.'

***

Holly and I were lying on the floor, looking at a board book, when Nick clattered through the front door a few hours later. I looked at the clock. Almost midday. It had been a long time since he came home at lunchtime. I tested a smile as his face loomed upside down, approaching from behind us. He was not usually one to hold a grudge, and he never had with me. Holly gave him her best gooey grin.

He returned hers but not mine.

Sinking into the armchair in the corner of the room, he cleared his throat. 'Sorry for interrupting.'

I shook my head. 'You're not. I was just going to show Holly my wonderful pig impersonation.'

I demonstrated a loud snort and Holly cackled with laughter. He frowned. 'That's not an attractive sound. Is she going for a nap soon? I just wanted us to talk.'

I frowned. 'We can talk. Couldn't it have waited until later?'

He shrugged. 'I couldn't concentrate at work.'

I rolled my eyes as he flicked a glance at Holly. 'She's not even managed one word yet. She's not going to be dissecting our conversation.'

He bit his lip. 'Fine. What's going on with us, Renee? Do you really think all those things that you wrote about me? Do you think I'm totally useless?'

I scrambled to sit up properly. 'Not really. Only a bit. Sometimes. Not useless ...'

'I think that's really unfair.'

I sighed. The argument seemed to be coming, whether I could handle it or not so I had nothing to lose. 'When was the last time you helped me with anything around here without asking for a ten-step plan first?'

He put his head in his hands. 'I don't help around here? I was living with your mother for who knows how long. Then it's this random teenager. You don't want anything to do with me but I keep my happy face on and try to think of nice things to do together. I'm busting my arse making sure the business is earning enough to provide for our family. It's hard work coming home and going straight into more stuff I have to do. But I guess you can't see that.'

'We agreed that I would be home for the first year. You were fine with it.'

He stood up. 'Yeah, I know. We agreed. I just didn't know it would be so ... separate.'

I stared at him. 'Separate?'

'Like it's me over here and you two over there and it doesn't really matter what I do so long as the money keeps coming in, right? Even Lauren's more involved than I am.'

'She's not here, you might have noticed.'

'Yeah, and no doubt you're more worried about that than you are about missing me.'

I picked Holly up and stalked to the kitchen. 'I'm not having this conversation.'

***

171

We stayed in the kitchen for almost an hour, watching birds dance on the trees outside the window. Nick would usually follow me in after a fight, to make a joke or reach for a hug.

This time, he turned on the television.

Finally, I heard the creak of the armchair as he stood and trudged out of the flat. I braced myself for the door to slam but he shut it gently. I stared at my phone. Should I call him and ask him to come back? What would I say?

I checked my watch. I had agreed to meet my mother for a walk in the early afternoon. There wasn't long to practise my brave face.

***

She was sitting on a park bench when we arrived, reading a magazine. She looked up as we approached and grinned. 'Darlings, it's so lovely to see you.' She had put another rinse through her hair and there were flashes of what looked to be green showing through the ends. She bent to kiss Holly's cheek. 'Shall we walk down by the water, maybe feed the ducks a bit?'

The sun was warm on my face, helping to push away the lingering chill of my fight with Nick. When was the last time I had been out for a proper walk? I had bought all the equipment to transport a baby around – wraps, slings, the stroller – but it often just seemed a little bit too difficult to get up and out the door. And although the woman in the shop had promised me that getting the wrap on would become second nature, I still ended up winding it around me until I felt like a huge sausage roll the couple of times I had tried.

My mum waved in greeting at an elderly woman who was walking towards us, firmly clasping the hand of a small child who was trying to chase a goose that strutted along the pavement ahead of her.

The pair stopped as they neared us, and the woman craned her neck to look at Holly. 'Marjorie. What an adorable little girl.'

I felt a flush of warmth wash over me. She really was, with her scrap of blonde curls, big brown eyes and those ridiculously long eyelashes.

The toddler who was with her leant over the stroller, too. She had a long string of something green protruding from her nose. I pulled the stroller back a little towards me as she extended her hand to touch Holly.

'This is my granddaughter, Holly,' my mother was telling her. 'Isn't she cute?'

The little girl nodded. I looked up at the swell of pride in my mother's voice. I could still remember the time I had overheard her at home when I was about nine, telling one of her friends that she didn't think she was cut out for motherhood. As if no one had noticed. I watched her gaze down at Holly, trying to shake Nick out of my mind. She was definitely trying. Maybe grandmotherhood was an easier fit.

'Still working on your pottery?' The other woman inquired.

My mother nodded. 'I'm semi-retired but you know, it's what I love to do so it's not really working, is it?'

They exchanged some more pleasantries as I focused on manoeuvring Holly just out of the reach of my mother's friend's granddaughter, who was surprisingly insistent on smearing something from her index finger on to Holly's forearm.

At last, my mother waved goodbye.

As they drew away behind us, I turned to her. 'Who was that?'

'I actually have no idea. But she seemed to know me, didn't she?'

I couldn't suppress a giggle. 'You've never been any good at keeping track of your friends.'

She smiled. 'Only the real ones.'

As we drew closer to the creek, she reached in her handbag and withdrew a plastic bag full of mouldy bread.

'What is that?'

She grinned. 'Sorry. I found it in the back of the cupboard. Birds won't care, though, will they?'

She took a handful and threw it towards the water. A squall of ducks descended on it, shrieking at each other. It reminded me of a Black Friday sale in a clothes shop, with people elbowing each other to get to the racks.

Holly giggled and waved a hand in their direction. Mum threw another handful, trying to land the bread nearer to us to draw the birds closer. One swooped down and perched on the end of Holly's stroller. She shrieked.

I leant back on my heels, feeling the breeze brush over skin that was usually clammy with sweat from holding Holly close. 'We still haven't found Lauren.'

Mum stopped and looked at me. 'Are you worried?'

I bit my lip. 'A bit. She's so young. And Mackenzie, too. I don't know if she's really got anywhere to go – it sounds like her mum is a bit of a shocker, not very supportive. What if she's roughing it somewhere?'

Mum touched my arm. 'She'd know she could come back to you if she was stuck. You can't fix everyone, you know. No matter how much you want to. We always muddled along okay, just the two of us.'

I watched as she threw another chunk for the birds. I pulled my phone from my pocket and snapped a photo. Quickly, I swiped to share it with the mothers' group. 'What's everyone else up to on this beautiful day?'

I'd deal with the responses later.

Holly had turned in her stroller and was focusing on something just out of the corner of my eye. There was a couple sitting on a park bench. I could tell immediately why she was interested – the man looked almost exactly like Nick. Right down to his bright orange workout gear. I looked again. There was no mistaking that jawline. 'What's he doing? I thought he was going back to work.'

My mum looked up but I was already halfway to the bench, fixing a bright smile on my face.

He looked up as I approached, the grin he was shooting the woman next to him still plastered across his face. 'Renee,' he spluttered, 'what are you doing here?'

'I could say the same to you. We've just come out for a walk.'

He shuffled in a way that almost looked as if he was slithering away from his companion. He gestured to her. 'This is Maia. We're just taking a coffee break.'

She shot me a very white smile. 'Needed to get away from the gym for a bit.'

It could not have been more than an hour since he arrived back at work from our place.

'Oh, sorry.' He seemed to remember. 'Maia, this is my partner, Renee.'

She extended a slim hand. 'It's lovely to meet you. That must be Holly.' She gestured to where my mother was watching us, one hand on the stroller handle.

I smiled despite myself. 'It is.' I turned to Nick. 'Do you want to see her before we go?'

Nick jumped to his feet. 'Of course. We need to be heading back anyway.'

They followed me back to where the stroller was now surrounded by angry birds. My mother had run out of bread.

She raised her eyebrows as Nick approached. I couldn't blame her. Maia looked like she could have stepped out of the pages of a fitness magazine. She was tiny, about ten centimetres shorter than I was, but looked like pure muscle. There wasn't a scrap of anything squishy on her that I could see. She had glossy, highlighted, chocolate brown hair and a light tan. It had been a long time since I had had time to get my highlights done and my skin felt like it had the distinctive pallor that you acquire when you spend almost your entire life indoors. Stay-at-home-mum tan, I'd taken to calling it.

Nick dropped to his knees next to the stroller, tickling Holly's cheek. She squirmed in delight.

When he slung his bag over his shoulder, his cheeks were tinged with pink. 'Have fun.' He gave me a dry peck on the cheek.

I nodded and watched as they trudged back across the park towards the street the gym was on. Maia gave me an awkward wave over her shoulder.

My mum looked at me, a question in her eyes. 'Who was that?'

I shook my head. 'I think I knew he'd hired someone new. She seems nice.'

She turned us back the other way. 'Yes. I suppose she does. Shall we walk around to the other side and get a coffee before we head back?'

I nodded mutely. Words and images kept zipping around in my head. Who was that? Why had he not mentioned her?

Mum had to stand on tiptoes to order our coffees from the coffee van. The woman manning the machine scrawled her name on two big disposable cups. 'Won't be long.'

Mum's gaze settled on something over my shoulder. 'Oh ...'

'What?' Before she could answer, a warm, wide hand clapped on to my shoulder. I spun on my heel. 'Oh!'

His face swam in front of my eyes, looking like David Beckham when he was going through his no-hair phase of the late 1990s. Dressed in a tailored blazer and khakis, he looked quite different from the last time we shared the air of a room, when he was dishevelled, with three-day stubble and an overgrown undercut.

'Jordan. What are you doing here? I thought you were working overseas.'

His grin was wide as he landed a kiss on each of my cheeks. No longer CK One, I noted. He had progressed to some sort of woody cologne that reminded me of how I imagined Don Draper might smell.

'I've been back home for a couple of weeks. You look great, Renee. Nice to see you, Marjorie.'

It was not so long ago that just seeing his name in my email inbox at work had immobilised me. One afternoon I had sat constantly refreshing my messages for hours, waiting for him to reply when I asked him out for a drink. Once, when we had been seeing each other for about a year, he went on a holiday without me, I went over to his house and collected some of his pillows so that I could sleep with his smell while he was away – then quickly washed his linen as an excuse for having done so.

But we hadn't talked in four years, six months and – I mentally ran the numbers – about two weeks. I was not prepared for this.

'What ... what are you up to these days?' I forced the words out.

'Still working in sales. I'm with a new fintech start-up, it's pretty exciting. And I get to live back home again, which is pretty great. What about you?'

I gestured to Holly. 'My daughter's taking a lot of my time at the moment.'

He seemed only to notice then that there was a baby with me. 'Oh, how gorgeous.' He turned to her.

I'd never seen him with a child before. Had I just assumed he'd be terrible? The thought twigged a memory – nope, he'd definitely said he didn't like them. Something about the noise and smell. But he actually looked interested in her, tilting his head to try to catch her eye.

My mum cleared her throat. 'I had better be going.'

I forced another brave smile at Jordan. 'Well, I've got to run my mum home. It was great to see you.'

He raised a hand to wave after us as we backed away. 'And you. Catch up sometime, maybe?'

Mum frowned at me when he was out of earshot. 'I've my own car here.'

I shrugged. 'I know. Panicked.'

***

At home, I balanced Holly on my knees on the bed so she was propped up facing me and pulled up the group on my phone. I tried to push all thoughts of Jordan out of my mind.

Three things were true: I had adored him once. He had hurt me. I loved Nick. It didn't really matter what he was doing now.

But that led me to my next problem.

'Advice, please,' I started my post. 'Would you be worried if your partner was having coffee in a park with a woman from work and didn't mention it?'

I pressed enter quickly to send the post to the group. Nick would probably be livid if he knew I was telling them but I didn't really care. The longer I looked at the words, the more twisted my brain felt. On one hand, it was just sitting in a public place, having a coffee. If he had been having a drink with Sam, I'd have thought nothing of it. But on the other, if he had time to stop for a break in the park, could he have stayed home a little longer and tried to work things through a bit more with me? Maybe a walk in the park together could have been what we needed. And why hadn't he talked about Maia, if she was close enough to him to be someone he wanted to spend a break with?

The replies were coming in already. Some were from the group regulars and I didn't even need to look at them to know what they would say. Maxine, a forty-something single mum from Essex, was adamant that I might as well have caught them in bed together and should change all the locks. But Fiona thought I was possibly being too harsh. 'It's normal for people to want some time out of work with their workmates, Ren. Especially if stuff's getting a bit stressful.'

I stared at the post as more comments rolled in. It didn't really matter what they thought, though, did it? What mattered was how I felt about it. And it wasn't great.

I clicked over to my private messages. Still nothing from Lauren. I sent her another message. 'Could you just let me know you and Mackenzie are all right? I'm still worried. Sorry to be a nag xx'

There were a handful of messages in a folder from people who weren't in my contacts list. I clicked it open. The name at the top was familiar. I realised with a jolt why – Lauren's mum.

'Could I come and talk to you about Lauren? I understand she's stayed with you recently. I'm very worried.'

It wasn't the type of message that I had expected to get from a woman that Lauren described as some sort of cross between a drill sergeant and the headmistress from *Matilda*.

'Sure,' I replied, giving her my phone number. 'If I don't answer, I'm probably just getting my daughter to sleep.'

The message below it was from a group member wanting a referral for a lactation consultant. I pulled up the numbers in my phone. They should have been in my speed dials, the number of times I had to send the contact details to people who were trying to win a battle to latch or work out why their babies never seemed to be able to get as much milk as they needed.

I clicked on the message below it and stopped. The name pulsed on the screen in front of me. Jordan Harrison. I let my finger hover over his name. Did I really want to give him any more of the space in my brain? I tapped on the message.

'Ren, it was so good to see you today. I was serious about catching up. Can we do that?'

Can we do that ... I turned it over in my head. This was the guy who had bailed two days before we were meant to move into a flat together. Instead, he sent his brother to collect the stuff he'd left at my place and I never heard from him again. I closed the message.

I stretched out on the sofa. Comment after comment was popping up on my post about Nick's strange coffee date. The verdict was that it was definitely weird. I would have to talk to him about it when he got home. It was starting to feel all a bit academic – it was like Nick and I were floating along in two different dimensions anyway, did it really matter if he was having coffee with someone else in his? Maybe he should have just tried to go out for dinner with her, too.

***

He arrived home as I was wrestling with a couple of reusable nappies that had turned inside out and velcroed themselves into an impenetrable ball in the washing machine. I'd bought them in a fit of conscience, worried about what I'd be tipping into the environment with every nappy change when every other person wants to tell you that having kids is the worst thing you can do for the planet anyway. But they weren't exactly cheap so I just bought two and used them in a haphazard way. The main problem with them was that they were so spongy and absorbent that I couldn't get them dry unless it was the hottest, sunniest day of the year.

As Nick walked in, I'd finally separated them and was contemplating attaching them to the ceiling fan and setting it going. At least they were cute colours – it could be some sort of new interior design trend.

He slung his bag on to the chair in the corner and wandered through to the kitchen, where he pulled a zero-sugar sports drink from the fridge. I gave myself a mental high five. I'd had an attack of the breastfeeding drought earlier in the day and had almost drunk it.

Returning to the lounge, he slumped on to the sofa. 'Where's Holly?'

I nudged the overturned laundry basket by my feet. Two little brown eyes stared out through the gap in the handle.

He slid down to crouch beside the basket, sticking his fingers through the hole. Holly giggled and grabbed one.

I stared at him. 'So ... do you and Maia go out much?'

He flipped the basket over, feigning surprise at finding Holly sitting underneath it. 'No. Just wanted a change of scenery today. You don't have to be weird about it.'

'Okay ...' I let the silence hang between us. 'And you don't need to be so defensive. You hadn't ever mentioned her to me before. I just thought it was a bit unusual.'

'Right.'

'What's that supposed to mean?'

He shrugged. 'Nothing. I said 'right'.'

'Yeah, but you said it like 'riiiight' like it's not actually all right at all.'

He leant back on his chair so the front legs lifted off the ground. 'Well, speaking of not mentioning ... how come you told my mum you were feeling low, but not me?'

'What would you have said if I'd told you?'

'I might have been able to help you, the way I got out of it.'

'Exactly. I didn't want you to tell me how you think I should fix it. I just wanted someone to listen.'

He shrugged. 'You know what I think.'

I threw the nappy inners over the back of the couch. 'Sure I do, as helpful as it is too.'

***

Nick
Age: Six months

I don't know why I bothered to go home for lunch at all. I'd been sure that Renee would be full of apologies, blaming hormones or whatever for her extremely public complaints about me. Instead, she doubled down. All I achieved was to make myself half-an-hour late for a meeting with an equipment hire company representative who wanted to part me from more of the business's cash. Wrangling salespeople had never been my thing. Sam just had to look at someone and they would offer half-off. But he was off somewhere, presumably attending to Project Baby. Even though I blustered my way through with as many 'mate's and 'I totally get it's as I could, I still ended up being offered a deal that was significantly more expensive than the current one and seemed to lock us in virtually for life.

My mood had darkened as I retreated to my desk.

Maia looked up from her desk in the corner as I sank into my office chair, rubbing my face with my hands.

'Tough day?'

'Nothing too unusual. You studying?'

She scooted over on her chair. Somehow, she made it look graceful, gliding from one end of the room to the other. I would trip over my own foot.

'A bit. Almost done. Anything you need a hand with?'

She made unwavering eye contact with me. Her eyes were sparkling – is that what happens when you get a normal night's sleep?

I shook my head. 'No, I'll get there. Thanks, though.'

'How's your daughter?' She gestured at the photo of Holly on my computer desktop.

'Very cute.' I involuntarily winked at the picture. 'Hard work, though. Keeping her fed and watered through the day seems to be about all that Renee can think about.'

'Still?'

'Well, you know she's not even seven months yet ...'

185

Maia ducked her head. 'I mean, what do I know? I've never done it. It sounds terrifying.'

I shook the dregs of an energy drink can left on my desk. Empty. I never used to bother with the things – full of chemicals and who knows what – but it felt like I had been awake for days.

Maia was still watching me. 'What have you got on this afternoon?'

I gestured at my desk. 'I'm going to make a protein shake and smash through this paperwork like a boss.'

She hauled me up by the arm. The touch took me by surprise and sent a warm tingle down my arm. 'I don't think so. Let's go for a walk. Molly's on reception. You haven't got any more clients.'

'How do you know?'

She shrugged. 'I checked.'

It had felt a little strange, walking next to her down the street, first to the deli on the corner for takeaway coffees and then to the park. But it was nice – when I'd first agreed I could probably find the time for a hot drink, I felt my neck muscles involuntarily tense, as if I was waiting for the usual, 'I wish I had time to have a coffee before it went cold,' response I'd get from Renee.

The excursion was short – maybe twenty minutes at the most. We were preparing to head back to work when I turned and saw those three familiar faces staring at me.

***

The pavement slapped the bottoms of my running shoes as I jogged away from the apartment block. Anger bounced in my chest. She was pulling me up on having a break with Maia, when she spent hours of every day online, complaining to thousands of strangers about me.

What else had she told them? Why couldn't she see how hurtful it was?

Was I not even allowed a half-hour to hang out with a workmate? I counted three more lampposts, sweat starting to drip over my eyebrows, then turned back for home.

As I trudged up the last few metres to our building, my phone bleeped. I reached for it – a message from Sam. He hadn't returned to work all afternoon. I was trying to be understanding but there was only so much time you could take off work for shagging purposes, wasn't there? The message was just a few words: 'I won't be in tomorrow.'

I had to hold my phone tightly to resist the urge to throw it across the road. Why was everyone suddenly so damn flaky? I pressed the icon to call him. It rang almost long enough to go to voicemail before he picked up. His voice sounded small and far away.

'What's going on?'

He was silent for a few seconds. 'It's all a bit of a mess, mate.'

'What's up?'

'Things aren't looking good.' He exhaled into the phone. 'My guys aren't doing what they should. Rachelle's egg count is low. We need to get some pretty significant help, it looks like. She's pretty cut up about it. Talking about quitting her job to reduce her stress to get things going.'

'Sorry to hear that ...'

He cut me off. 'Yeah. Need to hang out with her, take her mind off it. I'll try to be back the day after tomorrow, okay?'

When I hung up the phone, I switched over to my contacts and retrieved Maia's number. My finger hesitated over her name. Was it weird to call? Surely not. I needed her help to pick up the PT clients in the morning – I could do a lot of things for a lot of people but I couldn't train two clients booked in for solo sessions at the same time.

***

Renee

Age: Seven months

For weeks, I thought the only thing I was getting out of my antidepressants was a dry mouth and – if you can believe it – an even further increased appetite. But then, one day, I realised that something had changed. I was emptying the dishwasher, my back to Holly. The way our windows were positioned, we got the full glare of weak autumnal sunshine in the kitchen in the middle of the afternoon and it was surprisingly warm and a beautifully gold light that I hadn't really noticed before. She was sitting on the floor, examining a piece of apple, throwing it on the floor and then launching forward – tantalisingly close to commando crawling but not quite. She was muttering to herself and rubbing a squished bit of fruit between her thumb and index finger. Usually, the sound of her voice would make my back tense as I waited for signs of distress. But as I slid the last of the plates from the dishwasher to the cupboard, I realised she was babbling what would have sounded to someone who didn't speak English like a full, coherent sentence.

I sank to my knees in front of her. 'How are you, beautiful girl?'

She grinned at me.

'Boo.' I reached out and touched her nose. She screwed it up and seemed to try to repeat the noise back to me.

She leant out to grab a wooden spoon that was lying on the floor next to us and banged it on the floor.

'You can find interesting stuff anywhere, can't you?'

I stared at her. How could such a perfect little thing have come from someone so imperfect as me? If she could get so much enjoyment from a wooden spoon, just wait until she discovered real toys. Maybe instead of imagining a world where the environment would collapse around her into an apocalyptic wasteland, I could consider the possibility that she might use her clearly amazing brain to help find solutions. Was this what all those other mothers had been going on about? I kissed each of her cheeks.

My phone vibrated in the pocket of my cardigan. I knew without looking who it would be.

I hadn't replied to Jordan's initial surprise message. I'd told myself I'd just delete it and block him. Keep him out of mind permanently.

But I didn't delete it. Then, after three days of Nick and I only talking when it was absolutely unavoidable – I caved. What harm could it do?

In the two weeks since then, the communication had become more and more intense.

Now, we were trading messages virtually every other hour. He tried to impress me with a boat he had purchased for what he assured me was a fantastic price. I reminded him that I got horribly seasick. I was surprised he did not remember – he had bought me a whale-watching trip for a birthday and I had spent almost all of it lying down in the galley, drinking lemonade.

He told me he wanted to go back to university to train to be a teacher. I told him he could have saved himself twenty years if he had bothered to pay more attention the first time around. Had he forgotten he'd once told me everyone should be forced to stay home until they were eighteen, so as not to be a disruption in public places?

It was such an over-the-top display, it felt as though any minute he was going to claim to have spent the past year helping sick orphans or handfeeding blind puppies. But still, I felt a little ping of energy every time one of his messages arrived. There was no way I was going to let Nick know about it, though. He only vaguely knew about Jordan as the loser ex who had left me in financial disarray before we'd met. The guy who ignored the warning speech I gave them both – years apart – about how I'd rather be single than deal with any more flakiness in my life.

That morning, Jordan had sent me a detailed description of his memory of a day we had spent hopping from one pub to the next with friends from university, before sliding into bed in his dingy flat. 'When can we do that again?'

'What do you mean, do it again? I can't just muck around all day like that these days.'

He always replied virtually instantly. 'Not a pub crawl, then. Just an afternoon – the park maybe? I bet you're just as naughty as you ever were under all that sensible mum stuff.'

I rolled my eyes as I replied. 'I seem to remember you've always been the instigator.'

He sent me a wink emoji. 'You never complained.'

I looked up at Holly, who was still watching me. 'He'd be lucky. I think I'll just keep hanging out with my best girl, what do you reckon?'

She spat a piece of apple at me. 'Ba.'

***

I was washing Holly's hair when there was a knock at the door. This was not the sort of activity that you can easily interrupt. I had to hold Holly under the arms with one hand and frantically scrub her hair with the other while she twisted and turned, trying to get away. It was like trying to wash a particularly wriggly cat. Tilting her as far back into the bath as I could, I tipped a cup of water over her forehead to wash the last of the suds off. She screwed up her face and shrieked.

'What are you complaining about?' I tickled her under the armpit. 'None of that went anywhere near your eyes.'

I kissed her eyelids, wrapped her in a towel and, hoping there would be no cause to regret not having had a chance to put a nappy on her, propped her in my arms.

When I swung open the front door, the woman who had knocked was turning to go. She whipped back around and smiled. She had close-cropped hair, the kind of colour that could have been either naturally white or recently and carefully bleached. Her high cheekbones reminded me of someone, though I couldn't immediately place who it could be.

'Renee?'

'Yes?'

She extended a hand to me. She had a chunky white gold watch on one arm and a slim bangle circling the wrist of the other. She wore one delicate thin band on her ring finger. 'I'm Wendy, Lauren's mother. I'm sorry to turn up unannounced. I'm just so worried.'

I stopped. This was Lauren's mother? I had imagined some sort of dishevelled mess, greasy and unkempt, bumbling from one state of incoherent intoxication to the next, shouting obscenities at her daughter. Not this coiffed, calm person in front of me. When I'd told her where we lived, I'd half expected to never hear from her again.

'Hi,' I managed at last.

'Do you have time to talk? I hope I've not caught you at a bad time.' She gestured at Holly.

I stepped aside to let her in. 'It's fine, give me a minute and I'll just get this one dressed. Can I get you a drink?'

I internally checked myself. Did she know I knew about the drinking? She didn't seem to notice, settling on the couch and folding her hands in her lap. 'No, I'm fine, thanks. Take as long as you need. I so appreciate you being willing to help me.'

***

I watched Wendy's face as she talked. The picture Lauren had painted of her mother was starting to seem rather unreliable. From what I could make out, this wasn't a woman who was sponging off her daughter at all. If Lauren wanted to see flighty and unreasonable, she should read my teenage diaries' descriptions of my interactions with my mother.

'I have an idea where Lauren is.' Wendy's voice was careful. 'But I don't think it's going to be effective for me to turn up there. I was hoping that you might be willing to go and talk to her instead.'

I exhaled. 'Me?'

She nodded. Her eyes were hopeful. 'She seems to trust you. Look up to you. I am so worried, Renee. If someone could just go there and see that she's okay, it would just

mean the world to me. I keep picturing her somewhere ...'
Her voice trailed off.

'Where do you think she is?'

She consulted her phone. 'We think she's staying with
a friend from school, about five miles from here. But I
don't know how she's getting by – she won't be earning
anything, will she, and she doesn't have many of her things
for Mackenzie. I can give you money to give to her ...'

She broke off and studied her hands. 'I don't know how
our relationship's got this bad. It's been tough for a few
years – you know, just the typical teenage stuff and maybe
I've been a little overzealous about keeping her on track
since she fell pregnant – but for her to just totally disappear
like this, it's just taken me totally by surprise. While she
was with you at least she was replying to my messages ...'

I sighed. 'She mentioned feeling like there were a lot of
expectations at home ...'

Wendy didn't look up. 'I just wanted her to step up to
adulthood. Mackenzie needs her to be a mother, not a big
sister. If she were planning to study or anything, that would
be different but I won't just have her lying around all day
at home. She's got so much potential. Too much to waste.'

I nodded. 'She's trying. Even in the time she's been here,
I've seen a change.' I checked my watch. 'I should have
time to go there this afternoon and try to talk to her. Do
you want me to tell her to go home to you, or try to get
her to come back here?'

She spread her palms. 'I don't know. I mostly just want

to know she's safe and for her to know she can come back home any time. And find out whether she needs anything ...'

'I'll do what I can.'

***

I arrived at the address Wendy had given me three-quarters of an hour later. It might have felt like something out of a spy novel if I had not had a small child strapped to my front who kept simultaneously pulling my jumper down at the front with her hands, exposing the top of the lace of my bra, and up at the back with her feet, revealing a sliver of flesh around my hips that the carrier pushed down unflatteringly on to the waistband of my jeans. I frowned at her. 'It's far too cold to be disrobing your mother in public, my darling.'

The address was for one of a small row of terraced houses, with blank windows facing on to a quiet street. The sound of bass thumped from one of the front rooms of number 53. I walked past the house once, trying to look into the windows for a sign of Lauren or Mackenzie. On the second time, I tiptoed up to the door, trying not to let my steps make any sound. Not that I thought she'd try to get away if she saw me coming – it was hard to do anything quickly with a baby, let alone make a run for it, and besides, she had no reason to avoid me. Except that she might think I wanted her to pay for her half of our enormous power bill.

I rapped on the front door. Silence. I leant back on my heels and looked up at the top storey of the house. There was no movement in the net curtains. I knocked again.

There seemed to be a sound from further back within the house, then a rustle as someone came to the door and pulled it open.

Lauren took a quick breath as we locked eyes. She was holding Mackenzie against her shoulder. 'Renee.'

'Hi.'

'What are you doing here?'

I shifted Holly's carrier around so that she was on my hip and could see Mackenzie. The girls grinned at each other. 'I could say the same to you. Why did you just take off like that? Your mother is worried sick about you.'

She looked even younger than normal, her hair pulled into messy pigtails. 'As if. Probably just wants someone to pick her up a bottle of wine from the supermarket.'

'Don't start. We've met. She's lovely. Worried about you. I think you're being too hard on her.'

She stared at me.

I tried to keep my voice light. 'You need to get in touch with her and tell her you're okay. Imagine if it was Mackenzie doing a runner in twenty years' time. You'd feel awful, wouldn't you?'

She circled a protective arm around her daughter. 'She'll just want me to come back home.'

'And why don't you? What are you doing here?'

There was a crash from somewhere in the house. Lauren

shot a look over her shoulder. 'I'm just hanging out with friends for a bit, taking some pressure off. I need a break.'

'Please talk to her. I'm sure you two can work it out.'

She sagged against the front door. 'It's just too much. She wants me to be her daughter. But she wants me to be this amazing mum, too. Did I tell you she cuts out all the stories she sees about teenage mums who go on to have big businesses or whatever, and leaves them on the kitchen counter? It's exhausting.'

'You could have stayed with me, couldn't you? She seemed okay with that. We could set you up paying board or whatever for a month or two ...'

She took a step back. 'And get in the middle of your drama? No thanks.'

I watched her face. 'What do you mean?'

She sighed. 'Your mother's as flaky as anything. You and Nick skirt around each other as if you don't even want to talk to each other. It's stressful. At least here they just do their own thing and leave me to it. Remember that day we tried to watch a movie and you and Nick sat at opposite ends of the lounge? No thanks on that awkward sandwich.'

I felt heat rise to my cheeks. This was not how this was meant to play out. 'Can you just call your mother, please? Let her know you're fine. That Mackenzie doesn't need anything.'

She blew a piece of hair off her forehead and turned to stalk back into the house.

'Fine. See you around.'

I stared at the closed front door. Were we really that bad? Some of the women in the mothers' group had grumbles with their partners that were far worse than mine. I took a wobbly step back off the front stoop, reaching in my bag for my phone.

When I pulled up the messages. Jordan's name was at the top. I clicked on it. 'Tell me more about what you remember from that holiday.'

Chapter Six

Tricia Mullane, 8:37pm : 'How do you teach your kids to have a filter? We were out for dinner tonight and a man walked in with an eye patch. Mr 5 audibly gasped and literally yelled, 'Look, Mum, it's a pirate!' I could have crawled under the table. Same day he told someone in a wheelchair that they were too old for a stroller.'

Nick
Age: Seven months

I once told a group of friends that I'd rather be single than be the type of guy who has to beg for permission for a night out. Surely relationships are built on mutual trust and understanding, I'd ranted to the group assembled around a big wooden slab of a table at a rundown pizza joint. I was barely past my mid-twenties but already thought I knew everything – as you do before you realise how dumb you really are.

Then I grew up and had a baby. I felt less than useless at home most of the time, Renee and I were still barely talking and I was more like a third wheel than that time my mother made me entertain my cousin and his wife when they were on honeymoon from the US. But I still felt pressure to be home every minute that I wasn't working, unless I had an extremely good excuse.

It turned out that the next excuse I would get came from Sam. This was a guy who shared motivational posts online like 'live to work, don't work to live', but he was sitting at his desk at six o'clock on a Friday evening, literally shuffling paper. In a gym. Where he expressly asked that his job include 'no paperwork'.

I looked at him. 'What are you doing?'

He glanced up as if I had caught him in the act of stealing something from the work kitchen fridge. 'I'm just tidying. Paper mountain ...'

I cut him off. 'You are not. What's up?'

He put his face in his hands. A minute passed before I realised, with horror, that he was crying. The sort of weird quiet tears that men produced when they haven't been in the habit of crying for many years.

'It didn't work,' he spluttered at last then looked up. 'Sorry, man. Pathetic.'

'Don't be an idiot.' I slid into the chair opposite him. 'You mean the baby stuff. It didn't stick or whatever?'

He nodded. 'She's so upset. We had a month on those pills that are meant to get things moving but nothing doing except making her grumpy and sick. So, so grumpy. I don't even know what to do next.'

'I'm sure you're doing a good job. Not much you can do, I guess?'

'I feel so powerless. Like I just want to fix it, you know?'

I nodded. I did. When I heard Renee waking for the fourth or fifth time in the night for Holly, or puzzling over why she just threw on to the floor all the food Renee had cut up and arranged into pretty patterns on her plate, I wanted to come up with a solution for all the problems. But I had learnt my lesson about trying to offer helpful remedies.

'Do you want to get a drink? I can let Renee know I'll be home a bit late.'

He wiped the back of his hand over his face. 'That would be good.'

***

Three hours later, Sam and I were half a dozen beers in. The music had suddenly become thumpingly loud. We had settled on the pub around the corner from the gym – a place that we probably would have frequented more often were it not for the chance of being snapped by clients who expected us to aspire to higher health standards than they did.

After 8pm, the crowd was younger, less straight-from-work. I was contemplating another beer when a woman bounced over to our table in time to the music, her face pink with exertion, and possibly from the sparkling wine she held in her hand.

'Fancy seeing you here,' she said, grinning.

'Hi, Maia. What are you up to?'

She gestured across the room. 'Just out with a few friends. One of them quit her job today.'

'Oh ... congratulations?'

She nodded. 'Totally. What are you two doing? Rare to see you out.'

I could feel myself returning her smile. 'Just having a few. We'll head off soon. Don't get any ideas from your friends ...'

She pulled out the remaining chair at our table and slid into it. 'Course not. You guys are the best. Mind if I join you?'

Sam cleared his throat. 'What about your friends?'

She waved it away. 'They're all going home any minute.'

She rested her chin in her hands and looked up at me, wobbling slightly. 'It's so good to see you.'

My heartbeat had picked up as if I'd been chucking weights around at the gym.

A man in tight jeans and a slightly crumpled striped shirt ambled over to the table and put his hand on Maia's shoulder. She looked up. 'Oh, hi. I thought you'd headed off.'

'Hardly. The night is young!'

She gestured to us. 'These are my bosses, Nick and Sam. This is Mark.'

He mock-saluted us. 'Can I get you guys a drink?'

I was about to decline when Sam raised his empty beer bottle in acknowledgement. 'Sure, that'd be great.'

***

Two hours later, we had consumed three bottles of wine and at least four tequila shots between us, and had somehow agreed that it would be an acceptable idea to move to a karaoke bar. There was something about Sam and singing – every time he had a couple of drinks he decided he was going to be the next Tom Jones.

Maia was watching him, astonished, as he strutted across the tiny stage in the corner of the pub. Mark had disappeared – probably to the bar again. I turned to her and stretched my arm out along the back of her chair.

'You must wonder what you've let yourself in for, coming to work with us.'

She turned to me and smiled, resting her hand on my arm. 'I told you, you're both great.' Her speech was slightly slurred. 'I'm really enjoying it. I'm just sorry you've both got so much stuff going on at home. That's really hard. It's funny how the people you think have an amazing life always seem to have problems once you scratch the surface.' She made a little scratching gesture on the sticky tabletop. Sam hit a particularly screechy note.

'You think we have an amazing life?'

She blushed. 'Well, yeah. You seem pretty sorted from afar.'

I gestured at the empty chair where Mark had sat. 'You might get him across the line if you're keen for the whole bloke-and-kids thing.'

'What?'

'He's your boyfriend, isn't he? Seems pretty keen on you.'

Her blush had turned into a complete red flush. 'No!' She leant back and seemed to recover herself. 'I mean, it's not like that at all. Not at all.'

She shifted in her chair. I reached out for her. 'I'm sorry, I didn't mean to make you feel uncomfortable. You two just seemed like a thing ...'

She shook her head. 'Forget it.'

She played with the edge of her fingernail for a minute or two before looking up at me. 'Actually – could you come outside with me for a second?'

I shot a look at the stage. Sam had finished and was engrossed in conversation with the woman who ran the karaoke competition, probably picking his next number.

***

It was starting to rain more heavily as we huddled in the doorway outside the bar. Somewhere an alarm was going off and a group of what appeared to be uni students were shrieking at each other. Maia was flicking glances from me to the darkened windows of the shops across the road. I put my hand on her arm. 'What's going on?'

She looked at me. 'Does it really seem like Mark and I are hooking up?'

I waved it away. 'I'm sorry, I shouldn't have said anything. Forget it. Totally inappropriate for me to talk to you like that.'

She grabbed my hand. 'It's not that. It's just that, if I've got the hots for anyone, it's you.'

I felt my mouth drop open. She was swaying from one foot to the other, a streetlight casting a glitter of light over her dark hair.

She looked at the ground, where one of her heels seemed to have got stuck in a crack in the pavement. 'Now I'm sorry. I've had way too much to drink. I should go home.'

She turned to go back into the bar but I grabbed her hand and pulled her back towards me. She smelt of champagne and strawberries mixed with an odour of deep-fried chips.

Before I could talk myself out of it, I put my hands on her waist and pulled her in. And kissed her. She immediately responded, working her hands up the back of my shirt under my jacket.

A passing car hit the centre of the puddle next to us, snapping the energy, and we pulled apart.

We looked at each other in disbelief.

'Wow,' she exhaled. 'That was amazing.'

I laughed, my veins fizzing with energy. 'What do we do now?'

Before I could register what was happening, she had her arms around my neck, pulling me towards her. 'There's a taxi rank literally three steps behind me.'

'What about Sam?'

She nuzzled into my neck, drawing me along with her. 'What about him?'

I felt like a teenager bunking school. 'Just leave him here?'

'He's an adult. He'll be fine.' She was pulling my hand and I was not putting up a lot of resistance. Soon we were half-running. She opened a taxi door and we fell into the back seat, her hand up the front of my shirt.

I looked at her, trying to regain my breath. 'Where are we going?'

She kissed me forcefully. 'My place.'

The driver was half-watching us in the rear-view mirror as Maia curled up next to me in the back, occasionally giving directions. One of her long, slim legs was slung across my lap, her skirt hiked almost to her hip. Little fizzes of anticipation zipped across my skin as she dragged her fingernails over every inch of my exposed flesh.

We pulled up outside a big, white building. 'This is the one.' She grabbed my hand and pulled me from the car, waving her card at the driver.

Maia lived in one of those apartment buildings where all the floors look exactly the same and each unit is only big enough for two tiny bedrooms, a kitchen and half a living room. She fumbled with her key before pushing the door open to darkness, kicking off her shoes and pulling me in by the hand, turning on a table lamp as she guided me to the sofa. 'Drink?' She asked as she gently pushed me down, half climbing on top of me.

I shook my head, breathing in the scent of shampoo in the hair that hung down to brush my face.

She was kissing up the side of my neck, into my hairline, my hands drifting down her back, into the curve where the top line of her G-string rested.

She was loosening my belt when a photo on the wall opposite caught the light from the floor lamp. A woman was holding a baby in the waves at a beach.

I sat up straighter. 'Hey.'

She sat back, eyes wide. 'What's up?'

I shook my head, running my hands through my hair. The intoxication seemed to drain out of my body as the energy between us snapped. 'I shouldn't be here. What are we doing?'

She smiled and reached for my hand. 'It's just fun. You look like you could do with some of that.'

'I can't ...'

'You don't have to do anything. Just lie back and leave it all up to me.'

I stood up. 'I'm sorry. I need to go.'

The world had started spinning and I felt like I had when Elliott had convinced me to go on one of those theme park rides that throw you around 360 degrees at top speed. A cold sweat had broken out on my face. Renee would be at home waiting. What if she somehow knew where I'd been? What if Sam had got in touch and told her we'd vanished together? She could probably get on to my work computer and find Maia's address. There were steps on the landing – they couldn't be Renee's, could they? Rising panic shortened my breath.

Maia turned away. As I fumbled for my keys, checking I had my wallet and phone, I realised her shoulders were shaking with sobs. 'Maia?'

She pushed me away. 'I'm such an idiot. You must think ...'

I put my arm around her shoulders. The room was still in motion and nausea burbled away in my stomach. 'No. No. It's my fault ... we all just had a lot to drink. You're great.'

The floor seemed to lurch under me again. 'I've got to go. But you've nothing to worry about. Promise. Do you want me to call someone?'

She shook her head. 'I just need to go to bed.'

***

Renee
Age: Seven months

'Do you ever get those 'no possible answer' texts from your partner?' I wrote to the mums' group. 'Like why did you bother texting to ask me at all when you know I'm going to have to say yes whether I like it or not?'

Frankie was the first to reply. 'Our relationship's been so much better since we stopped texting totally. Speaking on the phone or in person means much less miscommunication, imo.'

Fiona was next: 'I find mine just texts whenever he's got something to tell me that he knows I won't like. Then turns his phone off quick.'

Nick had sent a message after work telling me that he wanted to go out for a drink with Sam – and was it all right? I couldn't do much but agree. But I didn't realise going out with Sam would mean crawling home at 5am.

Sam had been having some sort of ongoing infertility thing and it sounded as if it had failed again. I knew from my friend Matilda what that would entail – the devastation of having your period arrive just as you were counting down the days until you could do the test to determine whether anyone had taken up residence in your body.

But I had only just managed to have a shower at 5pm. The washing was sitting in the machine because I hadn't had a minute to look at it since the cycle stopped at 10am. I hadn't even had a second to formulate a thought on my own all day because Holly was going through what the baby book cheerily called a 'leap'. I called it a tiny mutiny against the world.

All our progress on sleep went out the window. Any food that she had started to eat was suddenly an abomination and any time I tried to put her down she would scream loud enough that I worried the neighbours would call social services on me.

I could just imagine them sitting in their flat – a very tidy one at that, I'd been invited in when we first moved over – and staring at each other. 'What is she doing to that poor child?'

The answer was usually trying to change a nappy or get her into a fresh set of clothes when she tipped a cup of water over her head. I shot a little message of thanks to my trusty bottle of pills. If she'd discovered this ability to argue while I was still battling the crushing existential dread, it might have been another thing entirely.

But I made it through the evening alone and had even managed to watch a decent amount of television before I fell asleep. I didn't allow myself to dwell on that thought too long. Since when had marathon TV binges been a success? As I surfaced, Holly demanding immediate access to my left breast, I could still hear Nick snoring from the lounge. I propped Holly on my chest and pulled up the messages from Jordan. There was a nagging question I couldn't shake.

'Why are you suddenly so keen on chatting to me, when I'm super boring these days?'

The minutes ticked by. He usually replied instantly. I checked the time – 8.30am on a Saturday morning. Probably too early. No doubt he was still in bed. Alone? Doubtful.

Finally, the little dots indicated he was typing something back.

'You're not boring.'

'I am. I went to bed at 8.30 last night after binge-watching three episodes of *Love Island*. I spend all my time wondering if Holly's eating and sleeping right. Why do you want anything to do with me?'

There was another long pause.

'If I tell you, you can't be mad.'

'No promises.'

'It's kind of "what might have been", right? When I saw you at the park with your mum, it made me think, if I hadn't taken off when I did, it might have been me and you and a baby.'

'You regret ditching me?' There was something about being on my phone that made me so much bolder than I could ever be in person.

'Yes.'

'I didn't think a family was something you ever wanted.'

'No. Or not then. But not never. I just wasn't ready to be an adult. But I shouldn't have given up on you.'

'But now you are ready?'

'I hope so.'

There was snoring from the living room. I flipped my phone face-down on the bedside table and inched over to the side of the bed.

Nick was crashed out on the couch, probably in the same spot I'd heard him fall into when he finally arrived home. His shirt was half undone, his hair pointing out at right angles from his head and his arms splayed across the couch as if he had fallen from a great height. It smelt as if he had spent the night crawling around on the floor of a bar. I stared at him. It was a bit like time travel. He had appeared in the lounge from a time that no longer existed for me. But no doubt, when the portal opened for me again, things would be totally different on the other side.

***

It was not until closer to 9.30am that Nick started to stir. For him, it might as well be midday.

He came into the bedroom, where we were tucked up in bed with picture books. His face was an unearthly shade of grey.

'Morning.'

'What happened to you?'

'We ran into some people.'

I nodded. Sam had been the instigator of several all-night one-more-drink-before-we-go-home events, especially if he was in a bad way. 'A big one then.'

He looked as though he was trying to say something. I reached for his hand but he leant away from me.

'I'm going to have a shower.' He pushed past to grab a change of clothes from the dresser. I watched him go.

'Fancy a coffee or something?'

He turned. His face was slack. 'Sorry, babe, I have to go into work. Some stuff I have to sort out.'

My shoulders sagged involuntarily. 'Okay.'

He seemed to shrink out of sight and around the corner. 'I'll come back as soon as I can.'

***

The house felt extra quiet without him. I lay back on the pillows and bounced Holly on my knee. 'What are we going to do now?'

She grinned gummily. I wriggled my legs. I had planned to get Nick to sit with her while I exfoliated my legs and conditioned my hair and did all the other things I couldn't find time to do during the week. 'You'll have to come with me while I have a shower.'

I set up a nest of towels on the floor of the bathroom and propped her on them, with an empty shampoo bottle to bash against the floor for entertainment.

'Five minutes, maximum, okay?' I yanked my top over my head and wiggled my pants down. Before the water was even warm, I jumped under the spray. As I closed the shower door behind me, Holly's face fell and her bottom lip started to wobble. I propped the door open and waved out to her. 'It's okay, darling, still here. See?'

She stared at me.

As I ducked my head back under the water, she wailed. I scrubbed frantically with the shampoo. 'Going as fast as I can.'

I towelled myself off and scooped her from the floor. 'I'll just pop some clothes on and we can find something to do.' She reached up and touched the hair behind my ear, pulling her fingers back and examining them intently.

I cursed under my breath. 'I forgot to wash the conditioner out. Okay, darling, thirty seconds, promise.'

***

Nick
Age: Seven months

It took a minute for me to remember why I was lying on the couch, wearing yesterday's clothes, when I opened my eyes.

Then it started flashing back. The bar. The drinks ... Maia.

I knew I should feel guilt. But the only thing I could concentrate on was the zipping energy fizzing in my body. She was so gorgeous. Like, objectively so. And she was keen on me? Unbelievable. Although clearly I couldn't allow anything to happen with her again. I tried to heave the idea out of my mind.

Holly and Renee were bustling about in the bedroom. I had to get out. I toyed with the idea of running to work, to try to burn off the almost anxious buzz that was bursting through my veins. But I'd probably need a marathon to get rid of it, and my hungover stomach would not be happy.

Instead, I took the bus, focusing intently on the ad

for a throat lozenge on the wall in front of me, pushing thoughts of both women out of my mind as much as I could. There were a handful of regulars on the main floor when I arrived, and a barre class in session in one of the small group fitness rooms. Our back office was dark. I realised I was disappointed. Had I really expected Maia to be there? I slid behind my computer and opened my emails. Did I need to contact her? Make sure she was okay after how we'd left it?

I'd been scanning news sites and social media as well as all our client files for about three hours when the door cracked open. I tried not to look up. If it was Sam he would come striding over, ready to tell me exactly what he thought of us ducking out and leaving him – assuming he could remember that he hadn't been consulted. There was silence. I opened an email and stared at it.

Soft footsteps tripped across the exposed wooden beams of the floor, closer to my desk. Definitely not Sam. I kept my eyes firmly trained on the programme on my screen until the footsteps stopped right in front of it. Maia cleared her throat. 'I wasn't expecting you to be here.'

I looked up. 'I had a bit to do. Are you meant to be working?' She was wearing a silky camisole top – through which the top of a lacy black bra was evident – and tight jeans. Her skin was dewy.

She cleared her throat. 'I actually came to pick up my stuff. I'm going to resign.'

215

'What?' I pushed my chair back. 'Why?'

She looked at her feet. 'I think I've made my position here untenable, don't you?'

I reached for her arm. 'No.' I tried to turn her to look at me. 'No, you haven't. Don't be silly. It was both of us.'

'We kissed. And you're my boss. And you're married.'

I ran a hand through my hair. It needed a cut. 'Not married and it's okay. Let's just chalk it up to a big night, okay? Please don't quit.'

She stared at me.

'Please don't. Sam would kill me.'

Her lips twitched in a small smile. 'Yes, he would.'

I watched her. 'I can help you get some of those PT papers done? I know you've got an assessment due.'

She sighed. 'Think you can trust me not to rip your clothes off?'

My body twitched involuntarily. I coughed to cover it up. 'I'm sure we can manage that. Listen, it was as much my fault as yours. Please don't feel bad.'

She stared at me. 'Really?'

I nodded. 'Really. I was a more than willing participant. Do not give it any more thought.'

Shifting my seat over, I pulled up another chair for her. She slid on to it, almost touching me but not quite. I made eye contact with Renee in the photo on my desk as Maia logged on to the online assessment system.

***

Nick

Age: Seven months

Six days had passed since what I was referring to in my head as 'D Day'. I did not know what I was expecting – perhaps that it would just be like a weird dream? That I'd wake up in a week's time and be back to my normal self, mildly pissed off that I never had sex any more but not thinking about it beyond that – much less the prospect of doing it with anyone else. But everything was different. I got to work even earlier than normal and watched the door until Maia walked in. I made excuses to get her to help me with PT clients. We had not touched again but every time we looked at each other I knew we were both thinking about it. I'd expected awkwardness but we'd slipped into an easy rhythm of what I was fervently telling myself was innocent flirting.

Even Sam had noticed something amiss – he bought the story she spun him about being unwell at the bar and me having had to help her home in a taxi, but he kept watching us and half-pouting like we were leaving him out of some secret club.

One minute I was cursing myself for not having gone through with it at her apartment, the next I was telling myself off for even considering it. It was exhausting.

My mum had sent me an email to ask if one of her friends could come and see me because she had been told she needed to exercise to ward off osteoporosis, but she was too nervous about going to a gym where she didn't know anyone. I only vaguely knew Marguerite but it seemed a straightforward proposition. Maia needed a chance to run through a workout with a client with more specific health needs.

Marguerite arrived about ten minutes before she was booked in for her initial assessment. Maia buzzed me from where she was filling in on the front desk. 'Scary lady here to see you.'

I collected my tablet, with the sheet we would work through loaded and ready. I spotted her as soon as I entered the reception area. While most of our clients were twenty through to the fifty-year-old rich-and-boreds, Marguerite would have been sixty-five at least. She had her hair in a severe bun and was wearing a pair of flowing linen pants and a fitted T-shirt. She looked like I always imagined a particularly severe ballet teacher would. She seemed to grit her teeth as I extended my hand in greeting. 'Last time I saw you, you were this high.' She gestured at her knee.

I grinned. 'Lucky I managed to have a growth spurt or two since then, right? Come through, we'll run through a few things to check where you're at and what you're hoping to achieve here.'

I caught Maia's eye over her shoulder. 'I was hoping it would be okay with you if Maia came with us? She's in training.'

Marguerite turned as if she had not noticed Maia was

218

there. 'Oh, of course. Not sure I'll be able to be much of a test case for you, though. I can barely touch my knees.'

Maia collected her notebook and scrambled to join us, her thigh almost grazing mine as we turned to walk towards the main floor of the gym.

I guided Marguerite into a couple of gentle side stretches. 'Do you have any fitness goals?'

She shook her head. 'No. I just don't want it to all seize up, if you know what I mean. I don't want to be one of those hunched old ladies you see in the supermarket.'

Maia giggled. Marguerite turned and raised an eyebrow. She recovered. 'Hardly, you look great.'

I passed Maia the tablet to take Marguerite's measurements. She recoiled when Maia produced the callipers. 'They're to measure your body fat.'

'I know I have it, let's leave it at that.'

'It'll help measure your progress.'

She sighed. 'Get on with it, then.' She turned to me. 'How's your baby?'

I shifted my weight from one foot to the other. 'Oh, she's great. Has Mum been talking to you about her?'

Marguerite nodded. 'All the time. And your clever partner, Renee, is it? Ellen's always talking about what a great mother she is.'

I looked at my feet. 'Yep, she is. She's very attentive.'

Marguerite chuckled. She was visibly softening. 'I've heard that line before. Not happy about being number two? It won't last.'

I looked up quickly. Maia was staring intently at her iPad.

'It's not that,' I managed at last.

Marguerite laughed again as if it was the funniest thing she had heard all morning. 'You're all the same. My husband used to complain and complain. When are we going to get our lives back? Why do you spend all your time worrying about the kids?'

I stood up as straight as I could. 'I'm happy that they have such a strong bond, it's great.'

She patted me on the arm. 'By the time she's two I bet she's shouting for you when her mum won't give her what she wants.'

***

We looked at each other after Marguerite had left the gym. At last, Maia exhaled.

'She gave you a bit of a hard time.'

I rolled my eyes. 'We're all the same, remember? Any woman who's had a crappy husband thinks all men are useless dads who only think of themselves.'

Maia was watching me intensely. 'Is that how you've been feeling, though?'

I turned the question around in my mind. 'I don't think it's just that. It feels like we've grown apart or something. All the ways we used to spark off each other in a good way are just things to argue about now.'

I cleared my throat and broke our eye contact. 'Anyway,

I don't think Marguerite thinks much of me, so I doubt she'll be back.'

She grinned. 'You did a great job. She was maybe playing hard to get.'

The innuendo stopped us short. We looked at each other for a little too long again. My skin glowed hot.

'Are you hungry?' I ventured. 'Could try that new sushi place for lunch?'

'I was thinking about asking if you wanted to try that new Greek café around the corner. I've been meaning to pop in there for ages.'

I bit my lip. The sushi restaurant was bright and open and right on the street. Anyone walking past would see us and say hi. It was just the sort of place that you might go for lunch with a workmate. The new Greek café, on the other hand, was down a flight of stairs in the basement. From what I had seen of it, it was all booths and low lights and weird drapey curtains. Very trendy but much harder to explain how we ended up there.

She sensed my hesitation. 'It's okay if you'd rather not.'

I shook my head. It wasn't a crime to go out for lunch with an employee, was it? It could be a performance appraisal, perhaps. A discussion about an upcoming client meeting.

'It's fine. Should we invite Sam?'

Maia looked at me, hard. 'I don't think so. Do you?'

***

221

Renee
Age: Seven months

I had got into a routine every morning. I woke when Holly did and turned over to allow her to latch on to the breakfast bar, lying next to me in the bed. I'd pop my half-an-antidepressant and down it with some water that I left on the bedside table. I'd open my phone and check through the Facebook group for any member requests or posts that had gone mad. You would be surprised at what people could get upset about when you stirred that potent cocktail of maternal love and serious sleep deprivation. Even a photo I had posted of Holly standing holding a walker had sparked an argument. 'Did you put her into that position?' one woman asked. Helen had joined in: 'It's best to wait until they can do it for themselves, really helps their development much more.'

Once I'd defused any drama, I'd switch to my instant messages to see what had come from Jordan overnight. He sent me a message before he went to sleep and again when he woke in the morning. We still hadn't even spoken on the phone but his messages were becoming more fervent. My phone was permanently face-down so Nick wouldn't see anything on the screen. Not that he was ever really anywhere near our bed, anyway.

Jordan knew about my reluctance to trust my mother's maternal renaissance. My already overwhelming dread at the prospect of having to make a decision about my return to work when Holly was one. He even knew about the weird varicose vein that I had developed where my thigh joined my bikini line. And he kept on sending me messages anyway.

I scanned the group. There was a post that was generating a lot of comments but it seemed to only be concerning a brand of car seat. I sent a private message to Mei, who looked to be winding up about whether a child should rear-face until two or not, telling her to be gentle. 'You never know what other people are dealing with in this group': it was one of my stock responses.

I switched over and clicked on his name.

'Morning,' the first message read. 'I dreamt we were back on that mountain in Switzerland, do you remember? With the flowers?'

I smiled. We had gone for a week and it had rained virtually every day, except for one where we had climbed a mountain and I'd picked a sprinkling of tiny flowers that had been brave enough to stick their heads out into the weather. Then I'd forgotten about them and had been hauled up by airport security when we flew into Australia and broke all their agricultural rules.

His next one: 'I've been wondering ...'

Was that it? Where was the rest of the message?

Another one flashed up.

'Whether you actually do want to meet up properly? Chatting on here is nice but it would be awesome to be

223

in the same room again. I've missed you. I'd love to buy you a coffee.'

The message seemed to flash at me on the screen. Holly snuggled in closer to my chest.

I stared at it. I wanted to see him again. I didn't want to see him. I plotted to stalk his house then I avoided walking past the building where he worked. There was something about this conversation that was like trading secret messages in the back of class. What if the magic bubble popped if we met in person?

'I guess we could do that,' I replied slowly. 'What were you thinking?'

I squeezed my eyes shut. This was the guy who dropped me without notice, remember? Even after spending years joking about my 'daddy issues'. When Nick and I got together, I'd been astonished that someone would make me a cup of tea and rub my feet when I was snappy about minor inconveniences like a towel left on the bathroom floor. Jordan had always fought every criticism as if that towel represented the very essence of his soul.

I switched to his social media profiles and scanned through the photos. He was definitely more worldly now than when we were together, and more confident, if that were possible. The sight of his grin brought back the rush of butterflies I used to feel every time he'd park his car out the front of my place and amble up the path after work, walking like he had all the time in the world, even if I had been waiting hours.

Jordan was still typing. 'Maybe we get a drink after work?'

'Baby, remember?'

'Oh right, sorry. Café in the afternoon? I can skive off for a bit. Or what about lunch?'

'When?'

'Today?'

'Can't do today.' I could, in truth. But I wasn't even sure if I wanted it to happen yet.

'Ren.' Another message popped up, this time from Felicity. 'Can you get some good posts going on the group? A PR chick for a mothers' health initiative is monitoring this week with a view to getting us some advertising. Be good to make a great impression.'

Snapped out of my conversation with Jordan, I switched back to the group. What else could I get them talking about? It felt like my ability to communicate like a normal human had vanished since I had my baby. It used to be that I knew a decent amount about a lot of things. I was even pretty good at pub quiz when I could find a team that did not descend into bitter arguments. But now it seemed that all I knew about was feeding, sleeping, and stimulating little baby brains.

I opened a message to Ruth. 'Ever done anything really stupid?'

She messaged back quickly. 'Does skipping the one-year-old's nap count?'

'I was thinking more like meeting an ex for a coffee.'

She replied straight away. 'Do you want to?'

I paused. 'I think so. Is that bad?'

'Not if it's just coffee ... is it just coffee?'

I closed the window and switched back to my post in the group.

Maybe sleep deprivation it would have to be. What did I know about sleeping? 'First thing you must do,' I tapped, 'Take all the sleep training books you've been given and put them in a pile. Next, set fire to them. Dance around them with your baby. This is the closest you'll get to the feeling of being in control of anything for a long time. How about you? How did you get through?'

I opened Jordan's messages. 'Where are we going to meet, if we go out?'

'Your place?'

'What?'

'Joking. I'll send you a link to a great little café. You won't be able to resist.'

I took a deep breath. That feeling was relief, right? Not disappointment.

***

Nick
Age: Seven months

There was a scuttle of footsteps on the pavement behind me as I left the gym for the evening, then a tap on my shoulder. I turned but the smell of her perfume had already told me who it was.

Maia's face was flushed, the cold evening air bringing the colour to her cheeks. She had a hot pink scarf wound around her neck which brought out the colour in her blue eyes. 'You left without saying goodbye.'

I laughed. 'I think I've left without saying goodbye more days than I've remembered.'

She fake-pouted. 'It's different now.'

'Is it?'

She blushed. 'Well, you know.'

I bit back a smile. Renee always made me feel vaguely inadequate but Maia seemed to permanently look up to me, and not just because she was a full head shorter than me. She reached up and kissed me on the cheek, her hair fluttering against my face as she bounced back down to her heels, pulling her coat around herself.

'You must be heading home soon?'

She nodded. 'Just got to do some admin stuff for my course. It's so boring. Wanna help? I'll buy you a drink over there.'

She gestured to a pub across the road where outdoor heaters were roaring over huddled tables of footpath diners. I paused. I should get home. I'd already managed the hard part of getting out the door. There were only so many days that Renee would put up with me not being there to help with dinner time.

But Maia was a staff member. And I was a good boss,

helping her get qualified so she could become an even more integral part of the team. Wasn't I?

'What do you need help with?'

'It's just some basic programme design stuff. Full body workout in the shortest amount of time possible. I'm sure you could do it in your sleep.'

'You probably could, too.'

'More fun with you ...'

Her smile was infectious. I reached for my phone to send a message to Renee. 'Okay, I guess I can spare you half an hour.'

***

An hour later, a waiter was stoking the fireplace in one corner of the pub's main dining room. Maia and I were seated at the long table in the middle. As we finished a wine each, we shunted the glasses to the side. A plate of antipasto followed. She had spread her coursework out in front of her and her hair caught the breeze each time the door opened. She tapped a pen to her lips as she noted hazards in the safety portion of the workbook. From the window in front of us we could see the gym, where one of our part-time staff was leading a group fitness class in the street-front studio. One of the women in the row closest to the window was completely out of time and would almost collide with her neighbour with every other beat. I nudged Maia. 'Spot any hazards over there?'

'Don't be horrible.' She swatted me on the arm. 'Okay, I'm going to switch to the sample workout.'

I watched as she made notes on a figure of a person that looked as if it might have come from a crime scene. 'I'll do squats for quads. Dips for triceps. Crunches for abs?'

I frowned. 'I think we're meant to have gone off those. Superman?'

She scrawled a note and then turned to fix with an unwavering gaze. 'What are we doing?'

My heart promptly started hammering as if it wanted to fly out of my chest.

'What do you mean?'

She sighed. 'You know what I mean. Is this sustainable?'

She broke eye contact quickly and stared at her feet, as if she hoped the slightly worn carpet beneath our feet would tell her what to say.

'Like pretending that nothing is going on. Maybe I should find a job somewhere else. It's taking so much of my brain power, thinking about you. Telling myself not to. Thinking about you again.'

This time my reply was instant. 'What? No. You're not going to work somewhere else. Especially not after all this time I've put into your training.' I tried to catch her eye to make her smile. Her face was steady.

'I was hanging on to see you this morning from the minute I arrived. That's not normal. Most people hate their bosses. Then I couldn't handle you walking out the door tonight.'

'So what do you want me to do? Make me hate you?'

I flicked a glance at the class across the street. The woman looked to have found her rhythm at last.

There was a long pause before she replied. 'Make me stop falling in love with you?'

I pushed back my chair involuntarily. Was that the word for the fizz in my bones? A whack of guilt slapped my chest. It had been a long time since Renee had used that word with me. We barely even spoke. Maybe I'd be doing her a favour if I let her be free to find her own happiness somewhere. She didn't seem to be happy with me.

Maia was still waiting for me to say something.

'You're right. We can't go on like this. Let's go somewhere and talk. Sam might come in any minute.'

She didn't call me on the implausibility of that. We'd both seen him go home earlier.

She put her hand on my arm. 'My place?'

I paused. 'Okay.'

***

The bus to her home was full. Standing together in the aisle, my skin would ping every time our arms brushed as we clutched a rail to remain upright when the driver lurched from accelerator to brake.

I kept my gaze fixed on my feet. I could probably explain to anyone who asked why I was heading west out of the city when I lived in the north but I'd rather not have had to.

After about ten minutes of rumbling through twisty streets, planting my feet on the floor like a surfer when the driver slammed to a halt at every red light, Maia nudged me. 'Here's our stop.'

***

I realised as she tried to put her key in the door that her hands were shaking, too.

I reached out and put mine over hers to help her, with confidence I did not really have. The apartment was empty again, the photo of her sister and child still on the wall. This time I held eye contact with the picture. A small Christmas tree with a scattering of tinsel stood in one corner.

She turned to look at me once we were inside. 'Can I get you anything?'

I shook my head and pulled her towards me. 'No.'

She buried her head in my chest, allowing me to stroke her long hair.

'I can't handle this,' she spluttered. 'It's like we're together. But we're not. Because you have Renee. But I spend all my time thinking about you and dreaming up ways to spend time together.'

I nodded. 'I know.'

She leant back. 'You need to cut me off. Let me move on. Or jump in.'

Was this on me? I hadn't tried to discourage her, it's true, and I had done a fair bit of encouraging as well since that first night when I had bailed. But I hadn't asked for any of this.

'I can't ... I mean, I want to but ...'

'Yeah, I know. You can't leave your family. But this isn't exactly ideal for them, either, is it?'

I pushed past her and sat on the couch.

She settled beside me. 'Do you feel something for me? Or is this just some sort of fun distraction?'

I shook my head. 'I'm not playing with you. I keep thinking about what it would be like to chuck it all and go and do something crazy together.'

She put her arm around my shoulders and rested her head against me. The weight was weirdly reassuring. 'I'm sorry. I'm not suggesting that you're messing around. I just don't know what to do. Maybe it's better for everyone if we just cut this off. Stop spending time together.'

I looked at her, her eyes wide and her forehead slightly creased. The urge to kiss her was overwhelming. How could I not see her again?

As I pulled back, I looked at her. 'I don't want to do that.'

She wriggled around so she was sitting on my lap. 'Great.'

She started kissing a line down the length of my torso, deftly undoing her jeans as she did so, then reached up to place a palm on my chest, gently pushing me back on to the couch.

She ran her hands down my sides, over the top part of my thighs. My skin goosebumped involuntarily.

I reached for her and pulled her face towards me, feeling

for her lips with mine. Somehow the awkward scramble ended up with me above her. Then there was a collapsing feeling in the base of my stomach. She was looking up at me in the same way Renee had when we first got together and used to spend all afternoon in bed at the weekend. Now I realised why she had looked so familiar.

What was I doing? New and fun and unpredictable is good for a holiday, maybe, but not when it meant chucking away the best thing in my life.

I sat up. 'I can't do this.'

She pulled a couch cushion down over her face. 'Not again, Nick. You're not running away again.'

I pulled my jeans back up on to my hips and stood. 'I'm sorry. Really. I just ... I can't. I need to not be a twit about this. We have to just be friends.'

She pulled her clothes around herself. 'Could you not have told me that at the beginning? Honestly, I have enough friends.'

I reached for her. 'Wait, Maia. I'm sorry. It's not like that. It's just ...'

'Ego trip. Attention-seeking. Whatever.'

'It was just – it was a mistake. I owe it to Renee and Holly not to bail.'

She was still staring at me. 'Right.'

'I'm sorry.'

She pushed away from me and made for the kitchen, where she pulled open the larder doors and grabbed a readymade protein shake, shaking it with a quick flick of her wrists. She was so different to Renee and yet what I liked about her most were the things that reminded me of her when we first got together. A pang of guilt punched me in the guts. Maia hadn't done anything except be a young, single, ball of energy rolling into my life. And I'd stamped on it.

Although perhaps that was giving me too much credit. The way she necked her drink and stared at me, almost forcing me out of her apartment with her eyes, seemed to indicate I hadn't dented her energy much.

'I'll see you at work, okay?'

'Yeah, whatever.'

***

I trudged into the gym at my normal time the next morning, my sight set firmly on the new punching bag we had installed downstairs. I thought I might feel a rush of relief when I left her place, but I didn't. All I could feel was crushing guilt.

When I had got home, I could hear Renee singing to Holly on the baby monitor and had to down a glass of water to battle the nausea.

Maia was leaving the office as I arrived. Her face drained of colour as she spotted me. 'What are you doing here?'

I took a step back. 'Coming to work?'

She gestured to a bag over her shoulder. 'I thought I'd be out before you got here. I'm clearing out.' She tossed her hair over her shoulder and seemed try to stand up a little taller. 'I've emailed you my resignation. It's not going to work – me and you here. I've just finished my certificate so you don't have to keep me around anymore.'

'Okay.' I gritted my teeth in an attempt at a smile. 'Thanks for all the work you've done for us.'

She paused. 'That's it?'

I shrugged. 'Yeah – you've been great. We'll miss you.'

She sighed and hitched her bag higher on her shoulder, pushing past me. 'You really are a piece of work.'

I waited until I heard the doors shut behind her before pulling out my phone to send Sam a text. 'We're going to need to hire someone to replace Maia.'

I made for the bench press machine, loading an extra 10kg on each side.

My phone bleeped. 'What the hell?'

'Long story, mate. I can fill you in when you're around.'

***

Sam stared at me, slack-jawed as I gave him the edited version of what had happened.

'You mean, you had a chance to sleep with her. And you didn't?'

I rolled my eyes at him. 'I have Renee, and a baby, remember? We can't be young and dumb for ever.'

He nodded slowly, as if turning the idea over in his head. 'But ... Maia ...' He opened his eyes wide. 'How did it even get to that point?'

I studied my hands. 'I'm not totally sure. I feel pretty rotten about it, to be fair.'

'So what are you going to do now, apart from hire a replacement?'

I took a sip of water. I hadn't allowed myself to ponder this thought much. 'I don't know.'

'You can't tell Renee, obviously.'

'You reckon?'

'No! She'd kick you out in a minute and then you'd have neither of them. Pointless.'

He was probably right. 'But living with a secret like that's a bit dicey too, isn't it?'

He shrugged. 'Price you pay, I guess.'

I swiped my phone to look at the photo of Renee and Holly. 'Maybe.'

***

Renee

Age: Eight months

It was still three weeks until Christmas but the shops were mayhem. 'Where did you park?' I messaged Ruth as I circled the parking lot for the third time. A car in front of me flicked its brake lights on. 'Never mind, I'm going in. See you in five.'

I slapped the indicator on and nudged forward. A car coming the opposite direction slowed. I glared. 'No, you bloody don't.' As the reversing car edged out, I pushed forward, fixing my gaze on the car park. The other car nosed towards it but, keeping the front of my car almost to the bumper of the one leaving the park, I squeezed into the spot.

The other car was still hovering as I pulled Holly from her seat. I kept my eyes on her face. 'No one takes my parking spot.' She grinned.

Ruth was waiting inside the door of the mall. 'What do you still need to get?'

She was pushing her stroller forward with one hand, then pulling it back with the other. She peered around the edge after a dozen repetitions and smiled with triumph. 'Asleep at last. You lead on.'

I tucked Holly into the carrier on my front. 'Let's not drag it out. I need something for Nick, something for his mum. Something for my mum. That's pretty much it.'

Ruth nodded. 'Any ideas for Nick?'

I shook my head. 'None at all. He just buys whatever he wants when he wants it, it's very frustrating.'

We walked in silence, Ruth manoeuvring around stalled shoppers and pot plants in her way with the precision of a figure skater. 'What happened to that coffee with what-shisname?'

I sucked in my breath. 'Nothing yet – I've been putting it off.'

'You're worried about seeing him?'

I pretended to look at a dress in a shop window.

She nudged me. 'Are you?'

I ducked to kiss the top of Holly's head. 'Not worried ... just wondering if it stops being just a bit of fun if we actually see each other in person.'

She was staring at me. 'I don't know – does it? Are you looking for more fun in your life?'

We plodded a few more steps to the next shop, a menswear outlet with house music blaring and an assistant rifling officiously through the rack out front.

I picked through one stripy shirt after the other. 'I don't think he needs any more shirts.'

'Activewear might be more useful?'

I snorted. 'You haven't seen his drawers. Honestly, he's the guy with everything. I'll have a look for weird supplements or something online later on. There's a book I want to get for my mum, that'll be easier.'

'Okay, we'd better go quickly.'

I looked up at the note of urgency in her voice. She was retreating from the shop at speed. 'What's going on?'

She gestured at the rack. 'Xavier's woken up. I didn't notice he was wiping his nose on the bottom of every single one of those shirts while we were standing there. That scary shop assistant will not be impressed.'

***

It was early evening when we arrived home. I'd spent the entire car trip reaching behind my seat to tickle Holly's feet to keep her awake.

My mum was leaning against the front door as I climbed the stairs to the landing, juggling Holly on one hip and my oversized nappy bag on the other. So much for the advertising claim that it would 'make outings a breeze'. I just seemed to end up carrying six mismatched socks, heavy wooden baby toys, and, inexplicably, three notebooks. It was heavy enough that it set off the seatbelt alarm on my passenger seat.

'I thought I'd come and cook dinner for you.' Mum gestured to some bags of groceries at her feet. 'I was just trying to find my key.'

I settled Holly into her highchair at the kitchen bench while Mum clattered in the cupboard under the sink, extracting first one saucepan, then another, and then the only frying pan I had that still had some of its non-stick coating.

'What's brought this on?' I watched as Mum dropped a slimy chunk of tofu into the middle of one of the pans. Even when she'd stayed with us, I'd never seen her cook more than a piece of toast.

'Just brushing up some skills. I thought you might be a good test subject.' She flicked me a smile.

'Brushing up skills for whom?'

She swallowed and ducked her head, running her finger down the recipe on her phone.

'Mum?'

She blushed. 'Henry is back in the country.'

'Henry! I thought you two—'

She batted me away. 'Go and sit down. Can't I just make dinner for my daughter?'

Holly stared at her, watching her long earrings wobble in time with her movements.

'You know it's probably only the two of us eating dinner tonight, right? Nick's been coming home from work late.'

Mum muttered something in response but her head was too far in the fridge for me to hear it.

I scooped a spoonful of baby food and waved it in Holly's direction. She frowned. It was pumpkin and apple. It's always pumpkin and something. Pumpkin and beef – kind of gritty weird orange stuff. Pumpkin and apple – lighter orange pulpy stuff. Pumpkin and banana – I don't know why you'd even try. Holly threw more of it on the ground than she ate but the fear of having a five-year-old who was still fully dependent on breast milk kept me trying. Xavier was eating whole rounds of sushi in one sitting. I was desperate for her to at least manage a jar.

Finally, the sink piled high with dirty dishes and cooking implements, Mum slid a plate of noodles in front of me.

She twirled some around her own fork. 'You've looked a bit like you're wasting away lately. I'm worried about you.'

'First time for everything I guess.'

She looked up. 'What?'

'Nothing, Mum. I'm fine, honestly.'

'Is Nick going to be able to get home a bit earlier soon? What's going on at work?'

I shrugged. 'You know about as much as I do on that front.'

***

When I returned from the bedroom after settling Holly to sleep, it was dark outside. Mum had gone and Nick was sitting in the living room, staring into the distance.

'Hey, love.' I settled on to the sofa next to him. 'How was your day? Another long one. Did you see my mum leaving?'

He turned and stared at me as if it took him a minute to realise who I was.

He coughed. 'Oh ... yeah. She said something about the dishwasher not having been turned on.'

'I'll check. Her clean-up can be pretty haphazard. I'm going to get a water, want anything?'

He shook his head.

'Hey, can you spare me a minute for a chat before bed?'

He whipped around to face me, his eyebrows knotted together. 'About what?'

I raised my hands in a peace gesture. 'Nothing major. Just wanted to run something by you that I've written.'

He leant back against the couch. 'Oh. Okay. Sure.'

I filled my water glass, watching the bubbles cling to the sides. We hadn't had another real blow-up but he was always either on edge and acting like he thought I was about to start picking on him, or over-compensating.

He was flicking through his phone when I returned to the lounge.

I sat next to him so our legs were touching. It was a closeness that we rarely had but the way his body sort of moulded into mine was comfortingly familiar.

241

'So ... I wrote something about co-sleeping on the group.'

He nodded. 'Like, you having Holly in our bed all the time.'

'Yeah, and I got a lot of response about how bad it is for our relationship.' I reached for his hand. 'You don't feel that way, do you?'

He let me hold his hand but didn't reciprocate with any pressure. 'It's okay, Ren. I don't mind the spare bed. She won't be in there for ever.'

I turned to try to make eye contact with him. 'But are we okay? It's like we hardly talk these days. You're always working, Holly's so full on ...'

He looked away and seemed to shrink into himself. 'I don't think we should be talking about this right now. I have an early start, clients all day tomorrow ...'

The ground seemed to be shifting underneath me. 'I really need you to reassure me on this one. Are we not okay?'

He inhaled slowly and seemed to hold his breath, looking at me. Then he released it.

'Nick.'

He opened his mouth, shut it, opened it again. 'No. I guess we're not okay.'

He looked as though he was going to cry.

I clutched his hand harder. 'What do you mean?'

He shut his eyes. 'I've done something really bad.'

I stood up. 'What? You've done what?'

'I've got into something with someone else, Ren. I was

hoping I could just forget about it and move on but I don't think I can.'

***

Nick

Age: Eight months

I have known Renee for four years and lived with her for three of them. I would have told you that I'd seen her in every possible situation. But as soon as the words were hanging in the air in front of us, I saw her crumple in a way that I'd never even imagined. Her face went white and her mouth dropped open. She sank down on to the couch as if she wanted it to absorb her.

She looked up at me blankly. 'Who? What?'

My stomach turned over, my adrenaline picking up. I should never have said anything. What was I thinking? I could have just shut up and said nothing and coped with the guilt and everything would have been fine. I just hadn't been expecting such specific questions.

'Maia.' I sank to my knees next to her and rested my head on her lap. 'I'm so sorry. I haven't slept with her. But ...'

'But what?'

'Um.' I shut my eyes. How could I explain?

'What?' Her voice was getting louder with every minute I was quiet.

'I went to her place. It got a bit intense. But I stopped it ...'

'Do you want to be with her?'

'No, no. I don't want to mess up our little family. You and Holly, you're the best thing in my life.'

She swallowed and pulled her legs back from me.

'And you've ruined it.' Her voice was cold and weirdly quiet. 'How could you do that? After what my dad did ...'

A moan forced its way out of my throat. I laced the material of her skirt through my fingers in an attempt to hold her close. 'I'm so sorry.' The material smelt like the oil she rubbed Holly with after her bath. What had I been thinking? There should never have been any doubt about this. I wanted to go back and slap myself.

'How could you?'

'I guess I missed you. It's been a bit lonely when you and Holly are this tight little unit ...'

'Weak. You're weak.' She stood, pushing me off. 'You couldn't handle a few months of coming second to a baby. Your own baby.'

'I know. You're right. What do you want me to do?' I watched her as she gathered her things and headed for the bedroom.

She didn't bother to turn. 'I literally do not care.'

I scrambled after her, positioning myself in front of the bedroom door so she could not get through. 'Please, can we talk about it?'

She gave me the most withering look I had ever seen, hatred mixed with the sort of disgust I remembered registering on her face when her elderly cat had become incontinent in old age and she sometimes stepped in its puddles first thing in the morning.

'I thought you were working late all this time,' she spat at me. 'But while I was feeding your daughter, cleaning your laundry, getting her to sleep, you were at her place, were you?'

I shook my head. 'No. It stopped a while ago. And there weren't many ...' The words choked in my throat.

She stared at me, her green eyes catching the light of the stereo in the corner of the room.

'Many times you had sex?'

'No, I told you – we haven't. I stopped it before it could happen.'

Her lip curled with distaste. 'I don't want to know. I don't care. Go back to her.'

'I don't want to go back to her.'

The lump in my throat was becoming hard to swallow. Sometimes it felt like we veered from a kiss in the morning to a quick snuggle after her bath but the idea of not being in the same house as Holly when she opened her eyes in the morning was gut-wrenching.

And Renee. Who else would understand why I still laughed when I saw a man in the street who looked like the landlord of the house she lived in when we met, who'd decided that I was a burglar creeping into her flat in the middle of the night and called the police?

I'd been so caught up in the buzz of Maia being

infatuated with me but I instantly saw it meant nothing. Just a stupid distraction when I could have stepped up and tried to be what Renee needed, instead.

'Please go.' Her voice was small but cold.

'Can we talk about this?'

She turned further away from me. 'I don't know what there is to talk about.'

'Please.'

'Just go.'

I pushed into the room and headed blindly to the wardrobe to find a change of work clothes to take with me. 'I'll go to work. But I'll call you tomorrow.'

I reached for her hand on my way back to the door. 'Renee. I'm sorry.'

She snatched it away from me. 'Get out!'

***

Renee
Age: Eight months

I waited for Nick's footsteps to fade away completely before I allowed myself to cry. I stumbled to the kitchen and reached for my phone. Ruth would still be awake. I sent her a message. 'You up?'

She replied straightaway. 'Sure am. What's up?'

'It's Nick. I think our relationship is over.'

There was no reply. I stared at the screen, waiting for her to respond.

'Over?' She typed at last. 'What do you mean? Did he freak out about the ex?'

'He's been seeing someone else.'

'What! Like sleeping with someone?'

'He claims not. But honestly, who knows?'

She paused before typing again. 'What a dick. Does he want to be with her?'

'Allegedly not.'

'Are you going to give him another chance?'

'I never want to speak to him again. I can't believe he's just like every other guy, after all.'

'Fair enough. So, nothing happened with that ex of yours then?'

I rolled my eyes. 'No. All that beating myself up about a few messages and whether it was bad to have coffee with him and Nick was already taking up with someone.'

I switched back to my main message list. Jordan's name was at the top. He'd sent me a cute GIF of a wet cat earlier in the evening when I'd struggled with Holly's bath time.

I opened a new message to him: 'You'll never guess what just happened.'

***

We ended up 'talking' until Holly woke for the first time in the night. Jordan had a fine line to navigate – he clearly

247

wanted to tell me that he thought Nick's behaviour was outrageous. But we both knew I had a strong suspicion that he might have done something quite similar when our relationship was in its final throes.

'I don't know how someone could do that when you've got kids together,' he offered as some sort of justification. 'It's time that some people knew how to grow up a bit. Don't you reckon? Put themselves second for a bit?'

I raised an eyebrow. I was still unconvinced that Jordan Harrison could tell anyone to grow up. This was the guy who put a pool table in his dining room instead of a table that one might eat at, because he claimed that it would get more use.

I finally fell asleep at about 1am, after watching a clip that Jordan had sent me of otters bathing in a stream, one sunning itself and sweetly rubbing its face – which he said was me – and the other turning over and over in the water like some sort of turbine, which he said was more his style.

***

When I opened my eyes, my room was already warm with sunlight. I could hear someone putting a kettle on in the kitchen. It had better not be Nick. Who else had a key? Ellen – that would almost be worse.

I rolled towards the edge of the bed.

Holly was lying on Nick's side of the bed. Her eyes blinked open at the sound of my voice and stared at me. 'Morning, darling.' I touched the end of her nose with mine. She grinned and rolled over, pushing herself back on to her haunches and then up into a seated position, catching the edge of her sleeping bag under her feet. I nuzzled into her neck. She always smelt vaguely sweaty in the mornings, perhaps because she spent each night with her face pressed up against mine. But somehow sweaty Holly smelt comforting and snuggly in a way that sweaty anyone else would definitely not. 'Not long until Christmas, my darling. What's that going to be like now?'

Mum stuck her head around the doorway. 'Morning, sunshines. Chamomile tea, Renee? Sure you're not ready for a proper coffee yet?'

I tried to force a grin, burying my face in Holly's hair. 'I reckon I can manage a little one. What are you doing here?'

She took a step towards the bed, extending her hands for me. 'Need to practise my breakfast-making too, don't you think? But darling, what's wrong?'

'Nick.' I struggled to spit the word out. The sadness that I thought had evaporated collapsed on my chest like a bag of potatoes.

'Is he okay?'

'I think it's over.'

She pulled back. 'What do you mean? I'm sure it's not, honey. All relationships go through tough times, especially with a baby. Your father and I—'

'Split up when I was like three months old. And then you found out about Veronica.'

She cut me off. 'Well, yes, but—'

'He's been seeing someone.'

She bit her lip. 'He told you?'

I nodded.

'A one-off? Drunken night thing?'

I sat back. 'No. Does it matter?'

She scrambled around to the other side of the bed and slid in beside me, pulling me into her chest in the same way I had Holly cradled in mine. 'No, I guess not. But Holly – your first Christmas together ...'

She started to draw circles on my back with her finger. It was what she used to do when I was an anxious child – usually fretting over something she'd done.

I lay, feeling the curve of her body against my back. Holly was watching me, puzzled. I kissed her cheek, tickled her toes, attempted to hum a nursery rhyme.

'We'll muddle through. Holly doesn't have any other Christmases to compare it to.'

After ten minutes had passed, I turned over to look at her.

'Aren't you going to say something?'

'Do you want to talk about it?'

'No.'

'Well then.'

The front door rattled and there were three heavy footsteps before Nick appeared in the doorway.

I felt myself suck in a lungful of air and scramble to sit up, trying to make myself 10cm taller in the process.

He coughed, blinking at the sight of three of us curled up in our bed. 'I've taken the day off. Can we talk?'

Holly looked towards him and smiled but he stared past her, intent on making eye contact with me.

I looked at my hands. The polish on my nails – from my trip with Ruth to a nail salon as the children sat in their strollers and cooed at the technicians – had been chipped off overnight. 'You can say whatever you need to say.'

He shot a glance at my mother. She shrugged and made to climb out of bed, reaching for Holly.

'I just wanted to say I'm sorry. Sorry doesn't cut it, I know.' He was stammering, a habit I hadn't heard since he tried for a speech at his brother's wedding and fell over every third word. 'I screwed up, so badly. I just wanted to know ... is there any chance you can forgive me? I've been going back and forth on this in my mind all night. I just can't bear the thought of this being it. I don't know why I let it happen with Maia. I'm an idiot. I got carried away.'

Even the birds outside seemed to fall silent. I stared at him. It was still Nick. The most familiar face in the world apart from my own. The smell I associated with home. But the usual warm burble of love that I would get in my stomach when I looked at him was gone. I didn't hate him – that was weird. I had expected to want to torch his clothes and slash his tyres or exhibit some other sort of Hollywood melodrama. I didn't even really feel angry, watching him with his big eyes and forlorn frown, standing like a gangly teenager in the doorway to what had been our bedroom. Everything had been so surreal since Holly was born, were we even the same people? I just felt cold, sad and empty, like every piece of my energy had been wrung out.

'I don't think so.'

I had to look away as the tears welling in his eyes made mine start to flow again.

'Please, Ren. I need our little family.'

'I think it's best you go. This is such a mess.'

He ran his hand through his hair. 'I am so sorry. Can we work on it? Get counselling maybe? I'll do anything to make it up to you?'

I watched him. 'I just don't think it'll work. We've changed so much lately. I can't even really blame you. What does that say about our relationship?'

He seemed to lose half of his height as his shoulders rounded. 'I wanted us to get it back together. Having a baby is hard work, everyone said that. But we're a unit.'

'Are we really? You were right when you said it's me and Holly and then you somewhere over there. I do everything for her. Honestly, I do. It's like you didn't even really try to be a full-time father. I don't know why I expected anything else, though, you've always left everything up to me, even before Holly came along.'

'Everyone said I'd be able to have a more active role when she was a bit older ...'

I waved him away. 'Yeah, everyone. Meanwhile I go out for coffee dates with my friends and their husbands are there with the baby in a frontpack.'

He took a step back. 'I need to get some things.'

My mother had arrived in the door and looked at him. 'I think you should go.'

He raised his hands in protest. 'It won't take a minute—'

'Go. I'll bring a box of things to the gym today. She's asked you.'

He looked as if he was about to protest again.

'You let her down. Now the least you can do is let her get on with it in peace.'

'I let her down? You are the last person ...'

I stood up. 'Can you two cut it out? I need to take Holly for a shower.'

***

I stroked Holly's head as she lay in the crook of my arm, gumming her fingers. Nick had skulked out, my mother on his heels to shut the door behind him. I still hadn't made it to the bathroom to wash. Outside my door, I could hear my mother talking to Ruth, who must have virtually collided with Nick on the landing. It was like a train station out there when all I wanted was a morning to myself. We were meant to be going out for coffee with the kids but I'd completely forgotten.

'She deserves so much better,' I could hear my mother telling Ruth. 'What was he thinking? Holly's so young.'

I pulled a pillow over my face. She had come to the defensive mother role relatively late in my life and it wasn't a good fit. He might have bailed on me at an awful time but her efforts hadn't been that much better – I'd almost missed my first 'real' exam at school because she forgot study leave had finished and didn't bother coming home after a night out with her friends to take me.

I sent Ruth a text: 'Just going to give Holly a quick wash then I'll be out.'

Holly had got used to the shower in recent months – the look of outrage as the water splashed on to her head replaced with a wince if it touched her forehead. Holding her on one hip, I slipped her onesie off with one hand and – transferring her to my other side – wiggled out of my own clothes. There should be some sort of internationally recognised competition for the things you could do while holding a baby. People definitely didn't give mothers enough credit.

I shimmied backwards into the shower cubicle so the water ran down over my shoulders and pooled on Holly's tummy. She looked up at me, water dripping from my hair on to my shoulders. I blew a wet raspberry on her shoulder, balancing on one foot as I reached down for her baby wash. I squeezed a few pumps into my hand and lathered her back, then her sides. She was becoming increasingly slippery as I tried to clean her bottom.

I pulled her into me. Sometimes it felt like the two of us were in a little bubble while the rest of civilisation rumbled on around us. Now that Nick was gone, the feeling of 'us against the world' intensified. I popped her on the floor of the shower to wash my own hair, trying to direct the spray of water away from her. She reached forward and supported herself on her hands and knees. Then, with one tentative hand and foot after the other, she propelled herself forward, through the shower curtain and out into the bathroom. All I could see was her soapy bottom disappearing out of sight. 'You did it!' I shouted somewhat desperately as I tried to get the last of the shampoo out of my hair. 'Well done, darling! Now just stay there while I grab my towel.' There was a crash as she reached the vanity cupboard. A box fell out and I could see tampons rolling out over the floor. One shot under the bathroom door and into the hall.

Mum knocked. 'Is everything okay in there?'

I turned off the water. 'She's learnt to crawl! No more commando.'

Mum pushed the door open as I was clambering out of the shower and bending to scoop her out.

'Well done, Holly, that's great!'

Ruth appeared behind her, then seemed to realise she was staring at me, completely nude. 'I'll see you when you get out.'

***

My phone buzzed as I struggled to pull my skinny jeans on over too-damp thighs.

Holly was now sitting on the floor, gumming an edge of the towel. There were three text messages on the screen, all from Nick.

'I'm sorry.'

'Can we please talk?'

'Alone?'

The icon indicated he was typing. Another shot through: 'Please? I'm sorry.'

I put the phone down again. He could wait. Everyone was so needy. Jordan. My mum. All the women on the Facebook group who needed 300 people telling them to take their kid to the doctor before they'd make an appointment. Even one of the neighbours had given me a look when I didn't immediately offer to help her carry her groceries like I would have before I was lugging a tiny human load of my own everywhere with me.

Now Nick had thrown a grenade of his own into our relationship and seemed to think it was my job to save him from it. The helpless infant in my life had become the least exhausting of the lot of them.

My mum opened the door and gestured in a way that was meant to ask whether I wanted a cup of tea. I shook my head. 'I'll be out in a second. Are Ruth and Xavier okay?'

'Perfectly. Take your time.'

My phone started to buzz. It was Nick calling. I pressed the button to decline it.

'Renee, please.' Another message beeped in. 'I can't handle this.'

I might have been thinking of going out for coffee with Jordan but I would never have kissed him. Let alone gone back to his place. I stabbed at the buttons to reply. 'That is not my problem. You created this. You can deal with it.'

'What do you want me to do?'

How did this man manage to run his own business? I stared at the screen.

Another message popped up: 'I'll stay at the gym for a few nights.'

I sighed. 'Okay.'

Chapter Seven

Fiona Harcourt, 5:32am: 'Has anyone else completely lost control of their music collection? I was driving, by myself, to my parents' this afternoon and flicked on Spotify – took me a full half a song to realise I was blaring 'Hakuna Matata', and singing along, top-of-my-lungs style. I did wonder why the guy in the car next to me was giving me an odd look.'

Renee
Age: Eight months

I've never been one of those people who loves Christmas. When my grandmother was alive, we would go to the house every year for a meal and presents and I remember the Christmas-morning excitement of waking up in her spare bedroom to a stocking full of gifts. But once she was no longer around, and it became evident that my mother could not be counted on to remember that it was coming until the night before, it lost some of its magic.

When I was a teenager I'd tried to take over some of the organising myself, putting up decorations wherever we were living, and arguing for a tree. But it's not the sort of thing that really works as a one-person exercise, is it?

Nick's family was different. His mother spent weeks planning the decorations each year, and went through magazines and cookbooks to put a menu together. She worried about every last detail. She even bought the expensive crackers so the little trinkets inside seemed like something you might want even though you usually just ended up with an expensive bookmark that got lost down the side of the bed or a teaspoon that didn't fit with anything else in the drawer.

Ellen had gently nudged, when she visited during the week, about whether Holly and I could still be there, despite the implosion of our relationship, but the idea of playing happy families made me feel faint. 'Maybe Granddad and I will come and visit on Boxing Day, then,' she'd said as she kissed Holly on the cheek. 'Two Christmases, you lucky wee thing.'

She turned to me and patted my hand. 'We'll miss you. You know you're always welcome with us, even if ...'

I looked at the floor. I'd only told her the bare minimum about what had happened and I wasn't sure if Nick had told her anything at all. She was kinder than to push me for the details. 'Thanks.'

She pulled me in towards her. 'You're part of our family, now, no matter what happens with Nick, okay? I'm your interfering, judgmental mother, too.'

I looked up. She was smiling. 'I never meant any of that.'

She kissed me on the cheek. 'Yes, you did. But I didn't mind. I am interfering. Never judging you, though.'

***

I put up with as many gaudy baubles and twinkly lights as I could. We even had a line of tinsel that I didn't realise Holly had swiped from a tree we had walked past in town. I settled on a couple of gifts for her – a big rocking horse that I figured would look impressive wrapped in bright paper, and a cute little winter jacket that I would have bought her anyway. But the two presents looked a little lonely under the expanse of fake-fir branches.

My mother arrived early on Christmas Day with a bag of croissants, wearing an oversized Santa hat and angel earrings. She flicked on the radio, which was running a too-small rotation of Christmas songs.

'I just brought you a few little things.' She grinned at Holly, pulling half a dozen brightly wrapped boxes from her carrier bag and pushing them under the tree. 'From me and Henry.'

'Henry? So it is serious, then?'

She smiled but ignored the question.

'And something for you.' She thrust another package at me. 'Is Nick coming over?'

I shrugged. 'A bit later, I think.'

'Do you want me to stick around, keep him from being a problem?'

I shook my head. 'Whatever happens is fine. I'm sure I can cope for one day.'

***

Nick turned up at the door with a big plastic carrier bag of presents just after lunch, knocking as if he was not sure whether it was acceptable to walk straight in, before he peered around the doorframe. Holly beamed as he scooped her up.

'Your gran sent me so many things for you,' he told her, his words muffled by the top of her head as he covered her with kisses. 'And I think there's more tomorrow. Has Santa been good to you?'

My mum gestured to the floor. 'She's got everything a little girl could wish for.'

'That's what I like to hear.' He was already lifting the wrapping from a present and waving the toy inside in Holly's face. She looked to me in alarm.

He pushed a small present towards me. It had been wrapped by someone in a shop. 'Thanks.' I forced a smile. I had never got around to buying him anything.

'Open it?'

'Maybe later. I might go and have a Christmas nap.'

***

262

Lying on my bed, I could hear him playing with Holly in the lounge. It sounded like he was doing the 'invisible motorbike' trick. He would sit her on his arms as if she was riding a bike and make the sound effects as he scooted from one room to the next, slamming on the brakes and taking hard corners.

I reached for my phone to tap out a message. 'Happy Christmas.'

Jordan replied a couple of minutes later. 'And to you. What are you up to?'

'Just at home. You with your family?'

'Just my sister and her crazy kids. Get anything good?'

I hadn't opened anything yet. 'Not sure. You? Get that car you were hoping for?'

'Sadly, no. Poor form on the family's part. Still hoping for that coffee date one day. That would be a good substitute.'

I grinned and settled further back into my pillows. Having an inane conversation with Jordan seemed easier than returning to the lounge to deal with Nick. 'Okay, fine. You win. Not tomorrow or the day after but maybe early next week. And it's not a date.'

'Book it in. I'll send you directions.'

I switched back to my messages and opened a new one to Lauren. 'Happy Christmas, sweetheart. Have you given any thought to giving your mum another chance? Bet she misses you.'

***

Susan Edmunds

Renee
Age: Nine months

I thought about cancelling on Jordan about fifteen times in the three days after Christmas. But even my mother thought I should go.

'It'll be good for you to get out of the house,' she said when she arrived first thing. She and Ellen had fallen into a pattern of alternating mornings. Once I got used to the rhythm of one unpredictable, chaotic one followed by a relaxing one, it was a nice balance.

'I don't want to get anything complicated,' I hissed at her, as I pulled a camisole top over my head. I was still in my breastfeeding go-to – skinny jeans with a white or black camisole and then a cardi or scarf thrown over the top. It wasn't going to win any fashion awards but it meant I could give Holly easy access without having to disrobe too fully. I was still recovering from the day she decided she needed to feed while I was wearing a shift dress on what I thought was going to be a quick trip into the bank. I – and a few of the other customers waiting in line, probably – couldn't quite believe that a human breast could be stretchy enough to go right to the top of a quite modest neckline.

'It's not complicated,' she said with a sigh. 'It's not a date. You're just going to meet someone you used to know for a coffee. Take your mind off ... everything'

264

I eyed her. 'Why are you so invested in this?'

She shrugged. 'I think sometimes being reminded that there are other people out there can be a good thing when everything goes a bit sour, even if you're not actually going to want to do anything about it. Have some fun, relax. Spend time with someone who will make you laugh.'

I raised my eyebrows and drew a thin, dark line along my upper eyelid. No doubt it would be smudged off by tiny fingers before long.

I smeared some concealer on my under-eye circles. 'Things are all firing with Henry, then?'

She blushed. 'Henry's been very sweet, actually. Most apologetic for the fight we had on the cruise. We've been having a really lovely time.'

She was avoiding my eyes.

'And ...?'

'And nothing! You might even get a visit one day.'

I handed Holly to her. 'Well, he more than knows what he's getting himself into, right? I'm just going to go and get a bit of stuff going on the group before we head out. You two will be okay for half an hour, tops? I'll come and grab her before I leave.'

She stared at me. 'You're taking Holly with you?'

'Of course. Not a date, remember? Just catching up with an old friend.'

***

265

I powered up my laptop and stared at messages flying in the group. There were at least twenty requests for membership waiting to be checked out. Someone had flagged a post as potentially inappropriate because it included some discussion about a nipple. A new mum wanted to discuss the finer points of two brands of baby sleeping bag. Another person wanted to take legal action because someone had screenshotted something and sent it to her boyfriend's sister.

I groaned. It was all a bit trivial.

'Hey, you there?' I opened a message to Felicity. She was no doubt running a PTA meeting somewhere or single-handedly catering a banquet dinner for twenty-seven of her closest friends. After a year of chatting, she still intimidated me.

She replied a minute later. 'Sort of, what's up?'

'Sorry. You're not going to like this.'

'Ugh, what now? Just ban them if they're being difficult.'

I drummed my fingers on my leg. Why was this so hard? It wasn't like she was paying me.

'I think I need to quit the adminning thing. I need to spend a little bit less time online. I'll still be in the group, though, backing you up when you need me. Just not sure I'm in the right head space for it at the moment, do you know what I mean?'

I picked at the end of a rough fingernail while I waited for her to reply. She sent a message at last. 'That's fine. You've lasted longer than I thought you would. I'll get Angela to step up. Thanks for your help. You've been a star.'

That was it? I stared at the screen for a minute the clicked my laptop shut.

***

My nerves were sparking as I walked into the café, toting Holly on my hip. What would this have been like if Nick hadn't had his meltdown? Would I have even gone?

As it was, the nerves were all anticipation. But I didn't really care what he thought of me, if I was honest. I didn't care if we had a good time. I didn't care if anyone saw us, or if Jordan decided he never wanted to see me again. I was going because I wanted to satisfy an itch of curiosity that had been burning for years. And it didn't hurt to get out of the house. He could turn out to be the most attractive man on the planet and I'd probably walk away feeling the same as if I had sipped lukewarm lattes and chatted about the weather for twenty minutes with my local MP, who, it must be noted, is not attractive in the slightest. Although I'm told she's a dab hand at crochet.

The café was busy. Young people with large bags stood in line to order. A group of what looked to be estate agents sat around one of the room's bigger tables, poring over some documents and laughing far too loudly for the size of the premises. Jordan stuck a hand in the air from the far corner of the room to wave. We locked eyes.

I ducked my head and wove my way through the tables towards him. He was on his feet as we approached and kissed my cheek. 'It's so lovely to see you,' he said before his face had properly left mine. He switched his attention to Holly. 'And your gorgeous girl.'

I positioned her on my lap as I sat so she could look at him if she wanted to. She reached for a sachet of sugar on the table. 'Can I get you a drink?' He was on his feet, reaching for his wallet.

'Sure, just a single shot vanilla latte would be great, thanks.'

He nodded and went to join the queue. I watched him out of the corner of my eye as he jiggled from one foot to the other. Had he improved with age? I checked myself. No doubt he was still as thoughtless and unreliable as he had ever been.

He grinned as he slithered back on to the chair in front of me. 'How have you been holding up?'

I looked at my hands. What was the truth? I veered from railing against the injustice of my life having fallen apart to feeling oddly indifferent.

'I'm okay,' I managed at last. 'I guess everything that's happened with Nick is a chance for me to think about what next. Going back to my job is going to be a bit hard as a single mum.'

He cocked his head and stared at me. 'Are you going to stay around here? Your mum is ...'

'She's still in her mad old house. Yeah, I'll stay, I think. I guess we'll have to put the flat on the market or something, I dunno. We haven't got to that yet. I'm putting it off for as long as possible. Adulting is hard enough anyway, let alone when you're trying to get it right for a kid.'

He nodded. 'It really sucks, Ren. I'm sorry.'

I shook my head. 'Let's not dwell on it. Tell me about you. Tell me more about what you've been up to since I saw you last.'

It felt like a rehearsed speech, especially since we'd already traversed most of it online, anyway. He'd spent a lot of time thinking about how he'd let me down. How he could have done better. He'd got a decent job. I had to fight to keep my face passive. Crediting me for the life turnaround was a bit rich. Surely it had more to do with that gorgeous Swedish woman he'd hooked up with shortly after we'd parted. I wasn't about to admit to online stalking him to discover that, though.

'I'm glad it's all worked out so well for you.' I managed a smile.

He put his hand over mine. 'I just wanted to apologise for the way I vanished on you. I knew it was a thing for you – not wanting people to just up and disappear. Then I turned around and did it.'

I took a deep sip of my drink. 'It's okay. I'm over it.'

He threw his hands in the air. 'Don't let me off so easily.'

'Don't give yourself too much credit.'

His face fell.

'I just mean, it's fine. People break up. Let's not tie ourselves into knots about it.'

He nodded. 'Are you loving being a mum?'

I looked down at Holly, who was reaching for the teaspoon that came with my coffee. I pushed it out of her reach. 'I am, now. It was a bit hard at the start. She didn't sleep well for a long time.'

He grinned. 'Good job you had a bit of practice with those all-nighters we used to pull.'

I smiled. 'I'd forgotten about that. I can't believe I used to stay up for fun. Now my idea of a good time is going to bed by 9pm and keeping my eyes open long enough to read a page of my book. It's pretty raucous, I must admit.'

He smiled at me. 'It really is so good to see you.'

Holly grunted and twisted on my lap. She was always desperate to keep moving constantly. I checked my watch. We'd been forty-five minutes. 'I think I might be pushing it with this one to stay out much longer. Better get her home to bed. It's been lovely to catch up, though.'

'You can't stay for another coffee? She might settle again.'

I raised an eyebrow. 'You've not spent much time around babies, have you?'

He looked sheepish and scrambled to his feet. 'I'll walk you to your car.'

I waved him away. 'Don't bother, we walked here.'

He scurried behind me, checking under the table for abandoned belongings and darting in front to shift chairs out of the way as I made my way to the front door of the café. He held it open as we walked out into the sunlight.

He put his hand on my arm. 'I'll see you again soon? Is that okay?'

I looked up at him. What harm could it do? He was a distraction, if nothing else. 'Sure.'

He beamed. 'Great. I'll message you.' He started walking backwards, gesturing to his phone. 'In fact, I already am.'

***

It took weeks for Nick to stop calling and texting three or four times a day. I just stopped responding. My mum organised weekend visits for him to see Holly and to get clothes to wherever he was staying. He assured me it was with Sam, not Maia, but who knew? I had expected to feel relieved when the incessant begging stopped but instead the silence felt a little empty. When Holly beamed at me with sand up her nose when we played in the sandpit on our balcony, and I snapped a picture on my phone, I only really had my mother to send it to. Jordan was true to his word and peppered me with messages but they were mostly about himself and his day or his job or subtle hints that he wanted more than just coffee next time he saw me. Any responses to messages about Holly were so generic I wondered if he was copying and pasting them from somewhere.

I was changing Holly's nappy when there was a clatter at the door. Nick back again? I slapped the tabs into place and hoisted Holly on to my shoulder. I slid back the bolts and pulled open the door. Lauren was on the doorstep, a bag slung over her shoulder and Mackenzie in a frontpack.

'Lauren.' I stood back to let her in. 'What are you doing here?'

She raised her shoulders and then let them fall heavily. 'It was getting a bit ridiculous trying to stay with them. Honestly. You'd think there were kids the way they stay up all night playing PlayStation games. Except they're usually drunk.'

I bit my lip. She was little more than a kid herself.

'You're going back to your mum?'

She shook her head, sinking on to my couch and putting her feet on the coffee table in front of her.

'Can I come and stay with you again for a bit?'

I frowned. 'She's really worried.'

'Yeah, I know.'

I wandered through to the kitchen to make tea for us both. 'You can stay, okay? But I want you to make a time to talk to her and at least try to get it sorted. Deal?'

She mumbled something I couldn't hear.

'You can arrange to meet her here if you want. I'll help you.'

I returned to the lounge and handed her a mug. She sipped it. 'Got any chocolate biscuits?'

I sat beside her. 'No. You can buy your own though.'

She blew her tea in the same way I might try to cool a forkful of Holly's mashed veggies. 'Haven't got any money.'

'Well then, another point in favour of talking to your mother.' She let Mackenzie down on to the floor where she and Holly sat, side by side, pushing blocks together with a satisfying clack. One block shot out of Holly's reach and she turned to look at me as if to ask what she was supposed to do.

'Why don't you try to get it?' I winked at her. 'I bet you can.'

She frowned and reached out an arm, waving it in the air when she came up short.

She wriggled around until she was facing the couch and, extending her dimpled arms, carefully pulled herself up to a standing position and edged along to the block.

Lauren and I watched her. 'You should know that Nick's not here at the moment.'

She looked at me. 'He's at work?'

'No. I mean he's not living here at the moment. We're ... well, we're separated.'

Her mug hit the coffee table with a clatter. 'What? Why? I thought you were just bickering like old married couples do.'

I waved it away. 'I won't bore you with the details. But we're having some time apart ... hey, look!'

Holly had let go of the furniture. She extended a foot and wobbled awkwardly. She looked at me, her arms wide with alarm, as if she could not work out what to do next. She landed with a thump on her padded bottom.

Lauren watched her. 'Cool. Mackenzie's still in potato mode. Probably won't move until she's two.'

I dropped kisses on to the back of Holly's head. 'Well done, my darling. Keep trying.'

Lauren frowned. 'Do you think it's a problem that Mackenzie's not moving at all? Like, literally, not at all? No crawling. Nothing.'

I shook my head. 'They're all different, aren't they? She's happy and healthy and fine. When I was worried about Holly having no interest in any food she had to chew, someone said to me that they're all walking and eating and using the toilet by the time they're twenty-five.'

Lauren seemed to accept that. Mackenzie had found part of a rice cracker that had slid under the couch and put it into her mouth.

'Are you going to divorce? Are you going to have to sell your flat? What about all his stuff?'

'We're not married and I don't know. At the moment I'm aiming to do as little as possible for as long as possible.'

***

Nick
Age: Nine months

My alarm always goes off with this awful screeching beep. Every day I decide I need to change the tone. But then I put it off, figuring I'll do it before bed, and then I fall asleep before I can be bothered to do it, so I wake again to the worst noise in the world and resolve to do something about it ... then repeat. I blinked and stretched. Some people leapt out of bed each morning no matter how little they had slept. You might think that being a personal trainer with a roster of clients that started at 5.30am some days, I would be one of them. You would be wrong.

I now live on the fold-out couch in Sam's too-small lounge. I stay at work until the last of the late-night squeeze-in-the-door-before-closing members finish their treadmill trudge, then I trudge back to the place he shares with Rachelle so I don't get there too early and have to spend the evening drinking a beer and pretending not to hear them bicker about their various attempts to fall pregnant. They are on to IVF now and the treatment sounds horrific. I'm not sure if it's the stress or the hormones she's injecting into herself every day but Rachelle is a mess.

One night they had a stand-up, apologise-to-the-neigh-bours fight about whose turn it was to pay the power bill. Sam and I were sitting on the couch afterwards, deliberately not talking about it, when Rachelle sent him a message summoning him to the bedroom.

'Got to do my duty.' He'd given me a mock salute as he stood.

'What? Like counselling or something?'

He grimaced. 'No. Like sex. There's still a week until they actually do the thing so if we can do it naturally ourselves in the meantime we can skip the whole egg transfer bit.'

'How romantic.'

He'd forced a laugh. 'Quite.'

I was still trying to get Renee to agree to let me see

Holly at a regular time in the weekends. As it was, I was hanging around waiting for her mother to give me word that there was an hour free. It was not like I had a packed social life but it would have been nice not to be literally waiting by the phone.

Holly had started walking, which was terrifying. I hadn't realised how much I depended on her remaining where she was put. But now I'd put her down for a second and turn to get a snack out of the picnic bag – supermarket sandwich for me, one of those fruit sachet things for her – and turn around and she would be halfway across the grass inspecting something that might have once been inside a dog.

I always used to roll my eyes at Renee when she tried to give me detailed instructions for every single detail of looking after Holly. But now I had proper sole charge of her each week and I realised the mental inventory that Renee must be carrying all day, every day. No matter how many changes of clothes I packed for her, I would never have the right thing in my bag. She'd drop a full sachet of yoghurt on her leggings, so I'd switch her into a new pair. Then we'd paddle in a puddle and I'd find myself having to roll up the legs because the only other things in her backpack were a cardigan and a swimsuit.

On one occasion, we met my parents for a coffee. Holly had just started doing this weird growling thing. It started off like a little quiet rumbling. The waitress taking our order paused. 'Is that your baby making that noise?'

'Yep, think so. I've told her she's human but she seems determined she's actually a puppy.'

The waitress shrugged. 'Cute.'

By the time the waitress returned with our drinks, the growling sounded more like a motorbike engine.

'Watch out for that one,' the waitress said, pointing at Holly, 'she sounds like something out of *The Exorcist* or something.'

Mum frowned. But as the woman was turning to walk back to the counter, Holly reached out and swiped my mum's latte glass. It teetered briefly then fell, hot milk running over the table, into my mum's lap. Then, while I thrust serviettes at my mum as fast as I could, she picked up a sticky handful of my dad's carrot cake and threw it at me.

Holly fell asleep in the car afterwards and we had to drive around for an hour, listening to the white noise app, because I was too scared to turn off the car, in case she woke up.

***

I scanned through my phone as I lay on the couch trying to find the energy to get up. My first client wasn't booked until 6.30am. Somewhere in the back of the house I could hear Rachelle and Sam rustling around. I switched to our shared calendar – he wasn't meant to be going into the gym until eight.

The door cracked open and he tiptoed into the lounge, exaggeratedly sneaking across the room. I coughed. 'I'm awake.'

He turned to look at me. 'Sorry, mate. Just going out to get Rachelle some breakfast before I go.'

I sat up. 'Okay ...'

'If she doesn't go to work today she'll probably lose her job – no leave left. I don't think our bank balance can handle that yet. I'm hoping a dirty takeaway breakfast might give her the stamina.'

I watched him shut the front door behind him before hauling myself up and heading for the shower.

When I returned, Rachelle was sitting on the couch where I'd slept, flicking through Netflix.

I waved the towel in the direction of my hair. 'How's it going?'

She looked up. Her face was pale, with dark bluish grey circles under her eyes. 'Not great. I feel rubbish.'

I perched on the arm of the sofa. 'Sick?'

She shook her head. 'Not really. Just stressed and can't sleep ever. Honestly, is it all worth it, really? I thought I wanted a baby no matter what but now ...'

An image of Holly's little face, with her wide nose and round pink cheeks, forced its way into my mind. The way she reached out for me when she realised I was in the room and giggled while she bashed away at the noisiest of musical toys the more sadistic of our friends had given us.

Then I thought of Renee, standing on the far side of the living room when I arrived to take Holly out for a walk, her face blank as she watched us leave.

'Yes,' I answered at last. 'It is worth it. But you guys are great, you'll be okay either way.' I tried to catch her eye. 'I've heard puppies are pretty good, too.'

She looked at me hard and seemed to be trying to smile. 'Yeah, I like puppies. You don't have to give birth to them either, which is a bonus, I guess.'

She shifted awkwardly. 'I'm sorry about what happened. I'm team Renee obviously but I hope you two can sort it out. You love her.'

I wiped at an invisible mark on the side of the couch. Sometimes it was best not to think too far into the future.

***

Renee
Age: Nine months

I'd dragged myself out early for a walk around the park with Ruth and Helen. As I loaded Holly into the stroller and watched them do the same with their babies, I had to fight back a giggle. We all had the same model of stroller, with an ergonomic handle that was meant to help your posture, moulded seats and extra hydraulics to help smooth a ride over bumpy terrain. We were in activewear that was almost matching, too – all clad in three-quarter tights and in the same grey adidas hoodies.

It had not been that long ago that I would have thought the idea of being part of a stroller group walking in the park was horrific. Nick and I had once sat and watched a group of women – my age, I now realised – wearing similar exercise gear and walking very intently around the lake, hands clasped firmly on stroller handles. None of them smiled and they seemed to be immersed in an incredibly serious conversation.

As we had watched them I'd asked Nick what they could possibly have to look so determined about. Back then I'd thought the mum life was just swanning about having a year off work and buying cute outfits for your kids. Now I was one of them. And I knew the old me should have offered those women a cup of coffee and a lie down, at the very least.

Ruth was a relaxing change from Lauren – whom I still hadn't managed to dislodge from the spare room, and who constantly wanted to know what was going on. If I wasn't with Nick any more, was I going to hook up with Jordan? As if those were the only two possibilities in my life.

Helen shot me a look out of the side of her eye as we walked, our footsteps falling into time, along the path that wound through the park. A cyclist had to divert on to the grass to get away from us.

'How are you coping?'

I shrugged. 'I've been better. But okay.'

We walked a little further. A family group was on the path in front of us, a mother and father swinging a toddler between them.

I had to look away. 'Do you think I'm short-changing Holly? Like with only one parent at a time, is she missing out?' My voice was croaky.

Ruth snorted. 'Don't even worry about that. You're a great mum. She's got everything she needs.'

I grimaced. 'Thanks.'

'Stuart, you know, Simon's mad son ... he's currently staging some sort of protest. Won't spend time with me and Xavier so the two of them are off all hours of the night doing whatever Simon can think of to 'bond' over. Xavi might as well just have a single parent at the moment.' She made little air quotes with her fingers.

Helen craned her neck to look around me at Ruth. 'That sounds really hard. I always thought you were brave taking on a guy with a kid like that.'

Ruth frowned. 'What could I do? I love Simon to pieces. They're a package deal. We used to get on really well.'

An uncomfortable feeling nagged in my stomach. 'What changed?'

'Stuart's mum. Apparently fine with the idea of us getting married. Not so keen on a baby. Keeps feeding him lines about how he'll come second best or whatever. What's the bet Xavier idolises his big brother when he grows up though? She's probably just scared they'll have a connection.'

Helen frowned. 'Bitch.'

Ruth giggled. 'She's not, really. Maybe just having a moment.'

I reached out to rub her back. 'Hard, right? All that blended family stuff? Nick had better not get a girlfriend till Holly's eighteen.' Saying it out loud made my breath catch in my throat. 'Helen's just lucky she doesn't have to deal with any of it.'

Holly was awake but staring at a toy I had strung from the rainhood, sucking her fingers.

Helen crossed her fingers and tapped her head. 'Touch wood.'

***

When I got home, Lauren and my mum were sitting at the kitchen table. Mackenzie was at their feet, batting a ball to her mother, who kicked it back when she noticed its arrival.

'How's the mum squad?' Lauren was a member of the online group but somehow none of the connections she made had turned into real-life meetings. She said it was because no one wanted to spend time with a single, teenage mother. I suspected it was because she kept telling everyone they were terrible people whenever they disagreed with her. When I tried to introduce her to Helen and Ruth, she had disappeared to read her phone in the spare room.

282

'Much the same. Tired. Over-caffeinated.'

'We've just been discussing your mother's new business empire.'

'Her what?'

Of all the things that my mother might be good at, business was not one of them. Anything that required her to do something she had promised with any regularity was sure to fall over.

Mum laughed. 'Don't be like that. It's a great fit for me.'

Holly was gnawing on the top of my Lycra singlet. Somehow she had moved my breast so that the nipple was almost breaking out over the top. I wiggled so that it slid back down again.

'I'm going to sell beautiful vegan cosmetics, help people understand how to use them ...'

'I'm going to go and get changed.'

She stood up, extending her hands to stop me. 'What? I know about that sort of thing. I'm caring. I'm artistic. It'll be great. Henry's daughter is going to sign me up. You can buy a kit from me, get wholesale prices ...'

She made an expansive gesture with her hand. 'Maybe you can come and do it with me, earn a bit of money while you're at home with Holly.'

I shook my head and made for the bedroom. 'No thanks. I know exactly how that pans out.'

***

Once the girls were asleep, Lauren, Mum, and I stretched out in front of the television. Was my mum hanging around to keep an eye on me, or on Lauren? It was hard to tell. It was the longest she'd been in the house since she shifted back out. It was weirdly comforting, if I allowed myself not to think about it too deeply.

'What shall we watch?' She scrolled through the options.

'Something light,' I offered weakly.

She was about to click on a romcom about young parents but Lauren sat up. 'Nothing about babies. I get enough of those all day.'

I rolled my eyes. 'It feels like they're all I think about.' I turned to look at her, expecting a conspiratorial smile. Her face had fallen.

'Honestly, I don't know what to do.' She looked as if she was about to cry. 'I'm getting a bit terrified.'

I sat up. 'What do you mean?'

She sank back against the couch as if she was looking for a hug. 'It's fine when we are all together, I can cope. But is this all we're going to do now? Like for years and years? And what about when you need me to move out?'

'I wasn't serious about you having to get out. Let's talk tomorrow about your options.'

She nodded. 'But you're right, I can't just go crashing on people's couches and hanging out in your spare room for ever. And the idea of being alone in a house with just the two of us is freaking me out.'

My mum patted her leg. 'It doesn't last for ever. I was

ancient before Renee finally moved out. You won't have that problem.'

She put her face in her hands. 'I know, I guess. But even a couple of years seems like a freaking long time when I haven't even really done a year yet. I'm either bored out of my mind trying to think of things to do to entertain her or I'm flipping out thinking that I've got it all wrong and she's hurt or I've neglected her or I'm going to make her grow up to be some kind of reject because she's just had me and not a dad ...'

I put up my hand as she took a breath to launch into another sentence. 'Lauren, stop!'

She looked up. 'Well, it's true.'

I reached across to pull her into an awkward hug. 'It's okay.' I used the same tone I would to talk Holly down from an inarticulatable disaster like having lost a piece of carrot over the edge of her high chair tray. 'It's okay. You're doing so well.'

She wiped her nose on my shirt. 'Easy for you to say. You've got it sorted.'

I leant back and raised an eyebrow. 'I've what?'

'You even ran the group where everyone basically just asks you for advice.'

'No one wants to listen to what I have to say, they just want some validation that they're not totally screwing up.'

'Still.'

'My relationship is totally dead.'

'You don't even need a guy, though, you're like Supermum.'

I watched her. It was like travelling back in time. Her face was creased in the same way that I remembered seeing my own in the early days. When I couldn't bear to let Holly out of my sight in case she stopped breathing. When I set an alarm but woke up five minutes before it every ninety minutes to make sure she was still alive. When I organised the thermostat in her room so that it was at exactly the WHO-recommended temperature.

But then when she woke and smiled at me, I instantly panicked about how I was going to keep her happy until her next nap time.

Even though Nick had turned everything on its head, those days where I couldn't shake the feeling of wading through jelly were gone. I would probably still have the worry about whether she was okay when she was thirty-five and had kids of her own. But I no longer seriously fretted that she was going to drop dead without warning. Instead I worried that I hadn't packed enough nappies when we went out for lunch.

'It's going to be okay,' I told her. 'I totally lost the plot at the beginning but the fog is clearing now. The same will happen to you. Promise. And you've got people you can lean on ... like your mum, remember her?'

Lauren wiped her face with her palms and nodded. 'Mum asked again if she can come and see me.'

'Good, that's great. Get her to come around tomorrow, if you like. I'll clear out so you can talk.'

She reached for my hand. 'Can you stay, talk to her? She likes you.'

'Sure. I'll do my best.'

Mum leant around and tapped Lauren on the knee. 'Maybe we could give her a makeover.'

I shot her a look. 'Mum!'

She pretended to be affronted. 'It's worth a try, isn't it?' Mum kissed Lauren on the cheek. 'Most mothers do want what's best for our kids, even though we don't always make it look that way.'

Chapter Eight

Lucia Monroe, 11:01am: 'So here's something I never thought I'd have to do – assure someone that I didn't, in fact, defecate on my husband's laptop. We were getting ready to leave the house and my husband was grring at me about my "crap" all over his laptop. Meaning my notebooks for work. Five-year-old turns around and, all wide eyes, asks deadly seriously, "Mum why did you poo on Dad's laptop?" As if that's something that I might actually conceivably do!'

Nick
Age: Nine months

I was demonstrating a deep squat to Marguerite when I realised she was staring at me hard.

'What? We can modify the exercise if you'd like to.'

Despite my initial prediction, she had booked in to come and see me every other Friday. For most people that wouldn't be enough to make any real difference. I'd turn down bookings like that because people would just blame me for their total lack of results. But Marguerite seemed to take my programmes seriously and assured me she was doing her 'homework' ever other night.

'I haven't had an update about your family lately.'

'Oh.' I coughed. I'd tried not to tell anyone of my clients about what was going on. The fewer people who knew, the less chance there was of it being true.

She raised an eyebrow. 'I talked to your mother.'

I snorted in surprise. 'You what?'

'We still catch up from time to time, you know. She mentioned that you and Renee are having a bit of a tough time.'

'Mmm.' I gestured to her to sit on a swiss ball and guided her back into a position to target her lower abdominal muscles.

'She mentioned a bit of postnatal depression.'

I avoided her eyes.

'I know you don't want to talk about it.'

'You're right.'

She put her hand on my arm. It looked almost exactly like my mother's. 'Just hear me out. When I was young, I had the twins. You remember?'

I nodded. Vaguely. Sporty, rugby-playing redheads, from what I could recall.

'The first year after they were born was the toughest of my life. Not just the lack of sleep. It was like something took over and sucked the joy out of what should have been wonderful. I never got that time back. Back then, we didn't talk about it like we do now. There was no help for people like me. I was just lucky that my husband believed me and helped me through it. I don't know where I would have been, otherwise.'

I watched her. Heat rose in my cheeks as I thought back to those years of counting down to the moment I could put on my running shoe and sprint away from what felt at the time like someone else's life. I knew what it felt like to wake up feeling smothered. 'I understand. I just don't believe that jumping straight to medication is the answer.'

I'd briefly considered trying antidepressants, until I saw the shopping list of possible side effects. Renee didn't understand the way exercise helped me mentally, though. She just saw the workout videos online and assumed we were all trying to hone the perfect pectoral, or something.

Marguerite fixed me with her piercing stare again. 'The medication may have made the difference between Renee going through hell on earth for who knows how long and actually managing to crawl out of it pretty quickly. Can you see that?'

I stared at my shoe.

'If she took it upon herself to fix it, to make herself well, and, as a result, to be a better, more engaged mother for your daughter, you should thank her for that.'

We looked at each other.

'Okay,' I said at last.

'Okay?'

'You're right. I agree with you. The same stuff isn't going to work for everyone. I should have been more supportive.'

She smiled. 'I didn't expect it to be so easy. So what are you going to do?'

'Do?'

'To fix it.'

'I have no idea.' I put my hands under her shoulders to take her weight. 'There's not much I can do, is there?'

She raised an eyebrow. 'I wouldn't have picked you as so defeatist.'

I grimaced. Clearly my mother had been a bit selective in what she told her.

***

Sam appeared in front of us as we were finishing our session, on his mobile phone, running his fingers through his hair and massaging his temples with the other hand.

'I'll have a chat to Nick and call you back, okay?' He hung up the phone as he got nearer. 'What's going on?

I waved to Marguerite as she headed for the changing rooms. 'I don't know what you're talking about.'

'We've got no money in the bank. Our equipment hire fee just bounced.'

I pulled out my phone to bring up the bank app. It was overdrawn – and by more than usual. 'I guess people haven't been paying their subs?'

He raked his hand through his hair. 'Who?'

I rolled my eyes. 'Why do you think I know? Why don't you pay some attention to your own business for once?'

'Don't we have someone who deals with this stuff?'

'No, remember, you canned her when you thought we could handle it ourselves and save money.'

He stared at me. 'So what do we do?'

I pushed a piece of paper at him. 'Check which of the members isn't paying their fees. Call them and ask them to. Advertise for new members. Repeat.'

'And what if we can't get the money in?'

'I guess we don't pay the rent.'

I pulled a water bottle from the fridge in the corner of the room and headed for the weights section. Why was everything so damn hard? Maybe I didn't want to be in business for myself anyway. It had all been part of the Renee-and-me dream. If it was just me, did I want the stress of paying rent, wrangling customers, paying staff, chasing payments? I could probably earn at least what I was getting from the business if I went to work for someone else. Apparently cruise ships paid their trainers pretty well. Not that Renee would ever let me take Holly with me, and there was no way I was leaving her behind.

***

Renee

Age: Nine months

Ruth was waiting in the café on the corner when Holly and I arrived. She had Xavier on her knee and was trying to hold her coffee high enough that it was out of the reach of baby hands but not so high that she could not drink it.

I slid into the seat opposite. 'You've got that down to a fine art.'

Ruth laughed, craning her neck for another slurp. 'I can think of a few things I'm a total expert at now. Picking stuff up with my foot when I'm holding a baby, for one.'

'Cooking dinner with one hand,' I offered. 'Offering a muesli bar from your mouth while you use both hands to clip a car seat.'

Ruth stirred her drink. 'He's started asking me when we should be trying for another.'

I spluttered, a sip of water threatening to come out my nose. 'Simon has? Already?'

'Yeah, well, as he so helpfully points out – if I fall pregnant right now Xavi will be eighteen months by the time another one came along. And last time it took us months.'

'He's not content with two of them already?'

'I think he thinks Stuart missed out not having a brother or sister to grow up with. And now the ex is starting to thaw a bit ...'

I nodded. 'Nick and I had talked about trying again when Holly's two.'

Ruth's smile faded. 'Sorry, mate. I shouldn't be complaining.'

I brushed away. 'Of course you should. Simon wants you to go through all this again already! At least it might mean you don't have to rush back to work when Xavier's one?'

She stroked his head. 'I guess there's that.'

I cringed. 'I'm not looking forward to it. I've been talking to Mum about how I can try to convince my boss to let me come back part-time. She's more optimistic than I am. But how can I juggle looking after Holly most of the time by myself with work? It's madness. Especially with the weird hours I used to work.'

There was a clatter as a group of men passing the café stopped in the street outside the window we were sitting in front of. Ruth looked up as one tapped on the glass. 'Is he trying to get your attention?' She gestured behind me.

It was Jordan. He was wrapped in a winter coat with a scarf around the lower half of his face, and I could only see his eyes. He stuck his head through the door. 'Renee, how's it going?'

I half-waved. It felt like every eye in the room was watching us.

'I can't stop – on the way to a meeting. But can we catch up soon? Maybe see that movie?'

'I'll message you.'

He saluted and disappeared back out into the street.

'Was that ... Jordan?' Ruth's eyes were alight.

I nodded.

She looked surprised. 'He's quite good-looking.'

I looked up at her. 'Maybe. I'm pretty sure I prefer him when he's at the other end of the phone.'

***

Holly and I got home a couple of minutes before my mother was meant to arrive for lunch.

I kept an eye on the door as Holly clambered on to my lap and attached herself to my breast. Even though she was well past the age where she was meant to be getting all her nutrition from breast milk, she had decided with renewed determination that was the only source that would do. She affixed herself with the strength of someone trying to suck a golf ball down a hose. I watched her swallowing furiously. Had my nipples lost their nerve endings?

The doorbell rang. 'Come in,' I shouted, 'it's open.'

There was a pause and then it rang again.

I twisted to unlatch Holly, who scowled at me. I hoisted her on top of my shoulder, the clasp of my breastfeeding singlet still hanging around my waist, the air cool on my still wet nipple.

I pulled the door back, making only a half-hearted attempt to cover my chest with one arm. 'You know you can just come in. I was feeding Holly.'

The courier driver who used to drop off all of Nick's weird internet purchases stared at me. He was fighting to resist the urge to stare at my breast, which hung limply out of the hole in my top. He was young. Perhaps he had never seen one on which the nipple did not point skyward.

I reached for the clasp and pulled everything back up and into place. 'Here.' I gestured for him to pass me the electronic pad to sign. 'Thanks very much.'

When I shut the door behind me, I looked at Holly, who

was staring after him. 'He got more than he bargained for, didn't he?'

My mum arrived a couple of minutes later, pushing open the door and falling through. 'I should have known it wouldn't be you so soon.' I reached out to take her hand as she tried to kick off a high heel that added at least 20cm to her usually diminutive frame.

'What wouldn't?'

I shook my head. 'Nothing. Eggs and soldiers for lunch?'

She grinned and tickled Holly under the chin. 'Whatever the little princess requires.'

She pushed ahead of me to the kitchen, where Lauren and Mackenzie were playing with rice in a plastic mixing bowl.

She nudged Lauren with the side of her foot. 'Forgiven your mother yet?'

'Found a proper job yet?'

Mum shrugged. 'Touché.'

Her perfume was new and the dress was one I had not seen before. There was less of the ombré dye than I was used to. It was almost a block red with only a slight pattern around the waist.

'You look well,' I ventured as I pulled my last matching cups from the dishwasher and placed them on the bench, teabags at the ready. I had propped Holly on the floor.

Mum smiled. I could see all her teeth. It was the first time in years that she had smiled at me without her hand over her mouth or her lips pursed.

I watched her mouth. 'Did you get something done to your teeth?'

She laughed. 'No. I'm just focusing on being less self-conscious. Henry says ...'

'Henry.' Henry was appearing in more and more of our conversations. Could this be her longest relationship yet?

She scowled at me, 'Yes, Henry. If you ever met, you'd not be so mean about it. Henry thinks I'm beautiful.'

I ducked my head. 'You are, Mum. Sorry. That's not what I meant.'

She patted my shoulder as she passed on her way to the fridge to pull out a couple of eggs to drop in the noisily boiling saucepan. 'It's okay, I know.'

Holly yanked open the drawer on her left. It was full of plastic storage containers. She extracted one and threw it at the floor. Giggling at the satisfying thwack, she reached for another, then another

Lunch cooked, my mum stooped down to scoop her up. 'You come up here, please. No one is ready for you to start destroying the house yet.'

We positioned ourselves around the dining table, me in the seat that Nick would normally have occupied had he been home, and Mum on the other side of Holly.

'I flashed my breast at the courier driver today,' I offered as I dunked some bread for Holly, who smeared the yolk over her face.

'What?' Lauren looked up, astonished, from her game

on the floor. 'If you'd told me you were that desperate, we could have gone out dancing.'

I swatted her. 'It wasn't on purpose.'

Mum coughed on her mouthful of tea. 'Ah well, I'm sure he's seen worse.'

As she winked at me, I saw she was wearing eyeshadow. 'Have you been out somewhere?'

She shook her head and blew on her tea. 'No, Henry came over for breakfast earlier on.'

I bit my lip. 'You really care about him.'

She smiled. 'It's not for Henry.'

I raised an eyebrow. 'Sure.'

'I know you don't believe it. Even when I'm alone, I sort of feel now like it's worth doing things that I like for myself that I used to maybe think were a bit silly. I burn my good candles, I have a glass of my expensive wine, I wear my going-out dresses that I was saving in case I was invited to a wedding.'

'On your own?'

I was still wearing grey leggings and maternity singlets most days.

She nodded. 'I don't have a baby to worry about, remember. But Henry just makes me feel like every day deserves to be celebrated.'

I sat back in my chair. Had I ever felt like that? When Nick and I first got together I'd had that humming feeling you get, like everything was brighter and more exciting when he was around. That had faded and been replaced with a comfy sort of warmth. When had it disappeared?

Falling in love is a funny thing. You meet some random stranger and decide you quite fancy each other, and then all of a sudden that person becomes the most important person in your life and is there virtually all the time. If you were to describe it to someone who had never experienced it or seen anything like it, it would sound utterly mad. No wonder I had only done it twice.

'I'm glad you're happy.' I patted my mum's hand. It seemed condescending but she didn't notice. 'You do deserve to be. I'd like to meet him.'

Lauren was jiggling Mackenzie back and forth, swooping her down towards the floor and then raising her over her head to make her giggle. She looked at me as she made aeroplane noises and hovered her daughter over the faded tiles. 'You're lucky. Both of you.'

'Baby Shark' was still playing in the next room. 'What do you mean?'

She gestured at a photo of me and Nick that remained on the windowsill. We were on holiday, drinking dodgy cocktails by a pool that had turned a cloudy blue from the sunscreen of a hundred holidaymakers over the course of the day. I was looking directly into the camera, smiling at the waitress taking our photo. Nick was focused entirely on me.

'You and your mum – you've both been really in love. What if I never get that?'

I dropped my serving spoon on the table. 'Don't be ridiculous. Of course you will. You're not even twenty.'

She kissed Mackenzie on the top of her downy head.

'Exactly. What guy my age wants an instant family? And when we're older they'll want someone who can start all over fresh. Maybe I've missed my chance. Louis was a loser. But maybe I should have tried harder.'

My mum fixed her with a hard stare. 'Don't you be ridiculous. You're a wonderful young lady and the right man will think Mackenzie is a benefit, not a drawback, of being with you. I promise. You've your whole life ahead of you. When I was a single mum, I used to think Renee was the best filter out there because if a man didn't ask about her, I didn't see him again.'

I shot her a look. That was news to me.

Lauren looked at me. 'How did you know Nick was the one you wanted to be with?'

I sucked in my breath. It hadn't been instant. Soon after we met I'd told a friend he would have been the perfect man if I was at all attracted to him. But he'd won me over, as the memory of Jordan's heady chaos faded. He turned up with pegs for my cat when I told him that he loved to chase them down the hallway. Then he'd written a note for every day I was away when I had to go on a work trip.

'It just worked,' I offered at last. 'Then I couldn't imagine my life without him.'

'But ...' Her voice trailed off.

'But here I am,' I finished for her. 'Yeah. I guess you never know what's around the corner, right?'

My mum coughed into her cup. 'Have you thought of forgiving Nick?'

I stared at her. 'You told me no self-respecting woman ever forgives that sort of thing. I was at home with our baby while he was with ... her.'

She nodded. 'Yes. It was an awful thing to do. But it's clear he regrets it and you were going through a ... tough time. He loves you. I just wonder if you'll regret throwing it all away. You're big on Lauren giving her mum another shot.'

I stood to clear the table. 'I can't think about that right now.'

***

After lunch had been cleared, I sat at the table. My mother had disappeared. Holly was sitting by my feet, tapping an empty plastic cup on an ice-cream container, sort of singing along with the rhythm it created. 'That's a good noise,' I said, and dropped her a spoon. 'Try with this, too.'

My phone's messages were open in my hands. Now Jordan was suggesting that we go on an island holiday together – with veiled references to swimming nude. How could I break it to him that even the idea of me in a bikini was probably much better than the reality?

'Lucky we've got a good six months until it's time to get near the beach again,' I tapped out at last.

'Hmm, maybe we could go for a skiing weekend?' The reply was almost instant. I rolled my eyes. I'd like to see how he expected me to manage an infant on skis. She was barely even walking. Imagine strapping her up and hurtling down a mountain.

He tried again. 'Or even a movie?'

There was a cough in the doorway. Lauren hovered, darting glances at me. 'Do you have a second?'

I patted the chair beside me. 'Of course, what's up?'

She slid into it. I put my arm around her shoulder and rested my head against hers. She turned to look at me. 'Remember I said my mother wanted to catch up.'

I nodded. 'I do. Is she going to come around here? I'm happy to just hover around if that would be helpful?'

She shook her head. 'Sorry. We actually had coffee today when you were out with Ruth. I didn't want to bring it up in front of your mum because she was on such a roll with—'

'Henry.' We finished the sentence in unison.

I stretched my hands out on the table in front of us, inspecting my nail polish. 'Don't be sorry, that's great. How did that go?'

She ran a hand through her hair. She was regaining some of the bits that fell out when Mackenzie was first born. 'It was okay. I apologised.'

I traced my finger through a drop of water on the tabletop. 'You did?'

'Yeah. I've thought a lot about what you've said. She just wants what's best for me. I was just too tired and stressed out to understand what she was saying.'

I bit my lip. 'That's really mature of you, to admit it.'

She smiled at me through her fringe. 'She wants me to

get sorted to go back and finish school next year. D'you think I can handle it?'

'Of course you can! You'll be great.'

'Also' – she paused –'she wants me to move in with them – with my sister and her partner, too. So they can all help me.' She caught my eye. 'Help me, not do it for me. I know what you're thinking.'

I watched her face. It had been a little trying from time to time, having her with us. She spent ages in the shower. She used up my good toiletries. She never bought the right things from the supermarket or had the money for what we really needed. But Mackenzie and Holly were good playmates and it was a relief to have someone to commiserate with when nothing went to plan. I was just getting used to having her around.

'Is that what you want?'

She sighed. 'I guess. I mean I can't live with you for ever. It wouldn't be fair. I miss my mum.'

I rubbed her back. 'Of course you do. Let's make it happen. I'll help you get your stuff over there as soon as we can get it sorted.'

She looked up at me from under her overgrown fringe. 'Thanks for looking after us. You don't know what it's meant to me.'

I kissed her forehead. 'Thank you for looking after me, too.'

Chapter 9

Karla Stevenson, 2:04am: 'I just reached over and stuck a dummy in my boyfriend's mouth in the middle of the night. He woke up and looked at me like I was nuts. Sleep deprivation is something else, isn't it? Yesterday I forgot my son's name at the doctor's and called him "whatshisname".'

Renee
Age: Ten months

It took some getting used to, living alone. Lauren moved quickly once she made up her mind. Her mum arrived to collect her and the questions started before they even walked out the door. Did she have enough summer clothes for Mackenzie? Was she eating a proper diet?

Lauren rolled her eyes at me over her shoulder as they walked towards the stairs down to the street. Her mum caught herself. 'Sorry, darling. I do know you know what you're doing. I'm just excited to have you back.'

I patted her arm and handed them Lauren's last bag. 'I think she secretly likes it.'

Mum still came to visit all the time – although she was yet to introduce me to this mythical Henry. Ruth turned up to drink cheap champagne for my birthday. Nick appeared every Saturday to take Holly out. He had developed a little fan club of women in the café on the corner who were desperate to tell him what a wonderful dad he was for spending time with his daughter. He had looked perplexed when I told him that mothers didn't tend to get that same type of praise for simply existing in public with their children.

We'd also started going out most Sunday mornings as a little family of three. I'd not been able to shake what my mother said about forgiving him from my brain. The further I was away from it, the more I could see our relationship had been a bit of a mess. We'd both made mistakes – though I still maintained his was much worse. But for Holly's sake I found I could soften towards him enough to spend a few pleasant hours together on a regular basis. Growing up, just Mum and me had been fine, but a little family unit had been my dream. I figured I should do what I could to give her something as close to that as possible.

He would come over after he had finished his session with the first client of the morning and we would go and get a takeaway coffee and sit in the park, or wander through the new growers' market that had popped up around the block. It was so pretentious you wouldn't believe but it gave us something to do other than confront the weird-ness between us. Nick and I avoided looking at each other, browsing the stalls. We tasted cheese, dipped small dried-out bits of bread in various olive oils, bought bunches of flowers to sag in the middle of my dining table.

We were halfway through a ten-minute presentation on the merits of hydro culture when I caught Nick's eye mid-smirk. I had to bite my lip. Holly was gnawing on the strap of the baby carrier, creating a waterfall of dribble that I could feel soaking into the side of my T-shirt.

'So it's better basil, this, than stuff grown in the ground?' He cut the stallholder off as I suppressed a giggle.

The man raised a 'have you not been listening to anything I've said?' eyebrow.

'We'll take two.' I thrust a note at him – these markets were the last place in the world where it was socially acceptable to want nothing to do with electronic payments.

'Crepe?' Nick gestured towards a caravan parked in the middle of the market. A gruff elderly man was swiping a knife across a hot plate, spreading batter in the same way I might smear butter on to a piece of toast for Holly.

'Definitely.'

He filed into the back of the line and regarded the chalkboard menu. 'Lemon and sugar?'

I nodded. 'Maybe a little Nutella one for Holly?'

307

She grinned up at me at the sound of her name, angling her weight back in the carrier so she could see us.

'Hey, how's Sam doing, with the baby stuff?'

Nick turned to look at us. 'I think they're putting it all on hold for a bit. It was getting a bit much for them to deal with.'

'Ah, well, maybe they dodged a bullet.' I forced a laugh.

He shook his head and traced the apple of Holly's cheek with his finger. 'Never.'

I kissed the top of her head. 'True. Sorry. Just ...'

He rubbed my back. 'I know.'

Another hand clapped my shoulder and a stubbly cheek brushed against mine as a kiss was landed somewhere to the right of my mouth. Startled, I took a step back and away from the cologne cloud.

'Oh, Jordan. Hi. Fancy seeing you here.'

He grinned and kissed the other side of my face. 'This is a nice surprise. Hi, Holly darling.'

Nick shifted his weight from one foot to the other beside me.

'Jordan, this is Nick, my ...' I faltered. 'Holly's dad. Nick, you might remember I've mentioned Jordan in the past. We were friends at uni.'

He extended a hand.

Jordan shook it too hard. 'It's like looking in a muscly mirror.'

I coughed. It kind of was. Jordan looked a bit like Nick would if he swapped the gym for an office job with a few long, boozy lunches every week. 'We're just going to get some breakfast and go and sit on the grass with Holly.'

Jordan nodded. 'Great you can spend time together after, you know ...'

Nick whipped around to stare at me.

I could feel I was turning pink. 'Yeah, so I'll catch you later?' The line was moving too slowly. Were we ever going to be served?

Jordan stared at me for another half a second before slowly shifting his gaze. 'Yeah, I'll message you. Maybe we go out for lunch this week? New place open near my work. Looks romantic.'

I nodded mutely, avoiding Nick's eyes as Jordan lolloped away.

'You didn't tell me you were seeing anyone,' Nick said at last.

I shook my head. 'I'm not.'

'I know who that is. You were barely over him when we met, remember?'

I turned to face him. 'I haven't seen him for years. I've met up with him once. We talk online. You know I don't have time to see anyone. I make Holly her dinner, eat what's left when she's finished throwing it on the floor, put her to bed, and, when I'm really cutting loose, try to make one glass of wine last all night while I hang out online. Unlike you, I don't get to go out and mess around with other people whenever I feel like it.'

I exhaled hard. How could he make me feel guilty for

having Jordan hanging around when he'd literally started a relationship with someone else?

He bent over Holly and kissed her cheek. 'I'll be off. I'll see you later.'

I reached for his arm. We'd made it to the front of the crepe queue at last. 'You don't have to do that.'

He shrugged me off and looked over my shoulder. 'Yeah, I do.'

***

Nick
Age: Ten months

My stomach was burbling as I got into my car as if I'd eaten a really bad burrito.

I tried to coach myself through it. Who was I to complain about what Renee got up to, after what I had done? But this guy hanging around, talking about going out ... it made me nauseous. He was someone she knew from uni. Not just some random fling. I put my face in my hands. Maybe it really was all finally over.

I slammed my fist on to the steering wheel. How could she have already given up on the whole idea of our relationship? And moving on with that guy. If I could have picked anyone in the world for her to end up with it would not have been him. I'd worried for years she was still hung up on him, comparing me unfavourably to his testosterone-overload alpha energy. He looked like the kind of person who'd try to sell you the couch you were sitting on. Was he spending time with Holly? More time than I was? I started the car, blinking back tears.

On autopilot, I drove to my parents' house. My mum appeared at the front door at the sound of the car and stood watching me get out of the driver's seat, her hands on her hips. She still had not completely forgiven me for the little she knew about what happened with Maia.

But her face softened when she saw mine. 'What's wrong, darling?'

I lumbered to the door and lowered my head on to her shoulder. 'It's all messed up.'

She leant back and looked up at me. 'With Renee?'

I nodded. She gestured for me to follow her into the house.

'Can I get you a drink or something to eat? We're just about to have lunch.'

I shook my head.

She went to the kitchen and returned with a bowl of grapes which she placed between us. 'Just in case. Now, can you tell me what's happened? Have you and Renee had a new fight?'

I shook my head. 'No. It's not like that.'

She waited.

'I told you I—'

She cut me off. 'Yes, I know.'

'And I guess I was hoping we'd patch it up. But I think she's met someone else.'

I balled my fist into my hand. Were they going to get married? Was Holly going to get his surname? Over my dead body.

Mum exhaled slowly. 'Are you sure? She hasn't mentioned anyone to me.'

'We ran into him at the markets this morning. They seemed pretty close.'

She bit her lip. 'It doesn't sound like Renee. She only ever talks about spending time with her friends. Even then, I'm not sure how much she actually does it.'

'I didn't realise how much I wanted to sort it out until I saw them together.'

Mum put her hand on my knee. 'I can understand. Have you told her how you feel?'

I shook my head. 'Who cares how I feel? It's all my fault in the first place. It's too late anyway, Mum. I just have to accept it.'

She pursed her lips. 'Do you? You know, it wouldn't hurt you to stand up for yourself a bit more often.'

I put my head in my hands. She was right. My ability to go with the flow and try to keep everyone else happy was something I had always thought of as a positive trait, even if Renee wasn't convinced any more. But maybe it was time for me to work out whether I could channel my own superhero when I needed to jump into action, too.

She bit her lip. 'Now, don't forget we've that trip booked

to see your sister in Dublin. Will you still be able to come? She'd love to see Holly, and Renee of course if she'd be willing?'

I leant back in my chair. 'I'd love them to come. I'll have to ask her and let you know.'

***

Renee
Age: Ten months

It was 11.30pm and Holly had been asleep for approximately seven and a half minutes. Sometime mid-afternoon, her nose had started to run. By 5pm, she had developed a hacking cough. Closer to bedtime, she was snorting. But at 8pm, an hour after her normal bedtime, she was grunting with the effort of breathing. I took a video and posted it on the Facebook group. 'Any tips to help with this?'

The responses came in quickly. Stand in a bathroom with the shower running so the humidity can help clear her lungs. Prop her up with pillows in the bed. Try a bit of tea tree oil on her feet. Put onions in her socks.

We stood in the bathroom for fifteen minutes but all it achieved was a fine sheen of spray over both of us. Holly was still hacking and wheezing. I settled her on to the bed with my pillows behind her head and propped myself up next to her. I stroked my finger down between her eyebrows. 'Go to sleep, my darling.' Her eyelids fluttered and she turned towards me. But as she tried to latch on to my breast to feed to sleep, a cough shuddered through her little body and she gulped at the air again.

'Try going outside, where it's a bit cooler,' another person suggested.

I trudged outside and loitered on the street outside the apartment block. The air still held the last of the winter chill even though it was almost spring. She gasped and coughed.

'Okay, honey, we're going back inside.'

I trudged a path from the front door, down the hallway, back to the bedroom, and out to the front door again. For two hours I walked, singing and shhing, patting and stroking. She finally started to collapse into my shoulder just after 11pm, still wheezing with each breath. I did another couple of circuits before I edged her off my shoulder and laid her like an undetonated bomb on my bed, her head elevated on the pillows.

I flicked the bedside light on to illuminate her face. Her little chest was sucking in and out rapidly, her stomach pulling in with the effort of each grinding breath, and grunting with the exhalation.

I traced my finger down her face. Her forehead was furrowed with exertion. Surely this wasn't normal? If she continued to fight for breath she'd be exhausted by the morning.

I reached for the phone. The afterhours helpline number

was still programmed in from when she was smaller and I'd worried that she'd had some kind of allergic reaction. Then, it had turned out that she'd just smeared some cherry juice on her cheeks. I pressed the number to call.

'What's happening?' The woman at the other end of the phone sounded bored.

'I probably should have called a while ago but I'd been hoping she'd fall asleep and come right.' Why did I always feel the need to apologise? 'My daughter's having some trouble breathing. I'm not sure what to do.'

'How much trouble?'

I tried to describe the concave chest, the funny grunting.

'Can you hold the phone up so I can hear? Can you also time how many breaths there are in a minute?'

I counted, one eye on my watch as I held the phone up.

'I've lost count.'

'I think you should take her to be seen. Is there an after-hours medical facility near you?'

I bit my lip. We'd have to go to the children's hospital a couple of kilometres away.

'She needs to be seen soon. If her lips go blue at any time before you get there, you need to pull over and call an ambulance.'

I hung up the phone and tucked one arm under Holly's head. 'Sorry, sweetheart.' I kissed her quickly as her eyelids snapped open. 'We've got to get in the car.'

***

The hospital's emergency waiting room was packed. A man sat slumped in one corner, his face grey, clutching his right hand in his left. A woman had her head in her hands, her arms propped on her knees, giving every sign that she was asleep. A small child leant against his mother, sipping from a drink bottle. I approached the receptionist, Holly under my arm.

'My daughter's having trouble breathing.'

The receptionist thrust some forms at me. 'Come around to the right once you've filled those in.'

Usually I'd curse the wait but somehow being hurried through was much worse. I scribbled my name and pushed the papers back to her.

A nurse was waiting in the triage booth. She placed a stethoscope on Holly's chest and listened intently. Strapping a small sticky plaster around Holly's big toe, she hooked her up to a machine that bleeped at intervals.

'Her oxygen saturation's still good.' She smiled at me. 'Her heartbeat is a little elevated but nothing to be too concerned about. I'll show you through to a bed. A doctor will be with you soon.'

***

Holly was heading into overtired delirium when a doctor finally pushed back the cubicle curtain. She looked no older than I was and had dark circles under her eyes. How long had she been on duty in this department? My eyes drifted to the smartwatch pinging alerts on her wrist.

'What's happening in here?' She smiled at Holly, who was grasping a shelf above the bed to pull herself up to stand, hacking like an old smoker with every movement.

I tried to explain the laboured breathing, coughing, grunting, but the doctor was already reaching around, stethoscope in hand, to listen to her chest.

'That crackly sound is tell-tale bronchiolitis.' She straightened up. 'It's something that happens to quite a few littlies in their first year. How long has this been going on?'

I tallied up the hours in my head. 'Maybe twelve hours since she first started to show signs? I just thought it was a cold.'

She nodded. 'Okay. The second and third day are usually worst so I'm going to admit you to a ward. Just in case we need to help her out with some breathing support. It's best if she's here just in case.'

I nodded. What would breathing support mean? How much worse was this going to get?

'Someone will be with you soon to show you up to the children's ward, okay?' The doctor smiled. 'She'll be fine.'

***

We didn't make it up to the ward until close to 3am. The room was in darkness, but snoring coming from each of the beds indicated there were at least three other kids – and parents – sharing the four walls with us. Holly had accepted a dose of painkillers from a nurse who looked a bit like Ellen. As we were guided into the curtained-off space around a thin bed, a metal-walled cot beside it, I looked at Holly. 'How am I going to settle you in there?'

She had not used her cot at home for months. There was no way I was going to be able to get her to lie down in an unfamiliar one and sleep, especially when she still had to fight for each breath. The nurse at my side wheeled in a glaring monitor. 'We'll just need to hook up her toe to this,' she said, reaching for the cord that still dangled from the plaster around Holly's big toe. 'It'll keep a watch on her oxygen saturation levels. If it gets below about ninety-three per cent at any time we'll need to look at what we do to help her.'

'And she's got to keep that on all night?'

The nurse grimaced. 'Sorry, I know it's not easy. She'll be tired though. Right? Should settle relatively easily.'

'She should try sleeping in an unfamiliar bed with her foot tied to a post, see how easy it is,' I muttered to Holly as I stretched out on the bed and let her snuggle up beside me, her bleeping monitor tail showing she was at ninety-six per cent saturation. After about ten minutes, her eyelids drooped closed and I felt her weight rest a little more heavily against me. I slid an arm under her and tried to manoeuvre her over the side of the bed and into the cot. I realised too late that the sheet that was meant to cover her body was tightly tucked underneath her. But it wasn't like she was going to get cold – the room felt more like a sauna than a bedroom. Her breathing was still a struggle.

Her chest looked like a runner's. But she was still, somehow, asleep.

I leant back on the pillow and allowed my own breathing to slow, sinking into sleep.

It wasn't long before I was jolted awake again. Something was beeping. I scrambled around the bed, searching for my phone under the pillows and beneath the too-tight crackly sheets. After a couple of seconds, I realised it wasn't my alarm but Holly's monitor. I peered into the cot. Her eyes were open, her mouth agape, readying for a cry. I scooped her up – somehow her toe sticker had come off. I squinted at the monitor screen. Which button would stop the noise? A child on the other side of the room was already starting to complain.

A nurse pushed back the curtain. 'Everything okay in here?'

I gestured to Holly's foot. 'It came loose.'

She reached for her toe and twisted the tape around it again. The beeping stopped. Holly recoiled and tried to burrow into my chest.

The nurse watched the screen. 'Saturation is getting low. How do you feel about giving her some breathing assistance?'

I held Holly closer to me. 'What would that mean?'

'There are a couple of options – I'll get a doctor to tell us what's best but maybe in the meantime we just run an oxygen line. It'll sit in the bottom of her nose and just help her get a bit more in her system.'

I looked down at Holly's pale face. There was definitely no way we were getting any more sleep that night.

***

Holly finally settled into a fitful sleep on the bed next to me, two little plastic prongs up her nostrils, as the sun started to come up and send shards of weak light into the faded grey of the hospital room.

I pulled out my phone and swiped through for Nick's number. All night, I'd been on the verge of calling him or sending a message but then had put my phone down at the last minute. After the situation at the markets, I didn't want to face him unless I absolutely had to. But he would have to find out where we were eventually and the longer I left it, the more upset he would be with me.

'Holly is in hospital,' I tapped out carefully. 'It's nothing major and we'll be home soon. I just wanted you to know. You don't need to do anything.'

My mother was on a long weekend away with Henry, scoping out some art trails in an obscure little coastal village. I could ring her and tell her but I couldn't decide what would be worse – if she dropped everything to come back, or if she didn't.

I clicked on Jordan's name. He'd sent me something ridiculous the night before about people who looked like their dogs. He was desperate to catch up again, wasn't he? Maybe this was his chance.

'Any spare time today?' I typed. 'In the hospital with Holly, could really do with someone to hold her while I go and have a shower.'

I took a photo of Holly, her arms thrown up above her head on the bed next to me, the oxygen line clipped around her nose. I sent it to the mums' group. 'Any tips on how to get through this?'

Felicity sent me a private message: 'What's going on?'

I gave her a brief summary. 'Hopefully we'll get to go home soon.'

She sent me an eyeroll emoji. 'Nothing happens fast in those places. Take care of yourself.'

The door to the ward opened, letting in a rush of noise, then swung shut again. A nurse was doing morning rounds. I shot a glance at Holly. The curtain was pulled back. 'How's everything going in here?'

I grimaced. 'She's not slept much.'

The nurse looked at the monitor. 'Okay. The oxygen seems to be doing its job for now. I'll get a doctor to come and see you soon. Can you move her to the cot?'

I stared at her. 'I ... no, I imagine she'd just wake up.'

'How are you going to stop her falling out of bed, though? You might fall asleep yourself next to her.'

I swallowed. 'I'm sure I can manage. She needs to sleep.'

'It's not hospital policy to let kids that age sleep in a bed. She needs to be in the cot.'

I shook my head. 'What she needs is sleep. I won't let her fall out. Okay?'

She looked at me, her sleek brown bob quivering slightly. She seemed surprised, weighing up whether it was worth fighting me. I was surprised, too. Maybe Lauren was right – motherhood really had given me an extra layer of courage. The nurse backed out of the room. 'You can talk about it with the doctor. I don't want anyone pointing fingers at me if there's an accident.'

I returned to my position curled around Holly, one arm across her body to hold her in place.

My phone beeped again. Jordan. I flicked the message open. 'Sorry, mate. Committed to a work golf game today – could pop round with a bottle of wine tonight if you're out by then, though? Take your mind off it ...'

So that was where I ranked in the order of importance in his life. Somewhere below a work golf game. I pushed my phone under the pillow. There was no way I was inviting him over for a drink, even if we did manage to get home. Of course, it was no surprise, really. He had always been an over-promiser and under-deliverer, and, really, had he given me any reason to think he had changed? It was easy to flirt with someone who would never actually be able to meet you for that drink, or take that tropical holiday. Easy to say the right things about being reformed and regretful when you knew you would never have to turn up and follow through.

I mentally slapped myself. Why did I fall for it again?

I stared at the ceiling, counting the weird dots in the panels. I'd used so much of my energy hiding from real life, trading messages with Jordan. Imagine if I'd spent that on Nick. Would things have been different?

***

When I opened my eyes again the insipid light of dawn had been replaced with the glow of real morning. Through the sliver of window visible from the bed, I could see low cloud hanging over the city, the sun fighting to get through.

I was lying on my back. How had that happened? There shouldn't have been space for me and Holly to lie prone. I flipped over, reaching out for her, and locked eyes with Nick, cradling our daughter in his lap..

I scrambled to sit up. 'Hi.'

Holly turned to look at me. 'Hi.'

Nick and I stared at each other. 'Did she just say "hi"?' I sat up, peering into her face.

'Did you say "hi", honey? Hi, Holly.'

She smiled. 'Gung.'

Nick laughed. 'Have to see if she does it again.'

He had Holly sitting propped in the crook of his arm, holding the tube of her oxygen flow out of the way of her kicking feet. She was grinning up at him, swatting at her face to dislodge the tubes.

'I told you you didn't need to come in.'

'Did you really think I was going to stay away?'

I swallowed. 'I thought, after the way we left it ...'

He frowned. 'That's crazy. You can have a dickhead

boyfriend if you want. It doesn't change me wanting to be there for Holly. I'm not going anywhere. You two are my family. Always.'

'He's not my boyfriend.'

'Whatever. Is he bringing you breakfast?'

I sat up. 'No.'

Nick reached under the bed. 'That's good because I packed you a bagel and a vanilla latte. I doubt the breakfast service has improved much from last time you were in here, has it?'

I took them from him. The smell of coffee made my mouth water. 'Doubtful. Thanks, that's really kind. Stick around and help me talk to the doctor?'

He kissed Holly's head. 'The doctor came in while you were asleep, actually.'

'You didn't wake me?'

'You looked exhausted. Anyway, I'm her dad, right? Not totally incapable. She said it's just a matter of riding it out. They'll give you an inhaler and see if it helps but you're in here until it starts to improve.'

I let out a long breath. 'Are you sure? Some of the women in the mums' group said that there might be some essential oils I could diffuse that might help her breathe better ...'

He frowned at me. 'I think you need to defer to the doctors rather than your mad mums on this one.'

I leant over to watch Holly's face. 'Maybe. I'm kind of quitting them, anyway. I just want to get her home. If someone told me painting my face blue would do it, I would try.'

He winked at me. 'Don't worry, I'll keep you entertained. How many bad jokes do you want to hear?'

Holly reached up for his face and he rubbed his nose against hers. A familiar warmth rumbled in my stomach, mixed with something else.

He looked up, seemingly feeling my gaze on him. 'What?'

'I'm sorry,' I whispered.

He raised one eyebrow.

'I'm sorry that I didn't let you in.'

He shook his head. 'I'm sure you knew I'd come if I wanted to. If you'd told the nurses to stop me on the door that might have been a bit different ...'

'I don't mean here. I mean, before ... with Holly. I'm sorry that I let everyone else in and left you ...'

'Outside.' He finished the thought for me.

I nodded, biting my lip. How could I have thought asking Jordan to come to the hospital was a better option? 'You're a good dad.'

He kissed Holly, who was trying to pull herself up to stand on his lap, her hands around his neck and her tubes tangling behind her. 'I'm not. I mean, I haven't been a great one. I left too much to you to handle and kind of told myself that you could just ask me for whatever you needed. But I can see now that's not really that helpful. Especially not when you're depressed.'

I had to squeeze my eyes shut to stop tears. 'Thanks.'

'And I'm the one who's really got something to apologise for, although I know you don't want to hear it ...'

I reached for his hand. 'It's okay. I know.'

***

Renee
Age: Ten months

It was two and a half days before the doctors agreed that Holly and I could probably manage at home. I'd been too honest with my answers. 'Do you have someone to help you out?' Not really, not all the time. 'Are you confident administering her inhaler?' Have you seen how she tries to wriggle out of the way? Nick had offered to come and stay with us but I couldn't bring myself to agree.

Finally, her breathing started to become a little less laboured and I began to master the fine art of holding her against my body with one hand, reaching around her face with the mask of the inhaler's spacer in the other, and clamping it over her mouth for six wailing breaths, then doing it again every four hours. They seemed to think we could survive in the wild again on our own.

By then, we knew every creaking inch of the lino floor that we walked up and down during the day, to stare out of the windows at the rescue helicopter landing on the helipad at one end of the building, and the open-air car park at the other. We'd visited the playroom multiple times, while I tried to push out of my mind the mental image of germs swarming on each of the wooden toys Holly stuck in her mouth. I'd chatted to the mother of the baby who fell off a slide and broke his leg. The doctors had subjected her to a twenty-minute interrogation to determine that she wasn't making that story up. The woman whose son had some sort of weird food allergy that no one could pin down and I shared horror stories about sleepless nights. I tried to give a reassuring wave to the parents who were wheeling their son in for some sort of surgery about which he seemed increasingly anxious.

A nurse thrust our discharge papers into my hand. 'Any problems, just come back to ED. Or go and see your GP. But she seems to be well on the mend.'

I kissed the top of Holly's head. Her breathing was coming at a more normal rate and she no longer seemed to be angered by the effort involved in each breath.

Nick was at my side. 'I'll come home and make sure you're settling in okay.'

It didn't feel like a question. 'What about the gym?'

He frowned. 'Don't worry about that. Sam's all over it. They can survive without me a bit longer.'

We teetered out to the car park. Three nights of limited sleep had turned my legs to gelatine.

'I got a taxi here so I can drive you.' He held out his hand for my keys. I paused.

He reached for my bag. 'You're in no state to drive. It wouldn't be safe.'

***

As soon as we were in the front door at home, I collapsed on to the couch. Holly clambered from her father's arms to the floor and crawled to her play gym, batting at her favourite oddly shaped zebra. 'She's happy to be home.' Nick smiled at her.

She pulled up on to the chair on the other side of the room and released one hand, then the other, wobbling slightly as she took the full force of her weight on her feet. She turned to look at us, her eyes wide.

'I'm not sure she knows how to get out of that position.' Nick laughed, holding out a hand for her to grasp. He turned to me. 'You go get some sleep, I'll watch her.'

I hesitated. 'Are you sure? Don't you need to be going?'

'I've got time. I have a client I should see this afternoon but if you manage to nap that long I can get your mum to come over. Or mine.'

I bit my lip. 'Thanks.'

He cleared his throat. 'Ren, I've been thinking.'

My heart started to beat faster. What was coming next? It had virtually been like old times at the hospital – and suddenly I desperately didn't want him to leave. Was he feeling the same?

'We've got that trip to Dublin booked with my parents.'

I'd almost forgotten. Nick's sister had moved there with her weird husband in his pursuit of a truly dreadful music career. Why they'd gone there and not, say, Los Angeles, I had no idea. I'd agreed to the trip just before Holly was born, when it seemed so far into the future that it was all a bit academic.

'Do you still want to go?'

I watched his face. What was the right answer to that? His sister and I had never really got on. Now I wanted to see Kat even less than I did previously. What did he want? I bit my lip. It was probably silly to even consider it.

'Might be a bit weird?'

His gaze shot to the ground. 'Yeah, you're right. I can maybe take Holly when she's a bit older. That'll be fine.'

I watched him. His shoulders had slumped. Maybe he had wanted to go. Why had it suddenly become so difficult to talk to him? 'Okay. I'll see you in a bit. Call me if you need me.'

The sheets on my bed had been changed. Had my mother done that? If she had, it would have been the first time in my memory that she had made my bed. I settled in, my pregnancy-purchased mattress topper feeling like an unfathomable luxury after the utility of the sliver of hospital bed left once it was shared with Holly.

I turned over and inhaled deeply, willing sleep to wash over me. A faint whiff of Nick's body spray tickled my nose. So it wasn't my mother who'd made the bed after all.

I starfished and closed my eyes again. Nick had wanted

to visit Grafton Street in Dublin with me and Holly. I'd been looking forward to that part.

I reached for my phone. Maybe we should have a go at a little family holiday. Try out some time together in a different setting. Ellen could maybe even babysit one night for us.

But there was already a message on the screen from him. 'I've let Kat and Mum know it'll just be me coming. They were fine. Sorry for bringing it up.'

I stared at the screen. There was something I should have done months earlier. I pulled up Jordan's name and pressed the little red circle next to it to delete his number. Then I switched over to my social media accounts and, one by one, blocked him from them. Each time his name disappeared, it felt like a tiny ping of victory. There was some delicious irony in being the one to ghost Jordan Harrison. No doubt he'd have no trouble finding someone else to promise bottles of wine and bikini holidays to, but I was absolutely sure that I would never again let it be me.

Chapter 10

Renee Campbell, 12.33pm: 'I think I'm more worried about Holly's birthday than I was about her birth. How do you make one-year-olds play party games? What if she gets cake smash cake up her nose? Would it be easier to have her birthday without her? Joking, I think.'

Nick
Age: Almost one year

'Can you believe it's only three days until Holly turns one?'

Renee tucked a couple of nappies into a tote bag and handed it to me.

Holly was wobbling across the lounge, pushing a trolley full of blocks in front of her.

We watched her. 'It's definitely gone quickly.'

'I thought we might have a little party.' Renee was

331

looking at me, her eyes sparkling. 'Just Mum, you if you want to come, your parents ...'

'Of course I want to come.' I couldn't imagine ever wanting to be anywhere else, actually. It was a bit like when we'd first met – I just wanted to breathe her in every time we were in the same room. When she looked at me and gave me that cheeky broad grin I knew so well, I felt an energy buzz run down to my toes.

She smiled. 'Great. I also wanted to check with you – Mum's offered to look after Holly when I go back to work part-time. Are you okay with that?'

I shrugged. I'd never had the concerns Renee had about her mother. 'Sure. My parents would like to help, too.'

She tucked a loose strand of hair behind her ear. She'd had it highlighted again.

'Okay, I'll work it out with the three of them. It sounds like I can do quite a bit of work from home, which is such a relief. You have no idea.'

I smiled at her. She'd started worrying about going back to work during the second week that Holly was in the world.

'What are you two going to do today?'

'I think we're just going back to Sam and Rachelle's. They've got a new kitten. Rachelle thought Holly might think she's cute.'

'Makes a change from the park?'

I nodded. 'Definitely time for a change of scenery.'

The week before, Holly and I had had the playground

to ourselves. I helped her to the top of the slide, then supported her as she zipped to the bottom. She was so excited that I didn't even notice there was a fresh dollop of bird poo at the bottom of the slide. As she perched on the end, waiting for me to tie my shoelace so I could take her back to the top again, she reached over and stuck her finger in the gloop, dragging it through like a TV chef preparing to taste icing. Before I could grab her hand, she'd put her finger in her mouth. When I got home, I spent several horrified hours online trying to work out how much damage it could have done. The list of potential diseases was short. Someone even suggested it might just be good for her immune system. Although the memory was still on repeat in my brain, it was one secret I was willing to sit on, at least until her twenty-first birthday.

Renee covered Holly's cheeks in a pattern of kisses as she handed her to me. 'I'll miss you. Keep safe.'

***

Sam and Rachelle were too kind to prompt me about when I was going to do something about moving off their couch. With Renee preparing to return to her job, we were probably overdue to have a conversation about selling the flat, but I was holding off until I could execute one last attempt at reconciliation.

The kitten was a birthday present for Rachelle. About the size of my palm and a little ball of grey fluff, it spent most of the day charging around the living room floor chasing a leaf brought in on someone's shoe or an imaginary dust flurry.

I pushed open the front door, Holly on my hip. She grinned, showing off her three teeth, when Rachelle raced up to us and lifted her from me. 'Hi!'

'Clever girl, talking already! It's so good to see you again.'

I caught her eye. 'We thought it was a fluke at first but she's been at it ever since. I'm coaching her on "dad" next.'

Rachelle rolled her eyes at me. '"Hi"' is much more useful. Come through and meet someone ...' She was already ahead of me, skittering into the lounge with the same excitement the kitten was deploying to power from one end of the room to the other.

Holly squealed with delight when she saw the bundle of fluff catapult after what looked like a battered ping pong ball. 'Hi!'

Sam appeared from the kitchen. 'Hey, here she is! It's great she could come over.'

Rachelle lowered Holly on to the ground, where she promptly crawled after the kitten, cornering it against the French doors at the far end of the room. The kitten cocked its head at her.

She reached out, her shiny wet fingers dangling in front of the cat's face. It extended a paw in reply. She recoiled and turned to look for me, readying to scream. Rachelle swooped down and collected her, passing her to me before the inhalation could turn into a wail.

'Do you think she'll want anything to eat?'

Sam was on his feet, heading back to what smelt like toast burning.

I shook his head. 'She should be fine for a bit. I might make her some sandwiches a little later on.'

'Sure?' Rachelle craned her head to look at me.

Sam smiled. 'She just wants any excuse to look after a baby.'

I inhaled quickly and looked at Rachelle. Wasn't baby talk off limits? But she was smiling. 'It's true.'

I felt my shoulders relax. 'Well, babies are superior to most human beings, so I understand where you're going with this.'

She nodded. 'We'll get to find out properly soon. Did Sam tell you?'

He was leaning against the doorframe, a grin stretching his face from ear to ear.

'No! What?' I looked from one of them to the other.

'We managed to score the goal.' Sam fist-pumped the air.

'Hey!' The volume of my voice startled Holly, who looked at me with wide eyes. 'That's fantastic. I'm so excited for you guys.'

'We couldn't believe it.' Rachelle's eyes were wet with tears. 'After all the drama and messing around, it just happened by itself.'

'That's so great.' I looked from one to the other of them. 'You guys will be awesome parents.'

Sam strode over to Rachelle and kissed her on the cheek. Holly looked up at them. 'Hi ...'

I had to look away. Eighteen months ago, that had been

me and Renee. What I wouldn't give to go back to that. That intense excitement mixed with stomach-turning anxiety about the impossibility of knowing what was to come.

'I guess you'll be wanting your space back then.'

Sam waved it away but Rachelle grabbed his arm and shot him a look. 'Eventually. But no hurry, Nick. We want to help you as much as we can.'

'Help me fix it with Renee?'

Sam backed out of the room, returning to his quest for food from the kitchen.

Rachelle scrambled over and sat next to me on the floor. 'Do you think it's possible?'

I leant back against the cold leather of their lounge suite. 'I really don't know. Some days I think so – when we were in the hospital with Holly it was like old times.' I turned to her. 'What would you want me to do, if you were her?'

She frowned and looked out the window. 'It's tough. I guess I'd want to know that you were really sorry ...'

'I am!'

She put her hand on my knee. 'I know, but you need to make sure she knows.' She traced a line through the pile of the carpet. 'And I guess I'd want to know that things were different. Like that if you guys hit a rough patch again it wouldn't happen. Does that make sense?'

I wound a piece of Holly's hair around my fingers. 'I think so.'

***

Renee

Age: Almost one year

There are some things that you just kind of assume you'll probably become quite good at once you have a baby. Changing nappies. Singing nursery rhymes. Baking birthday cakes. As soon as I knew I was pregnant with Holly, I started thinking about the iced confection I would present her with at her first birthday. Which is weird, because I hadn't done baking of any sort since I was at school. But in my mind, I'd definitely become some sort of domestic goddess who could whip up a two-layer cake with cute Peppa Pig icing with the most minimal effort.

Never mind that she was still not eating much more than banana, rice crackers, and toast with any regularity – and I was trying to keep her away from most sugar.

As the day drew nearer, that birthday took on more and more importance in my mind. I was determined that it was going to be fabulous, even if I had to stay up all night the night before, icing cakes and hanging decorations.

The afternoon before her birthday, I dropped a full cup of flour into the mixing bowl, sending a puff of dust up into the air. Holly looked up from the playpen I had set in the corner of the kitchen. She grinned. 'Hi.'

'What do you reckon, little one?' I added some sugar. 'Chocolate will be okay, won't it?'

She picked up a block and stuck it in her mouth. Perhaps I should have found a wood-flavoured option.

There was a clatter through the front door. 'I've got bunting,' my mother called. 'I'll hang it in the living room, shall I?'

I dusted my hands and peered around the door. It was bright pink and glittery. 'I didn't pick you for the princess grandmother type.'

She smiled. 'The only other options were 'happy retirement' or 'get well soon'.'

I returned to my bowl. The mixture was gloopy like the muddy sludge we saw at the bottom of the duck pond on our weekend outings.

Mum appeared behind me, slinging her bag on to the kitchen bench and sinking on to a bar stool on the other side. She poked her tongue out at Holly. 'How's my big girl doing? Excited for your birthday?'

'She has totally no idea what's going on. Still, it'll be fun. And I'll show her the photos later on.'

Mum nodded, reaching across to put the kettle on. She was flicking glances at me.

I raised an eyebrow, adding a bit more flour into the bowl,

When I looked up, she was looking at me again. I put the container down. 'What?'

She cleared her throat. 'I wasn't sure whether to tell you ...'

I looked up. 'Yes?'

'I saw Nick at the mall when I was picking up the decorations.'

I nodded. 'He'll be at the party. It's fine, Mum. We're okay now.'

She cleared her throat. 'He was coming out of the jeweller's. With a bag of something. What's that about, is he seeing someone? We both know it's not for his mother.'

I closed my eyes. Was that why he was so keen to accept that Holly and I wouldn't go with him to Dublin? Mum was still looking at me.

'I don't know. He doesn't have to report to me, does he?'

She looked at her hands. 'Sorry. It's just ...'

'What?'

'I guess I was hoping you'd get back together. Is your friend Jordan coming to the party?'

I shook my head. 'Definitely not.'

She clattered a spoon into two mugs of tea and handed one to me. 'No loss.'

I laughed. 'What?'

She bit her lip. 'You can do better than him, darling. Both of you. How do you feel about Henry coming tomorrow?'

'Oh.' I still hadn't met him. But then I hadn't expected him to hang around quite so long, either. 'Sure, that would be nice.'

***

Renee

Age: One year

'What kind of games do you play at a first birthday party?'
I asked the Facebook group.

The responses started to roll in. 'Do a cake smash for
some cute photos?' 'None, you just drink all the wine to
celebrate making it through a year.' 'Maybe get some finger
paints for the kids?'

I looked at Holly. 'What do you want to do?'

She was pulling at the headband I'd bought to match
her outfit. The dress was layers of hot pink tulle – like
something a ballerina in a film might wear, with a cute
sparkly cardigan over the top. She seemed to hate it. It
was not well suited to crawling – every time she tried
to get anywhere in a hurry her knee would get caught
in the skirt and she'd be stuck. She still wasn't walking
without her trolley. She looked gorgeous, though, all big
eyes, cheeky grin, and hair that had started to frame her
face. Once I had taken a few photos I'd probably let her
get back into her leggings.

I cut some tiny club sandwiches into baby-sized pieces.
Among her haul from the mall my mother had bought
trays of little moulds to make tiny cupcakes and minus-
cule frittatas. Nick was bringing a couple of bottles of
champagne, though we had debated at length whether it
was appropriate to have alcohol at a child's birthday party.

'Let's be honest,' he had said over the phone the night before, 'it's more a party for us, isn't it?'

I wasn't sure about that – if I was planning anything for myself it would involve a whole lot more wine, some expensive cheese and someone offering free facials and massages. And no invited guests at all except perhaps a babysitter to play with Holly at the park for a few hours.

'Do you want to stick around afterwards and have dinner with us? Once everyone's gone?'

'That would be great. I'll cook.'

'You'll cook?'

He coughed theatrically. 'I'll have you know I'm a great cook, thanks very much. I'll make something even Holly will approve of.'

'We'll see about that. She's a tough crowd. Is this a newly developed skill?'

For a new mystery woman? I couldn't stop the thought before it shot out into my brain.

'I just thought it was something I should get a bit better at. You know, self-improvement and all that. I left it too much to you.'

'Okay. Well, I look forward to seeing the results.'

***

The guest list for Holly's party was small. My mum. Henry. Nick, his parents, Ruth, Fiona, Helen, and Lauren. People who didn't have kids joked that Holly would be more interested in the wrapping paper than the presents inside, but it became apparent early in the day that even that was a stretch.

It seemed a little pointless, buying her a present on her birthday when I had bought her almost anything she could want or need throughout the year preceding it. But I presented her with mine as we lay in bed first thing. She regarded the shimmery gold wrapping paper, reaching out a hand before turning away and burying her face in my chest.

'Shall I open it for you?'

She watched with one eye – the other still in my cleavage – as I slid the Sellotape off the paper and retrieved the box inside. It was a small wooden xylophone like I'd seen her playing with at Ruth's house.

She rolled over and sat up. 'Up.'

'Hey! A new word. You're on a roll, my darling.'

***

The party was meant to start at 10am but the first knock on the door came at ten to. Nick didn't bother to wait for me to open it but collapsed inside, reaching out his arms for Holly, who squealed with delight. 'Da da da!'

He buried his face in her hair. 'I haven't got you a present as such.' He reached for an envelope in his pocket and held it out to her. She ignored it and tried to climb on to his bent knee. 'I got us some tickets to see Peppa Pig on stage. It's going to be amazing. I promise.'

I snorted. 'You haven't really, have you?'

He looked up, his face a picture of faux outrage. 'Of course I have. What do you mean?'

'I just thought it might be – you know, your idea of hell.'

He smiled. 'Ah, probably. But she'll love it, won't she?'

I shrugged. 'No doubt.' I thrust a bag of party hats at him. 'Give these to people as they come in, would you? See how many people we can get photos of in silly hats.'

There was a sharp knock on the door. 'Come in,' I shouted. 'It's open.'

Mum slid it open and peered around.

'What are you doing knocking? Just come in.'

She stood aside. There was a tall woman behind her with the sort of shaggy bob that I always wished I could pull off but was never brave enough to attempt. She looked like Helen Mirren if she was a model for one of those high-end clothing shops aimed at older women – cream, perfectly tailored trousers with an electric blue shirt and tasteful but obviously complementary jewellery. Her hands, clutching a present she held out to me, were perfectly manicured. Beside her, my mother looked like some sort of strange witch, in a sparkly multicoloured maxi dress, an oversized fake flower behind her right ear. I stared at her, waiting for an explanation.

She blushed, shifting her weight from one foot to the other. 'Renee, this is Henry.'

The woman stuck out her free hand to shake mine. Her skin was warm and soft.

'Oh.' I felt my mouth hanging open. 'I wasn't ... I mean, I thought ...'

She smiled. 'Your mum didn't fill you in on what Henry is short for, I guess.'

Nick appeared at my shoulder. 'It's nice to meet you.'

I met my mum's eyes and smiled. Her face relaxed into a grin. She mouthed an apology, but I waved it away.

Mum gestured to Nick. 'This is Holly's dad.'

Henry didn't offer him her hand. 'I've heard about you. Nice to put a face to the name.'

Nick shot me a look, his eyes wide. Clearly, she didn't approve of him. I felt a pang of sympathy for him. He wasn't as bad as all that.

'We've got a giant Elmo arriving in about half an hour to try to entertain the kids for a bit.'

Mum raised her eyebrows. 'Whose idea was that?'

'Natalie. She couldn't make it.'

'That family, always throwing money at stuff to make it go away.' My mum was helping Holly unwrap her present. It was a pair of teddy bears – one brand new and fluffy and the other a little squashed and threadbare.

I took a step closer. 'Is that my bear?'

Mum looked up at me. 'It sure is. I found it in a box of stuff I kept from when we spent those years in the camper, do you remember?'

Holly tucked a bear under each arm and leant back on my mother. How had Mum kept track of that? She had barely known where her car keys were when I was growing up.

'What can I help with?' Henry was on her feet.

Nick gestured for her to follow him. 'I think we could get some of this food spread out – my mad family will be here before long and you never know how much my dad is going to eat.'

***

By 10.30, there was still no sign of Elmo.

Ruth and Xavier were sitting on the floor, with Helen, Max, and Holly in turns tottering and crawling between them. Lauren and Mackenzie had settled next to them and were making small talk about teething. I winked at Lauren. She was doing well to hide her fear of mum cliques. 'Get Helen to tell you what it was like studying in Manchester, Lauren,' I called across the room.

Lauren blushed. 'I've still got to finish school first.'

Ellen looked up. 'You're going back?'

Lauren nodded shyly. 'Give it a go.'

Ellen grinned. 'Nonsense, you'll be wonderful.'

Mum hovered next to me, watching them. 'Max is walking well, isn't he?'

I frowned at her. 'He's two weeks older than Holly. They all do it at their own pace. Some kids don't even walk until eighteen months and they're totally fine.'

She frowned. 'No need to be defensive. I was just making an observation.'

Nick circled around the room, a plate of baby-sized frittatas in one hand and adult-sized savouries in the other.

He appeared at my arm. 'Eat?'

I shook my head.

'Too early to crack that bubbly?'

'Yes! Wait till midday at least. I can't have everyone thinking I'm drunk in charge of child on a regular basis.'

He smiled. 'No one would think that. You're a great mum.'

I swallowed. Six months earlier, I would have argued vehemently. 'Thanks.'

Fiona stuck her head around the door from the kitchen. 'Renee, can I bother you for a second?'

I dusted myself off, leapt to my feet, and followed her through.

I gasped when I saw what she was trying to show me. The cake, which had been finished that morning with Peppa fondant, wasn't on its cake stand on the bench. It wasn't even on the bench. It had been upended on to the floor, one layer having slid off the top and a small footprint in the middle of the other.

'Oh no ...'

She bit her lip. 'I'm so sorry. Luka and Max were in here earlier but I didn't even consider that they could have reached the cake.'

I hadn't either. 'They aren't tall enough, surely.'

She regarded the bench, assessing its height. 'I guess they could kind of knock it over if they tried really hard.'

I put my head in my hands. Nick appeared behind us. 'What's going on? ... Oh.'

I couldn't look at him. 'This is all going so wrong. I haven't made enough other food to cover for not having a cake. And what kind of birthday doesn't have a cake?'

He dropped to the floor, scooped the pieces up, and dropped them into the sink. 'Give me twenty minutes and I'll come up with a replacement.'

'How are you going to do that?'

He frowned at me. 'Don't question it. I've got this.'

I trudged back into the lounge. Mum looked at me inquiringly. 'It's okay,' I mouthed to her.

Lauren looked up at us. 'What are we going to do about the missing red hairy dude?'

Ruth grinned. 'I've got one of those at home if you need one.'

'She means Elmo. We were meant to be having a visit and he's not turned up. I haven't really planned any other entertainment.'

Lauren waved it away. 'They're one, they won't care. Just grab some pots and pans and they can bash away on those together.'

'Good idea.' Ellen, who hadn't taken her eyes off Holly since she walked in the door, made for the kitchen.

Nick reached out for her. 'Mum, don't worry. We'll work something out. I don't know if the flat is big enough for a

347

kitchen orchestra. I've just got to pop out but I'll be back in a minute and it'll all be sorted. Promise.'

He gestured to his father, who had positioned himself in the corner, a big mug of coffee in one hand and three or four pastries in the other. 'Come with me, Dad?'

***

Nick

Age: One year

I threw my car keys at Dad. 'I'm going to go and get a cake. Can you please go to the shops and find a costume? Any sort of costume will do. Just make sure it'll fit someone who's six foot.'

'You know, when you were kids, we just thrust some sweets at you and let you run amuck.'

'I'm sure, but this is important to Renee.'

He ducked his head and took the keys from me. 'Okay. Meet you back here in half an hour.'

***

The woman behind the café counter stared at me. 'A what?'

'A whole cake. I need to buy a whole cake.'

'We usually sell it by the slice ...'

'I know. But I'm desperate. Please?'

'I'll just need to go and talk to the manager.'

She disappeared out the back. I surveyed the cabinet. The only cake that hadn't already had a slice taken from it was some sort of boysenberry jelly confection. I could imagine what the kids' faces would look like after they delved into that.

She returned. 'Okay. We can do that. It'll be £60.'

'How much?'

'Well, you know, if we sold it per slice ...'

I shook my head. 'Whatever. Let's just get it into a box so I can get back to the party.'

***

My father was pulling up outside the building when I returned. He had a large plastic bag over one arm, through which flashes of blue and red were evident.

'Spiderman was the only thing I could find in adults' sizes.'

I exhaled hard. Would she even know who Spiderman was? Wasn't Holly scared of spiders? Whatever Renee had been dreaming of for Holly's birthday, I was willing to bet big money that it had not involved a man in a skintight outfit with artificially inflated abdominal muscles.

'Take the cake.' I thrust it at Dad. 'I'll get changed and follow you up. I cannot mess this up.'

***

There was a hubbub from behind the front door as I put my hand on the doorknob. The suit was a little bit too small and the seam between the legs had uncomfortably settled between the cheeks of my bottom. I pulled the mask down over my face.

As I opened the door and stepped into the room, Renee looked up and screamed.

'I hear someone's having a birthday,' I shouted desperately. Holly looked up and giggled. I did a little jig, hopping from one foot to the other. 'Spiderman is here to rescue you.' I picked her up and jumped around the room.

She laughed and clapped her hands. A little girl sitting next to her looked up and chortled. Only one baby, a small boy at the end of the room, looked horrified and scurried for cover under his mother's legs. I did another circuit. 'Did someone call for a Spider!'

I swooped Holly down to Renee's mother's lap. 'Happy birthday, Holly!'

***

Renee
Age: One year

Holly was asleep almost as soon as we lay on my bed, her little face blotchy from the excitement of the party. I still could not believe that Nick had pulled it off. None of it was what I would have chosen – an overpriced cheesecake that none of the kids had eaten, instead of my Peppa chocolate cake, and Spiderman, who was a complete mystery to Holly. But he'd managed a good half an hour dancing around the living room, singing and shouting and making the kids giggle. Holly had smiled the whole time.

Nick was sitting on the sofa when I emerged, a bottle of champagne open on the coffee table in front of him and a plate of cheese and biscuits laid out with some of the expensive quince jelly stuff that I used to love before I tried to go on a budget to get through maternity leave.

I realised my heart was racing. A year ago, I would never have dreamt that talking to Nick would make me so anxious. I settled on the sofa beside him and took a deep sip of wine.

'Well done.' He grinned at me. 'The party was a success.'

I shrugged. 'I guess. You saved the day. Without you it just would have been a group of overexcited babies bumbling around eating sandwiches and my mother coming out to our family.'

He extended his arm along the back of the couch. 'Yeah, that was interesting.' He clinked my glass with his. 'Cheers, well done on your first year of motherhood. She's beautiful.'

I blushed. 'Thanks.'

We sat in silence, listening to the birds chirp in the tree that overhung the balcony.

I coughed. Best to just get it out. 'Hey, I was wondering ...'

He looked up.

'Do you want to move back in? Try again? I mean, I know it's probably going to be different, you could just be a flatmate if you wanted to, but be around Holly ...'

His eyes were wide. 'Are you serious?'

'Yeah, I mean, if you want to. I know we both went a bit mad for a while there, but I thought it would be good for Holly to have you here. If you want.'

He pulled me to him. 'God, Ren. You know how much I'd take it all back in a second.'

I leant against his warm chest, listening to his heartbeat. 'Is that a yes?'

He paused. 'No.'

I sat up. 'No?' I felt colour rush to my cheeks. What had I been thinking?

He grabbed my hand. 'No, I don't want to just move back in and be flatmates.'

He reached around to his pocket and pulled out a small box. He flicked it open. Inside was a small, white-gold and diamond, vintage set ring. It was like one I had admired when we were on a holiday in Rome before Holly was born.

'If we're trying again, I want it to be all in – sickness and health and stinky gym gear and clean, and all that.'

His voice trailed off.

Tears made my vision blurry. 'Wow. I thought you didn't believe in all that stuff.'

He spread his hands. 'I've had to rethink lots of things in the last little while. Now I'm asking – is that a yes?'

I swallowed. 'Yes. Most definitely a yes.'

He kissed me and I felt his weight guide me back on to the sofa. As we settled back on the cushions, his body increasingly urgent on mine, there was a cry from the bedroom.

He groaned into my chest. 'Some things never change.'

I kissed his cheek as I rose to get Holly.

'Some things get better.'

THE END

Acknowledgements

Thanks to my husband, Jeremy, for not minding me ignoring him for many hours while I write and rewrite, my parents for their ongoing support, my editor, Hannah Todd, for being so endlessly encouraging, Tilda McDonald, my children, for making me laugh every day, Liz Campbell, Mary Novak, and the Brilliants.